BY JOHN FEINSTEIN

The Sports Beat Series
Last Shot: Mystery at the Final Four
Vanishing Act: Mystery at the U.S. Open
Cover-Up: Mystery at the Super Bowl
Change-Up: Mystery at the World Series
The Rivalry: Mystery at the Army-Navy Game
Rush for the Gold: Mystery at the Olympics

The Triple Threat Series
The Walk On
The Sixth Man
The DH

Foul Trouble
Backfield Boys
The Prodigy

THE
PRODIGY

JOHN FEINSTEIN

THE PRODIGY

SQUARE
FISH

FARRAR STRAUS GIROUX
NEW YORK

SQUARE
FISH

An imprint of Macmillan Publishing Group, LLC
120 Broadway, New York, NY 10271
fiercereads.com

Square Fish and the Square Fish logo are trademarks of Macmillan and are used by
Farrar Straus Giroux under license from Macmillan.

Our books may be purchased in bulk for promotional, educational, or business use.
Please contact your local bookseller or the Macmillan Corporate and Premium
Sales Department at (800) 221-7945 ext. 5442 or by email at
MacmillanSpecialMarkets@macmillan.com.

Library of Congress Cataloging-in-Publication Data

Names: Feinstein, John, author.
Title: The prodigy / John Feinstein.
Description: New York : Farrar Straus Giroux, 2018. | Summary:
    Seventeen-year-old golf prodigy Frank seems ready to blaze his way into
    Masters Tournament history, but his college plans are jeopardized by his
    father's sponsorship plans that threaten to ruin Frank's amateur status.
Identifiers: LCCN 2018001428 | ISBN 978-1-250-21154-5 (paperback) /
    ISBN 978-0-374-30597-0 (ebook)
Subjects: | CYAC: Golf—Fiction. | Fathers and sons—Fiction. | Conduct of
    life—Fiction.
Classification: LCC PZ7.F3343 Pr 2018 | DDC [Fic]—dc23
LC record available at https://lccn.loc.gov/2018001428

Originally published in the United States by Farrar Straus Giroux
First Square Fish edition, 2019
Book designed by Aimee Fleck
Square Fish logo designed by Filomena Tuosto

3   5   7   9   10   8   6   4

AR: 5.8 / LEXILE: 840L

*This book is dedicated to the memory of David Sattler,
who didn't love golf, but who absolutely adored his children.
It was an honor to call him my brother for twenty-seven years.*

ACKNOWLEDGMENTS

You will notice a number of real people mentioned in this book. They are there because they're friends who I hope will enjoy their fictional selves as much as I enjoy them in real life. Among them: Mike Davis, David Fay, Tom Meeks, Pete Kowalski, Rory McIlroy, Jordan Spieth, Phil Mickelson, Zach Johnson, Justin Rose, Kevin Streelman, Brandel Chamblee, Davis Love, Joe Buck, Paul Azinger, Brad Faxon, Mark Loomis, Steve DiMeglio, Jerry Tarde, Larry Dorman, Mark Steinberg, and Guy Kinnings. I have fictionalized everyone connected to Augusta National because, well, it's Augusta National.

Thanks also to all my friends and colleagues in the golf world, notably to Dave Kindred, who hangs out with me whether he likes it or not at golf tournaments, and to all the folks I had the pleasure of working with at Golf Channel for the last nine years.

Thanks also to Wes Adams, my editor at FSG, who liked

the idea from the beginning and was willing to let me write a sports novel that isn't about football, basketball, or baseball. Thanks also to his two assistants during this process, Megan Abbate and Melissa Warten.

Then there is my agent, Esther Newberg. This is my thirty-ninth book and Esther has been involved with all thirty-nine of them—something she no doubt regrets almost daily. She got the first one sold in 1985 after five publishers rejected it, and she continues to be my staunchest advocate even when I infuriate her—which is often. She also has a knack for hiring brilliant assistants. Most recently both Zoe Sandler and Alex Heimann have brought to the table the thing Esther and I both lack most—patience, which is greatly needed in dealing with both of us.

Finally, my family. My sister, Margaret, and her two sons, Ethan and Ben, suffered the crushing loss of my brother-in-law, David Sattler, in December after a long, sad illness. My brother, Bobby, will no doubt be upset that this book isn't about a fifty-something low handicapper who suddenly "finds it," and wins the Masters. His wife, Jennifer, and two sons, Matthew and Brian, know I'm not exaggerating. Thanks also to my in-laws, Marlynn and Cheryl, and to, as my daughter Jane calls her, "Grandma Marcia," my dad's widow, Marcia Feinstein.

Last, not even close to least, my remarkable wife, Christine, and my three fantastic children, Danny, Brigid, and Jane. I will close with that because as Jane—now seven—likes to say to me, "Daddy, you've written enough for today."

As usual, she's right . . .

—J.F., Potomac, Maryland

PART I

1

THE BALL WAS ALREADY IN THE AIR WHEN FRANK Baker yelled, "Last chance to save a dozen if you quit now!"

"No way!" came the answer from Slugger Johnston in the golf cart on the other side of the fairway. Which was exactly what Frank had expected his teacher to say. In truth, it was what Frank had hoped Slugger would say.

The ball cut through the dewy early-morning air and landed about 20 feet short of the flag on the 18th green at Perryton Country Club. It took one hop, then rolled forward before skidding to a stop somewhere inside five feet. Frank couldn't be certain how close the ball was to the hole because the green was slightly elevated and the flagstick was near the back of the green. He didn't need to see it, though, to know it was close. The shot had felt perfect coming off his club.

Slugger had already hit his second shot into the right-hand bunker, which was why Frank had been willing to give him a chance to concede his victory and only have to buy Frank a dozen Dunkin' Donuts on the way to dropping him at school.

During the school year, this was their weekday morning routine: Slugger would pick Frank up and they'd arrive at the club by five-thirty, hit balls for thirty minutes, and then jump in a cart and play a quick nine holes. They would play for a dozen Dunkin' Donuts. Each press—starting another mini-match if one player fell two holes behind—was worth another six. Frank usually won and always shared his winnings with kids in his first class of the day, which was the only way his skill at the sport had ever earned him much admiration among his classmates.

If Frank's putt for birdie went in, he'd shoot 34—two under par. Slugger, who had been the golf pro at Perryton CC for five years—and Frank's swing coach for almost as long—was still a good player at the age of thirty-two, but when Frank was on his game, Slugger couldn't beat him.

Frank had already closed out the dozen-donuts match, and Slugger had pressed for six more on the 18th tee. Frank's offer to let him off the hook wasn't so much about showing mercy as about making Slugger give up with the ball in the air—which Frank knew Slugger would never even think about. It was Frank's way of taunting. You didn't get to taunt while playing golf too often.

Frank had only been 147 yards from the flag when he hit his second shot. He'd brought his putter with him so he could walk up to the green. It was only a little after seven, but the air was already warm and the bright blue sky was cloudless. Frank and Slugger both wore golf caps and sunglasses to protect themselves from the already-blazing morning sun.

When they'd teed off on Number 10 at six o'clock—they

alternated nines each morning, today was a back-nine day—the sun was up, but there was still a hint of coolness in the air. Frank loved this time of day and loved being on the golf course at such an early hour.

Most of the time, he and Slugger had the place to themselves, could still see some dew on the grass, and, as they drove off the tenth tee, could see most of the back nine—the trees overhanging the fairways, the pristine bunkers, and the water hazards were fun to look at from a distance as long as you kept your golf ball away from them.

Sunrise and sunset were great times to be on a golf course.

That was especially true for Frank Baker—whose full name was John Franklin Baker, after the early twentieth-century Baseball Hall of Fame player John Franklin "Home Run" Baker. Thomas Baker was a baseball junkie with a passion for the history of the sport. He had once dreamed that his only kid would be a baseball star, and had called him "Home Run" when he was little, but now he was completely immersed in Frank's golf career.

Frank was not quite seventeen, wrapping up his junior year at Storrs Academy. He was being recruited by every college in the country that had a big-time golf team. He had no idea where he wanted to go to school. In fact, at that moment, he had no idea *if* he was going to go to college.

As he walked up the slope to the green, he saw two men—one his father, the other someone he didn't recognize but who instantly raised Frank's concern meter. *Who shows up at a golf course at seven-fifteen in the morning wearing a suit?*

"Nice shot, Frank!" his father shouted. "Three feet, Slugger! That good?"

"Hell no," Slugger answered, digging his feet into the bunker. "It's more like four feet, and he has to putt it. Donuts at stake here."

The man in the suit laughed—a bit too hard, Frank thought—at Slugger's little joke.

Slugger's bunker shot rolled to within ten feet. A nice shot, but not good enough. Now that both players were on the green, Frank pulled the flagstick from the cup and set it off to the side, out of the line of play.

"Frank, putt that out if Slugger insists and then come on over. I want you to meet someone," his dad said, looking at Slugger, who nodded, even though he was away, indicating it was fine for the kid to putt first.

Frank took his time. For one thing, the putt *was* four feet—no sure thing. For another, he was in no rush to meet his dad's friend.

But he did knock the putt in.

Then he and Slugger, as they always did, took their caps off to shake hands. Slugger was a stickler for proper golf etiquette—whether on an empty golf course early in the morning or in the heat of a big tournament.

After replacing the flag and collecting their equipment, Frank and Slugger walked over to where the two men stood.

"What'd you shoot?" his father asked.

"Thirty-four," Frank said.

"Not bad. What'd you hit in here to eighteen?"

"Nine-iron."

"One-fifty flag?" his dad asked, slipping into golf jargon. *One-fifty flag* meant 150 yards to the flag for his second shot.

"One-forty-seven," Frank said, nodding.

Without pausing, Thomas Baker turned to the man in the blue suit and said, "Frank, I want you to meet Ron Lawrensen. He's a VP at Double Eagle Inc., and reps some of the upcoming young guys on tour."

Frank hadn't ever heard much about Double Eagle, but he knew that reps—agents—handled all the business details for pro golfers: getting them into tournaments, drawing up contracts, arranging travel, handling media appearances and sponsorships. They did all the boring stuff so that players could just focus on golf. And they were well paid for it, sometimes taking upward of 20 percent of an athlete's income.

"He's a pro—kind of a pro's pro," his dad finished.

Lawrensen's face lit up with a smile, and he put out his hand. Frank started to shake it, but Lawrensen twisted it into a bro-shake and pulled Frank in for a shoulder bump—a very awkward shoulder bump.

"Been wanting to meet you ever since the Amateur last year," Lawrensen said, the smile still plastered across his face. "I thought for sure you were going to Augusta."

Augusta National Golf Club was the site of the annual Masters Tournament, held every year at the start of April.

Frank said, "I never led in the match and I lost on sixteen, so I don't know why you thought that."

His father gave him a sharp look.

Frank didn't really care. The guy had just met him and had already brought up the most disappointing day of his golf career—his semifinal loss in last summer's U.S. Amateur. If he had won, he would have qualified to play in the Masters, since both finalists received invitations. But Rickie Southwick had beaten him handily in the semis.

Frank changed the subject. "This is Slugger Johnston," he said. "He's the pro here, and he's my teacher."

Mercifully, Lawrensen didn't go for a bro-shake or shoulder bump with Slugger. In fact, he said nothing to Slugger beyond "Nice to meet you."

Slugger, being polite, no doubt, but also looking for information, said, "What brings you to town, Ron?"

The agent gave him a no-big-deal shrug. "A few of my guys are playing an outing down at River Highlands," he said. "Media-day type of thing for the Travelers. Then I head to Memphis and from there on to Erin Hills. The circus never stops."

He gave a world-weary shake of his head after ticking off the next stops on the Professional Golf Association Tour. Memphis was this week; then the U.S. Open was at Erin Hills in Wisconsin the following week, and then the Tour came to Hartford after that, with the Travelers Championship being played at River Highlands—which was about 20 miles south of Perryton.

"I thought it might be interesting for you to spend a little time with Ron, hear about what might be in store for you," Thomas Baker said. "We can grab breakfast inside—"

"Dad, I have to get to school," Frank protested.

"First period is at eight-thirty," his dad said. "I'll drop you off this morning. We're ten minutes away, and it's not yet seven-thirty. Slugger can pay off those donuts tomorrow. Right, Slugger?"

"Sure thing, Thomas," Slugger said. He didn't really care about the donuts, and neither did Frank.

"Thanks, Slugger. Come on, Frank. Let's get some food in you."

He and Lawrensen turned in the direction of the clubhouse. Frank looked at Slugger.

"You coming?" he said.

Slugger shook his head. "Wasn't invited."

"*I'm* inviting you."

"Just go," Slugger said softly, putting his hand out for Frank's putter and nine-iron. "We'll talk later. I'll take care of the carts and the clubs."

2

KEITH FORMAN ROLLED OVER IN BED, STARED at the ceiling, and took morning inventory.

The first question, and the most crucial one: *Where am I?* His instincts quickly told him he was in yet another Courtyard Marriott. But where? It came to him: Germantown, Tennessee, a suburb of Memphis.

It was Tuesday at—he rolled over slightly so he could see the clock—6:35 a.m. Time to wake up. Tuesday was a big day for him at a golf tournament—any golf tournament. Tuesday was the day players first showed up and, since they had no official responsibilities until the next day's pro-am, they usually had time to talk to reporters like Keith.

He picked up his cell phone off the night table and glanced at it. There was one message on the screen: **Commie, call me ASAP.**

Slugger.

Forman groaned. What in the world could Slugger Johnston want with him? They had been classmates at the

University of Richmond and teammates on the UR golf team ten years earlier. They'd stayed in touch some through the years since both were still in golf—Slugger as a club pro in Connecticut, Keith as a golf writer. But they'd barely talked since Donald Trump's inauguration because Slugger kept sending him emails that started, **MAKING AMERICA GREAT AGAIN.**

Forman had stopped responding because, as a dyed-in-the-wool Boston liberal, he had been sickened by the outcome of the presidential election the previous November. That was why Johnston called him "Commie." It had been his college nickname because everyone else on the golf team was, as he liked to put it, "so far right, they were almost left."

Slugger had earned his own nickname in college, too—after an ill-advised locker-room fight with a guy from the football team.

Now, after almost six months of radio silence, Slugger wanted something—and he wanted it ASAP. Forman sat up and smiled. He knew what Slugger wanted: U.S. Open tickets for one of his members. Made sense. The Open was a week away.

Forman was thirty-two and once upon a time he had aspired to be part of the traveling circus that was the PGA Tour, just not *this* way. He had gone to the University of Richmond as a scholarship golfer with dreams of playing the Tour someday, of being a player like Phil Mickelson, Ernie Els, or Vijay Singh. Heck, he'd have settled for being the next Geoff Ogilvy, the Aussie who won the U.S. Open in 2006—the year Forman had graduated—and who hadn't done much since.

He didn't think once about being Tiger Woods because he *knew* he'd never be that good. No mere mortal was that good.

He'd had a reasonably good college career and had graduated with a degree in history, making him different from most of his teammates. He'd hoped that a few years of playing golf full-time, whether on mini-tours or the Hooters Tour or even the Web.com Tour, would get his game to a level where he could play with the big boys. The Web.com was one step from the PGA Tour; the Hooters Tour was two steps away. The mini-tours were the low minors, but players did occasionally work their way up the ladder from there to the big bucks.

Forman had gotten married shortly after graduating. He'd met Julie McCoy at a golf team party when both were juniors. They got married in her hometown, Asheville, North Carolina, and Julie's dad told Keith he'd loan him fifty grand to get him started as a pro.

"You pay me back when you begin making the real money," Julie's dad had told him. "The only interest I want is for you to take good care of my daughter."

Forman had failed to pay off the loan or the interest. He'd spent three years playing mini-tours in Florida and had made a total of $27,116. His biggest check had come when he tied for ninth at an event in Sarasota and brought home the princely sum of $2,811.

That money was barely enough to pay for his expenses—which included a small apartment he and Julie shared in Orlando and paid for with his tiny checks and her salary as a bank teller. The plan had been for her to go to graduate school and get an MBA once Keith started to make real money.

The real money never came. Three times Forman went to the PGA Tour's Qualifying School, a three-step grind, which, if all went well, led—back then—to the PGA Tour, or at least to the Triple-A Web.com Tour. Twice, Forman made it through the first stage but hit what players called "the second-stage wall." Second stage had a lot of good players—some who had been on the PGA Tour but had fallen to that level. Others were future stars on the way up. Jordan Spieth had once failed at second stage. That's how tough it was.

After Forman hadn't even made it to second stage in his third Q-School try, he drove home from Tampa to find Julie and her father waiting at the apartment.

"I was hoping we could go to dinner to celebrate you making it," his father-in-law said. "Let's go out and get a good steak anyway."

Forman knew that his golf-sponsor/dad-in-law hadn't flown down from Asheville to celebrate getting through first stage. Second stage—maybe. But he'd just flunked first stage.

They went to Charley's, a truly great steak house on International Drive in Orlando. Walking in, Keith felt a little bit like a convict about to have a great last meal before being executed.

With Julie sitting there, blue eyes glistening, her dad laid it out for Forman.

"Keith, I know how hard you've tried and I know how hard you've worked at your game," he said. "I also know you've spent the fifty I loaned you three years ago and, if anything, based on what happened this week, you're farther from the Tour now than you were starting out."

Keith started to respond, but the older man put up a hand to stop him.

"Let me finish," he said. "Keith, there's a time and place in life when you have to cut the cord on a dream. I know how hard that is—I know we all think we're close, that we're about to have a breakthrough. I was like that as a baseball player until I got to college and couldn't get the ball out of the infield.

"You play golf a lot better than I played baseball. But—forgive me for being blunt—it's not good enough. After three years, it isn't bad luck and it isn't because you've been injured. You've given it your best shot. It's time for you to find a job, spend more time with your wife, and start thinking about a family."

Deep down Keith knew that everything his father-in-law was saying was right. But he just didn't feel ready to give it up. For what? Law school perhaps? The thought of all the research made him feel sick. Money managing? He'd sooner rake bunkers for a living than do that.

He looked at Julie. "Do you agree with this?" he said.

She looked him right in the eye. "That's why my dad is here," she said. "I didn't think I could say the words to you, so I asked him to do it."

To this day, Forman remembered the moment vividly. He remembered sitting back in the booth, just as his massive porterhouse steak arrived. He knew what he said next would change his life—one way or the other.

"I'm sorry," he finally said, looking at Julie. "I'm just not ready to move on with my life. I still think there's another act left in golf."

. . . . .

The last act wasn't any better than the first three had been. Keith and Julie separated, quietly divorcing a year later. There wasn't any real animosity in the divorce, especially since there were no real assets to fight over. There was regret on both sides, but they both knew it had to happen. Keith was twenty-five. He wasn't ready for a nine-to-five life *or* children.

He actually played a little bit better on the various Florida mini-tours and got to second stage of Q-School again. But on the final day of second stage he hit four balls in the water, stubbornly trying to make an unreachable shot to the 17th green, just like Kevin Costner in *Tin Cup*, and went from three shots outside the cut to nine shots out. At that moment—a year too late—he knew he was done.

He still wasn't ready for nine-to-five or law school or any other kind of grad school. He thought briefly about going to work for a political campaign, but realized—finally—that golf was still his real passion. He started a blog, writing mostly about Web.com players and Hooters Tour players. He found stories about guys who'd made the big Tour, then slid back.

Occasionally there was a piece about a guy who finally made the breakthrough to the big money—or at least the semi-big money.

Because he'd played, even if it had just been on the mini-tour level, he could talk to golfers like a golfer. They opened up to him. People began to notice some of what he was writing. Eventually, *Golf Digest* bought the blog and brought him in to write regularly on its website. Now he occasionally got into the print magazine itself. He wasn't getting rich, but he was making enough money to afford rent on a decent-sized two-bedroom apartment in Boston's Back Bay within walking distance of Fenway.

He was on the road more than he liked, although being single, he didn't mind too much. He'd been in a lot more Courtyard Marriotts than he cared to think about, and he still drove more often than he flew because it was easier and because getting upgraded to first class had gotten harder and harder with the airlines flying smaller and smaller planes.

It was okay, though: he wasn't in an office chained to a desk.

He finished breakfast and poured another cup of coffee to take back to his room. Once back there, he decided to return Slugger's call before he showered. Even though he was fairly certain the call was about tickets, there was an urgency to the message that made him just a little bit curious.

He dialed.

"About damn time," Slugger answered.

This wasn't about tickets, Keith realized. Slugger would be a lot nicer if it were.

"I'm on central time," Keith said. "In Memphis. It's seven-fifteen. What in the world is so important?"

"I've got a problem," Slugger said. "And I need you to help."

"Too late. You voted for the guy, so you have to live with your conscience."

Slugger grunted. "You wish that was it," he said. "Listen, I'm serious. I've got a kid here at my club who has a chance to be a real player—I mean, he's legit. Not like you and me. Much, much better than that."

"So why is that a problem?" Keith asked.

"Because his father wants to grow up to be Earl Woods."

That brought Keith up short. Earl Woods had been Tiger's notoriously controlling, money-chasing father.

"Whoo boy," he said. "That *is* a problem. But how can I help?"

"I'll tell you when you get here."

"Get there?"

"Yeah, you're coming to Hartford right after the Open, right? Stop here on Monday on your way down from Boston."

That certainly wouldn't be difficult, although that would mean one night at home between the Open and Hartford as opposed to two.

"Tell me again why I'm doing this?" Keith asked.

"For the kid. Not for me. For the kid."

"Let me think about it."

Keith hung up, took his shower, and walked to his car in what was already almost ninety-degree heat even though it wasn't yet eight o'clock. It was fifteen minutes to the golf course. He waved at the rent-a-cop posted outside the parking lot, who put out a hand to stop him.

"Parking pass?" the guard said.

It was hanging from the rearview mirror. Keith pointed at it. The cop nodded sullenly. No doubt he'd been hoping to turn him away. Most of the cops who worked golf tournaments were friendly and helpful. There were always a couple of exceptions.

"Thanks, Barney," Keith said, rolling up his window to drive away. That was his name for any of the unhelpful ones, after the bumbling deputy Barney Fife in the old *Andy Griffith Show*. Barney was the ultimate cop-wannabe.

Keith parked the car, got his computer bag out, and began walking in the direction of the clubhouse. It would be another long, hot day on the PGA Tour. It occurred to him that Slugger might be offering him a break from the grind. Or maybe not.

Either way, he decided he should find out.

3

TWELVE DAYS LATER, FRANK BAKER STOOD IN
the middle of the ninth fairway at Perryton Country Club,
hands on hips, staring in the direction of the green. It was rated
the hardest hole on the course: a long, tree-lined par-four with
a gentle dogleg to the right, uphill to a well-protected green,
bunkers left, water right. It was 7:20 a.m., and he and Slugger
were finishing their early nine holes even though school was
out and Frank had plenty of time to play.

They were on the course that early for two reasons.

First, the humidity was already hanging in the air like an
invisible curtain even though the sun had only been up for a
couple of hours. Frank's shirt was damp with sweat, and the
mugginess was only going to get worse as the day wore on.

Second, his swing coach's friend Keith Forman was supposed to meet them for breakfast at seven-thirty. Frank's dad
had already told him that he was bringing a golf equipment
representative to the club to meet him at nine. This way, there

would be time for Frank, Slugger, and Forman to talk before the equipment rep showed up.

Frank knew this was going to be a long week. The PGA Tour was in town, the Travelers Championship being held at River Highlands. Frank had been going to the Travelers for as long as he could remember and always enjoyed watching the pros, occasionally getting to meet one—if only for a minute or two—and collecting autographs. He was too old for autographs now, but he still liked the idea of hanging around on the range checking out golf swings—Slugger always called a player's swing his *action*, as in "I love his action"—and walking the golf course.

He hoped the weather would cool off later in the week. He had tickets, thanks to Slugger, on Thursday and Friday.

"What are you looking at?" Slugger asked, driving up after hitting his second shot from the right rough. "Are you gonna hit or just stare into space?"

"Sorry," Frank said. "I was just making sure my dad wasn't back there somewhere."

"He's not here until nine," Slugger said. "We've got time. Keith just texted me he's coming up the drive to the clubhouse. So hit your shot and let's go."

That got Frank's attention. He already had his seven-iron in his hand. He abandoned any pretext of his pre-shot routine, swung smoothly, and sent the ball sailing high into the blue sky. It stopped, checked up quickly on the still-soft green, and ended up about ten feet left of the cup.

"Pre-shot routine is overrated, huh?" Slugger said.

Frank laughed and jumped in the cart. Slugger was in the front-right bunker. He hit a good shot to about eight feet. It didn't matter. Frank rolled his putt in to win the ninth-tee press.

"You keep hitting it like this, and you're going to have to give me shots," Slugger said as Frank plucked the ball from the hole.

"You keep losing like this, and I'm going to weigh two hundred pounds eating all the donuts I keep winning, coach," Frank said, laughing. That wasn't likely. Frank was six foot one and weighed a wiry 165 pounds. He had light brown hair and an easy smile. Only in the last year had he started to feel confident about talking to girls, at least at the club where he was well known. At school he was still pretty invisible—except when he had a boxful of donuts in his hand to break the ice.

Watching Frank laughing with Jenna Baxter—a standout tennis player who was a year older than him—outside the pro shop one afternoon, Slugger had commented to Frank's dad that it appeared Frank had finally discovered girls. "He discovered them a while ago," his dad had answered. "Now they're starting to discover him."

His dad, in the right mood, had a quick, dry sense of humor.

Five minutes after finishing on 18, Frank and Slugger walked into the clubhouse and found Keith Forman sitting by the window.

Slugger had told Frank about Forman a week earlier. Frank had actually read some of his stuff and had seen him on Golf

Channel when he made occasional appearances there. Most kids Frank's age spent their free time either texting or playing video games. Frank watched Golf Channel—while texting or playing games on his phone. The fact that Forman had played golf in college and had been a pro for a while didn't really impress Frank. His stories on the *Golf Digest* website were well written and "inside"—which Frank liked. But they didn't impress him that much either. Seeing him on a set with Golf Channel analysts Brandel Chamblee, Frank Nobilo, or David Duval? *That* was impressive.

Now, though, Forman was sitting at a table overlooking the 18th green and appearing a little bit bleary-eyed, drinking coffee.

He stood up when they walked over, and he and Slugger hugged briefly. Slugger introduced Frank.

"I honestly don't care if you can play or not," Forman said. "I just had to meet someone named after Home Run Baker." He paused and then added, "And no matter what Slugger tells you, I did *not* see Baker play."

That, Frank thought, was funny. He liked Keith Forman right away. He was about six feet tall and maybe a few pounds overweight. He had brown hair, brown eyes, and a low-key vibe. As the three of them sat down, Polly, the usual morning server, came over to the table. There was no one else in the dining room at that hour—a blessing as far as Frank was concerned. The fewer curious members who came over to interrupt, the better.

"Who's this on?" Polly asked after they'd ordered.

She had worked at the club for as long as Frank could remember.

"On me," Slugger said.

"Pro shop number or personal?" Polly asked, referring to the fact that Slugger sometimes charged things to the pro shop's club account, other times to his own.

"Mine," Slugger said.

"How'd it go this morning?" Forman asked as Polly walked off.

"He beat me three ways," Slugger said. "Normal morning nowadays."

Forman smiled. "So tell me, Frank, you want to turn pro sometime soon?"

"Not really," Frank said. "I have another year of high school, and then I'd like to go to college for at least a couple of years. I'm not really in a big rush."

"But your father is, right?"

Frank and Slugger both answered the question at once: "Right."

. . . . .

It was never easy for Frank to describe his father to an outsider. Keith Forman made it easy, though, because, as he put it, "I've never met your father, but I know your father."

Frank's parents had divorced when he was very young, and his mother had moved to Japan for her job—her desire to do so being one of the thorny issues between his parents, he'd later learned. Frank remembered a judge asking him if he wanted to live with his mom or his dad and answering, "Not in Japan." Soon, his mom had remarried and made a whole new life on the other side of the world. Thomas Baker had been a single parent for more than a decade, completely devoted to his son.

Growing up, Frank and his dad were very close, best friends. His dad loved baseball but also golf. He and Frank would go out to play late in the afternoon all summer and on weekends in the spring and fall. At first, Frank was interested only in driving the cart. But as he got older and began to play the game well, it became more about trying to break 100. Then 90 and then 80. By the time he was fourteen he was a 1-handicap and his dad, a good player who was about a 5 at his best, had turned him over to Slugger for lessons.

Frank loved working with Slugger. He told funny stories about his "failures" as a player even though he had once been very good. When they were on the practice tee, though, he was all business. He was working. He expected Frank to do the same.

It had all been fun until Frank's surprising run at the U.S. Amateur the year before. Having just turned sixteen, he'd been the youngest player to make it through 36 holes of stroke play into the 64-man match play field. Then, in a shock to everyone—including himself—he'd won four matches to make it to the semifinals. All of a sudden he was seeing stories on the internet labeling him the "Perryton Prodigy," a word he had to look up to understand the first time he saw it.

Until then, his dad had been his biggest cheerleader. No coaching, no questioning what he was doing, no talk of anything but playing golf. It had all changed at the start of this school year, when he'd come home a star after his performance in the Amateur.

Agents were calling. So were equipment reps. And college coaches—lots of college coaches. Clearly, his dad was enjoying the attention, and the possibility of early retirement. His dad was fifty-five and had never especially enjoyed buying and selling stocks for other people, although he did fine at it from his office in the attic of their house.

"You make it big," he'd said one night, "and we'll get a place in Florida. You'll be able to practice year-round once you're out of high school, and I can retire and get really good at golf and drinking at the bar after golf."

"What about college, Dad?" Frank had asked.

"If you're as good as Slugger and I think you are, you don't *need* college." He laughed. "Pass Go, collect two hundred dollars—or more." The reference was to their favorite board game. In simpler times he and his dad had played Monopoly for hours.

Frank spent what felt like a long while laying this out for Keith Forman.

Twice they were interrupted by members coming in to eat. Both apparently recognized Forman from his TV appearances and came right to the table.

"So, Slugger, you got a celebrity in town," Bob Dodson said, interrupting Frank in midsentence as if he were invisible.

"Old college teammate," Slugger said. "He's in town for the Travelers and dropped in for breakfast on his way down there from Boston."

Dodson shook hands, introduced himself, and added, "Why does Brandel always criticize Tiger the way he does?"

Forman shrugged. "Maybe because he thinks he deserves it."

"Well, I just think it's wrong for someone who isn't close to the player Tiger was to criticize him," Dodson continued.

Frank could tell by the look on Forman's face that he dealt with this sort of thing pretty regularly.

"If that were the case, then no one would be allowed to criticize Tiger," Forman said. "Except maybe Jack Nicklaus."

"I met Jack once—" Dodson started to say.

Mercifully, Slugger cut him off. "Bob, Keith's got to get down the road to Hartford here pretty soon, so . . ."

"Oh yeah, sure," Dodson said. "You go right ahead. Sorry to interrupt."

He half walked, half stalked away.

"They're never sorry to interrupt," Forman said. "If they were, they wouldn't interrupt."

Frank liked that line—especially since it was true.

A moment later, Ted O'Hara, a real slimeball who had lost the club championship match to Frank two years earlier, also stopped by uninvited.

"Sorry to interrupt," he said.

Frank couldn't resist. "If you're sorry, Mr. O'Hara, why are you interrupting?"

Frank couldn't stand Ted O'Hara and didn't care if he knew it.

O'Hara stared at him for a second, then continued. "Mr. Forman," he said, reaching across Frank and Slugger to shake Forman's hand. "I'm Ted O'Hara. I'm club champion here."

"Congratulations," Forman said. "You must be pretty good if you beat Frank."

O'Hara's face fell. He looked at Slugger and Frank almost pleadingly, as if begging them to keep his dirty secret.

"I didn't play here last summer," Frank finally said.

Now it was Frank and Slugger looking at O'Hara to see if he'd fess up. Instead, he told Forman he enjoyed reading his work and fled.

"Let me guess," Forman said. "You aren't eligible to play in the club championship until you're eighteen."

"You're half right," Slugger said. "Frank beat him—what, four-and-three, Frank?—two summers ago when he was fifteen. *Then* O'Hara and his buddies pushed through a rule saying you couldn't play until you were eighteen."

"What a shock," Forman said.

Frank had known Keith Forman for less than an hour. He already felt comfortable with him.

. . . . .

Keith had been a little cranky making the drive down to Perryton. Waking up at five did that for him. His coffee thermos was empty before he was out of Boston, and he was craving more caffeine and a Danish the last ninety minutes of the drive but resisted.

As soon as Frank and Slugger started talking—without interruption—the weariness washed completely away. He could feel his adrenaline getting started.

There was no way to know how good a player Frank Baker was going to be. Making it to the U.S. Amateur semifinals not long after turning sixteen was impressive. Plus, Keith trusted Slugger's judgment on all things golf. Slugger was the son of a golf pro and had been around the game all his life. He knew what was real and what wasn't.

Slugger believed that, if all went well, Frank would be ready to take a shot at the PGA Tour in three years—one more year of high school and then two in college. He could literally go to college anywhere he wanted—his grades were good, his board scores excellent—and he would make any team he joined an instant national title contender.

Slugger wanted him to go to Stanford because its golf tradition was virtually unparalleled. Frank liked the idea of Stanford but was intrigued by two other schools: Harvard, because it was Harvard, and Oregon. The coach there was Casey Martin, who had fought the PGA Tour for the right to use a cart due to a rare disease that made walking almost impossible for him. The case had gone to the Supreme Court, and Martin had won a 7–2 decision. Frank had read a book about Martin and had come away thinking he'd be a great person to play for at the college level.

"He can't possibly go wrong," Slugger said. "Great schools, great coaches. There's just the one problem."

"Dad," Keith said.

They both nodded. While Frank had been reading up on Casey Martin, his dad had read both of Earl Woods's autobiographies. If you read those books, you would come away thinking that Earl's son was just along for the ride, that it was Earl's genius that had made Tiger into arguably the greatest golfer of all time.

"What aspect of Earl does your dad admire the most?" Keith said.

Frank smiled. "All of it," he answered. "The money, the planning, the control he had over everything. How tough he was on Tiger. The whole package."

"Mostly the money," Slugger put in.

"It isn't quite that simple," Frank said. "My dad is a good guy, really he is. He's been a great father. Raised me alone since I was six. He's just got so many people in his ear telling him how rich he can be that it's kind of overwhelming. Now he's gotten defensive about it, at least in part because I've told him I'm going to college—period. He wants me to at least think about turning pro next year."

Keith knew exactly what Frank was talking about. He had dealt with plenty of fathers like Thomas Baker, both as a player and as a reporter. The only difference between Earl Woods and thousands of other pushy stage fathers was that Earl had been lucky enough to have the son whose talent was so extraordinary he could succeed *in spite* of Earl.

What's more, Earl's teachings might have helped Tiger a little bit as a competitor, but they had also helped to mess him up pretty good.

Keith was starting to explain that to Frank and Slugger when they saw a man with salt-and-pepper hair walking across the room in their direction. Keith guessed that he was in his fifties and, judging by the look on his face, he wasn't coming over to tell Keith how much he admired his work or to apologize for interrupting.

"Let me guess," he said quietly to Frank. "Your dad."

"Brilliant deduction," Frank hissed back.

The two men stood up to greet Thomas Baker.

"Must have somehow missed my invitation to breakfast, Slugger," Thomas Baker said. "Who the hell is this?"

4

IT WAS 8:40 WHEN FRANK SAW HIS FATHER walking in the direction of their table. He had already figured out that their discussion wouldn't be over before 9:00—when his dad was scheduled to arrive with the rep from Brickley. He was fine with the notion of his father meeting Keith Forman—even liked the idea—so the early arrival didn't bother him.

But his father's opening salvo to Slugger—"Who the hell is this?"—made him wince. He already had the sense that Forman wasn't a backdown kind of guy, and he *knew* his father wasn't a backdown guy either—especially nowadays if he sensed that someone didn't fully agree with his grand plan for Frank.

If Slugger was ruffled, he didn't show it.

"Mr. Baker, good morning," Slugger said. "Want you to meet an old friend, Keith Forman. We were teammates in college about a hundred years ago."

Grudgingly, Thomas Baker shook Forman's proffered hand.

"And what brings you to Perryton?" he asked.

"Please, sit down and join us," Slugger said before Forman could answer.

Frank saw his father's face soften—if only for a moment. He sat in the one empty chair at the table and waved at Polly for coffee. She already had it in her hand and poured refills for Keith and Slugger while giving Mr. Baker a fresh mug with the club logo on it.

"Anything to eat?" she asked.

"Not yet," Frank's dad said, and then caught his son's eye. "We have a *separate* meeting with someone at nine. I'll eat then."

Polly left and Thomas Baker took a sip of his coffee, leaned forward, and said, "So, Mr. Forman, you were saying?"

Forman shrugged as if he'd been asked what time it was.

"I'm in Hartford this week," he said, also taking a swig from his coffee. "Just got back from the Open late last night, so I'm a little bleary-eyed, but I'm supposed to meet up with Rory around lunchtime today. Slugger's been telling me about Frank, so I thought it'd be nice to meet him since you guys are pretty much directly on my route from Boston to River Highlands."

Frank loved the way Forman dropped Rory McIlroy's name. He suspected it was his way of saying *I'm big-time, pal, so don't think you can intimidate me.*

The name-drop momentarily slowed Thomas's charge.

"You know McIlroy?" he said.

"Pretty well," Forman said casually. "He and I kind of came on tour together eight years ago. He arrived as a star. I arrived as a writer—couldn't get there as a golfer. He's a terrific guy. You'd like him."

"You ever meet Tiger?" was, not surprisingly, the elder Baker's next question.

"Sure, a number of times," Forman said. "Can't say I *know* him because no one really knows him. I'm not sure *he* knows himself."

"So if he walked in here right now, he'd know your name?"

"Absolutely," Forman said. Then he added, "Though he'd probably turn and walk in the other direction."

Frank saw his father's face darken—a look he recognized.

"What do you mean by that?" Mr. Baker asked.

"I mean he doesn't like me much," the reporter said.

"How come?" Frank asked.

"Because I've written that his father pretty much ruined his life—which happens to be true."

Frank took a deep breath. It hadn't taken long for the battle lines to be drawn.

. . . . .

Keith saw Frank go a little bit pale when he made his comment about Earl Woods. He also noticed the trace of a smile on Slugger's face. Clearly, to some extent, this had been a setup. Slugger knew there was no way that Thomas Baker was going to want to hear anything he had to say—unless there was some kind of challenge involved.

All the agents and equipment reps in the world weren't going to begin to tell this kid's father the truth. Keith would, because—unlike the agents and reps—he had nothing to lose.

Keith looked at his watch. Whoever the Bakers were meeting at nine hadn't arrived yet.

"What in the world does that comment mean?" Thomas Baker said.

"It's what I believe, Mr. Baker," Keith said. "Tiger Woods is about as rich as you can be. He's won fourteen major titles and, in my opinion, is the greatest player in the history of the game."

"Better than Nicklaus?" Frank asked, unable to resist the question.

"Nicklaus has the greatest *record* of all time," Forman said. "Eighteen majors to Tiger's fourteen. But at his dominant best from '97 to '08, Tiger did things no one's ever done. He won the Masters by *twelve* strokes, a U.S. Open by *fifteen*. He had nine years in which he won at least five times. Those numbers are impossible."

"So how can you possibly say Earl ruined his life?" Frank's dad said. "You just said he's the greatest player ever."

"And he's not a happy human being, in my opinion," Keith said. "Earl raised him to believe that only two things mattered—winning and being rich. He raised him to not care about anyone but himself and to never do anything that didn't benefit him in some material way. And, most important, he raised him to trust no one—except for Earl.

"And then he betrayed his son by cheating on his mother—repeatedly. So Tiger did the same thing, and the rest is supermarket tabloid history. Everyone knows the trouble he's put himself and his poor kids through. Forget the divorce—that's the least of it."

"So you don't like him because he's driven."

"That's not what I mean at all. I don't dislike him, I feel sorry for him. And I blame Earl."

Baker opened his mouth to respond, but something caught his eye and he turned around. A tall man with thick blond hair and wire-rimmed glasses was crossing the room with a huge, phony smile on his face.

Keith knew him: Tony Morton, who worked the Tour for Brickley, one of Nike's big competitors. He was the kind of guy who laughed too hard at jokes told by people he considered important and had no time for anyone or anything that didn't involve promoting his company in some way.

Generally speaking, Keith's conversations with Morton usually started and ended with a curt nod or a brief hello. They never even reached *How's it going?* most of the time.

Now they had no choice.

Since the others stood to greet Morton, Keith stood, too—grudgingly. Morton put his arms out to hug Frank's dad as if they'd been separated in a war zone.

"Thomas, it's been forever, hasn't it?" he said as they disentangled.

"The Amateur last year," Baker said. "Frank, you remember Mr. Morton, don't you?"

"Um, sure," Frank said, clearly not remembering Morton at all. "Good to see you . . . again, Mr. Morton."

"Come on, Frank, it's Tony. You know that," Morton said.

"Sure . . . Tony."

Frank looked miserable. Keith didn't blame him.

"Tony, this is our pro here, Slugger Johnston," Frank's dad said.

Morton acted as if he were being introduced to Jack Nicklaus. "Slugger, know all about you," Morton said, slapping Slugger on the back. "Heard you've done great work with our boy Frank here. Nice to finally get to meet you."

Slugger managed, "Same here."

There was a brief, awkward silence. Clearly, Baker had no desire to introduce Keith to Morton.

Finally, Slugger said, "Tony, I don't know if you know Keith Forman—"

"Of course I do," Morton said, hand extended. "You get lost on the way to Hartford, Keith?"

"Was going to ask you the same question," Keith answered.

Their hostility simmered just below the surface.

"Well, I know you want to get down the road, Mr. Forman," Baker said. "Lot of work to do at River Highlands."

"I better get to work, too," Slugger said. "I know you two want to talk. Frank, you gonna go and hit some balls?"

Keith knew his friend was trying to provide Frank with an escape hatch. The father was having none of it.

"Now, Slugger, you know Tony didn't come out here just to talk to me. Frank will stay. I know Tony's got some fun stuff to tell him about."

Fun stuff, Keith thought. What could be more fun for a seventeen-year-old than talking about why the new Brickley driver was the best thing to hit the golf market since Titleist first made a golf ball?

There was another round of decidedly unenthusiastic handshakes, and Keith and Slugger left.

After an hour inside the air-conditioned clubhouse, they were blasted by the humidity once they were outside again.

"So what do you think?" Slugger said.

"I think that kid is about to be pushed off a cliff," Keith said. "I feel bad for him. He seems like a good kid."

"He's a great kid, not a good one. The dad isn't a bad guy, Frank's right about that. But he's under the spell of frauds like Tony Morton who keep filling his head with dollar signs."

"Yeah, I get it," Keith said. "All Frank wants to do is play golf and these guys are already planning the first marketing campaign. He needs a buffer—maybe more like a brick wall— between him, his dad, and all these guys."

"Someone who doesn't have to worry about losing his job if he says something the dad doesn't want to hear," Slugger added.

Keith looked at Slugger. "I'll see what I can do."

"You'll go to L.A. for the Amateur in August?"

"I said I'll see what I can do."

Slugger clapped Keith on the back. "Thanks, pal," he said.

"There's one more thing," Keith said.

"What?" Slugger asked.

"Morton's a big Trump guy. He's one of *you*."

Slugger didn't miss a beat. "All the more reason for you to protect the kid from guys like him . . . and me."

Keith shook his friend's hand and headed for the car. He needed a shower. And it wasn't because of the humidity.

5

RIVIERA COUNTRY CLUB WAS ONE OF GOLF'S
most prestigious spots. Located about twenty minutes west of
downtown Los Angeles, in Pacific Palisades, a few miles east
of the Pacific Ocean, it had opened in 1926 and had an illus-
trious history. It had hosted three major championships—
including the 1948 U.S. Open won by Ben Hogan—and had
been the host of the PGA Tour's annual L.A. stop fifty-four
times.

Frank Baker had never laid eyes on the place until he,
his dad, and Slugger arrived there on the Saturday prior to
the start of the 2017 U.S. Amateur. There were 312 players
in the field, and they would play 36 holes of stroke play beginning on Monday. Because the field was so big, two golf
courses were used during stroke play. Frank was scheduled to
play his first round at Bel-Air Country Club, which was about
15 miles east of Riviera.

He and Slugger had decided to practice at Riviera on
Saturday and Bel-Air on Sunday. Slugger's theory was that he

was better off playing Bel-Air on back-to-back days to try to get off to a fast start.

Only 64 of the 312 players would advance from stroke play to match play—which would begin on Wednesday, with all the matches at Riviera. The Amateur wasn't just a test of nerves, it was a test of endurance: the final was 36 holes, meaning that to win, a player had to play nine rounds of golf under extreme pressure in seven days.

That was one reason why Slugger had insisted that Frank walk every day when they played back home rather than take a cart, beginning in mid-July. And why he had been making Frank jog the four miles home after their second session at the range every evening.

Frank was excited to get to Los Angeles. They had arrived at lunchtime Friday and, since neither golf course was available for practice until Saturday, they had decided to make Friday a rest day. They ate at the Palm on Friday night. Frank was awed by the size of the steaks and the sight of some of the stars who were in the restaurant, most notably—at least to him—Davis Love III and Brandel Chamblee, who came in together. Love was working for Golf Channel during the Amateur. There were about eight others in their party, but Frank picked out Love and Chamblee.

The only problem with the dinner was the company—or some of the company. Tony Morton, the fast-talking Brickley rep, was there, and so was Ron Lawrensen, the agent from Double Eagle. Frank had already met about a half dozen agents and another half dozen equipment and apparel reps courtesy of his dad. He didn't like any of them. And Keith Forman had told him his instincts were right.

Frank and Forman had been communicating regularly by email since their June breakfast meeting. He had come to trust Forman—even though he'd spent only one hour with him— in the same way he trusted Slugger.

Unfortunately, Forman wouldn't be at the Amateur until Wednesday, meaning Frank had to survive stroke play in order to make the trip worthwhile. At that moment, Forman was in Charlotte at the PGA Championship. He would fly to L.A. the following Tuesday.

As Slugger and Frank walked to the range at Riviera on Saturday—it was straight down a massive hill from the huge clubhouse—they shared a laugh, remembering Thomas Baker's reaction to seeing Brandel Chamblee and Davis Love walk into the Palm.

"Can you believe that?" Frank's dad had said to the table, but mostly to Lawrensen and Morton. "Why would Davis Love go to dinner with Chamblee? All Chamblee ever does is put players down—especially Tiger."

"Actually, Thomas, he says a lot of good things about players—including Tiger," Slugger said in a polite tone. "It's just that players and agents tend to only focus on the negative."

"What's that supposed to mean, Slugger?" Lawrensen said defensively. "Chamblee is pretty awful."

Frank saw Slugger give Lawrensen the same phony smile he put on for club members he couldn't stand but had to deal with anyway.

"Just what I said, Ron," Slugger said. "If I had a dollar for every good thing Brandel says about players, I wouldn't have to work."

Frank laughed out loud. Since he watched Golf Channel constantly, he knew Slugger was telling the truth.

Chamblee and Love were being led to a table in the back. As they were walking past, Chamblee braked to a halt.

"Frank Baker, right?" he said, looking at Frank.

"Um, yeah," Frank answered.

"Brandel Chamblee," he said, putting out his hand. "I'm guessing you recognize Davis Love. Didn't cover the event last year, but watched a lot of it on television. Thought you showed remarkable poise for someone just turned sixteen. Looking forward to seeing you this week."

Love also shook Frank's hand while Frank searched for his tongue. It was Slugger who rescued him.

"Hey, Brandel, I'm Slugger Johnston. I'm the pro at Perryton Country Club in Connecticut."

"Yeah, that's right," Chamblee said. "I heard the guys talking about you last year. Congratulations on your work with this guy." He smiled. "The Perryton Prodigy, right?"

Everyone laughed. Slugger then introduced the other three men at the table.

"We know one another," Lawrensen said, not smiling at Chamblee. "Davis, it's always good to see you."

If the obvious snub bothered Chamblee, he didn't show it. The steaks were arriving. Chamblee and Love moved out of the way. "Good luck," each of them said, shaking Frank's hand again.

Someone at another table was waving at them. They departed.

Slugger looked at Lawrensen. "Boy, you're right, Ron," he said. "That Chamblee seems like an *awful* guy."

Lawrensen said nothing.

Frank thought it was about the funniest thing he'd ever seen.

· · · · ·

Frank had difficulty with the *Poa annua* greens at Bel-Air on Monday, the first day of stroke play. *Poa annua*—the Latin name for annual bluegrass—grew in the turf on the West Coast whether you liked it or not. Unlike the bent grass greens at most East Coast courses, *Poa annua* greens tended to get bumpy very fast, because the grass grew irregularly during the sunniest part of the day. Playing later on Monday, Frank missed a number of putts he'd been sure he would make and struggled to a 74—four over par. That put him in a tie for 96th going into Tuesday, meaning he needed a good round at Riviera.

The first hole at Riviera was a par-five, and Frank bombed his drive there, hit a four-iron onto the green, and rolled in a ten-foot putt for eagle to start his second day. He had an early tee time, and the greens were considerably smoother than the ones he had played on in the afternoon at Bel-Air. Buoyed by the eagle, he went out in three-under-par 32. He decided to try to drive the short 315-yard par-four tenth. The tenth at Riviera was one of golf's most famous risk-reward holes. It could be driven, but if you missed the green in the wrong place, a bogey—or worse—was very possible.

Frank figured he had some margin for error at that point and, with the hole playing slightly downwind, only needed a three-wood to reach the green. The three-wood was his favorite club. Slugger, caddying for him, didn't argue for a second when he asked for the three-wood. He didn't want to say anything to dent Frank's confidence.

Frank hit a high fade that started left of the narrow green, drifted to the right, bounced just short, and rolled to the back fringe. The cup was cut near the back, and Frank had a fairly easy two-putt birdie from 30 feet. Except he promptly rolled the eagle putt in, provoking a roar from the couple hundred people following his group. The eagle put him at five under for the day and one under for the two days.

He and Slugger had figured the likely cut for match play would be around two over par, and anyone over that was going home. He was now well inside the number. He made two birdies and one bogey the rest of the way to shoot a 65—low round of the day at Riviera. His 74–65 total for the two days put him comfortably into match play as the 16th seed.

That meant he would play his first-round match against someone named Gil Beltke, who was the 48th seed. All Frank knew about Beltke was that he was a twenty-year-old rising junior at Oklahoma State University. If he played for the Cowboys, he was a good player: OSU was one of the elite Division I college golf programs in the country.

Still, that match didn't scare him. His potential second-round match did: it would likely be against Rickie Southwick, the same Rickie Southwick who had dusted him in the semifinals a year earlier and gone on to become the Amateur champion.

Southwick had decided to return to Oregon for his senior season rather than turn pro, in part because he wanted to try to help the Ducks win a second straight National Collegiate Athletic Association title but also because he had to remain an amateur in order to use the exemptions he received into the Masters, the U.S. Open, and the British Open—or, as it was called in Great Britain, the Open Championship.

Having finished tied for 19th at the British Open a few weeks earlier, Southwick was already being touted as the next young star on the PGA Tour. He was going to turn pro after the Amateur and was expected to receive sponsor exemptions into just about all the fall tournaments once the new PGA Tour season started in October.

Frank had liked Southwick when they played each other. The guy already had a coterie of agents and shoe reps following him around because a lot of money was being thrown in his direction if he opted to turn pro. At one point when Southwick holed a long birdie putt and one of the agents screamed, "Way to go, Rickie!" Frank saw him shaking his head.

"Who was that?" Frank had asked as they walked to the next tee.

"His name's Sam something," Southwick said. "He thinks I'm going to sign with him and turn pro next week, which I'm not." As they reached the tee, Southwick put his hand on Frank's shoulder. "They're going to start chasing you in a couple years when you get to college. Remember one thing: they are *all* the same in the end."

Frank had remembered that when the agents and shoe reps began showing up—invited by his dad—at Perryton. He just wished Southwick had been right that it would be a couple of years and that it hadn't started so soon.

He'd seen some familiar faces following him the last few days, especially after his front nine at Riviera. When word had gotten around that he'd shot three under on the front nine, they started popping up on the back nine, almost like magic. The last few holes, every walk from green to tee was a little bit like going through a receiving line. There they all were with a word of encouragement.

Three words popped into his head in response: *Please go away.*

He knew they wouldn't, if only because his father wouldn't let them. More and more he wished he was ten again, when the thing he loved most in the world was playing a round with his dad and then getting treated to a burger and an Arnold Palmer at the 19th hole afterward.

· · · · ·

Frank had to talk to a handful of reporters after he signed his scorecard on Tuesday. A year earlier he'd become a story as he made his way through match play because he'd been one of only two players under the age of eighteen to make it to the round of 64 and, since his birthday was in July, he was the youngest player in the field.

The week before flying to L.A. he'd talked to Keith Forman on the phone about dealing with the media. Forman's advice was a good deal different from what he'd heard in the past from his father, the agents, and, for that matter, Slugger.

"Just be yourself," Forman counseled. "Don't give them *Bull Durham* BS."

Forman had asked him early on if he'd seen the old minor-league baseball movie and, of course, he had—being the son of a rabid baseball fan.

The difference between Forman and his father was that his dad saw Crash Davis's speech on how to handle an interview with the media as gospel. Forman saw it as blasphemy. In the movie, Crash Davis, the beaten-up old catcher played by Kevin Costner, explains to Nuke Laloosh, the phenom pitcher played by Tim Robbins, only to speak in clichés. The basic message is to never say anything. Crash counsels Nuke to say that all he wants to do is help the ball club, give 110 percent every day, and thank God for the opportunity he's been given.

"You don't have to be outrageous, predict you're going to win, stuff like that," Forman had said. "Just be honest. If you think of something funny, say it. Reporters love funny."

The Amateur, Forman had explained, wasn't like a professional golf event. There wouldn't be that much media there.

"Mostly it'll be golf insiders," Forman said. "Guys like me, to be honest. Golf magazines, bloggers, some local media from Southern California. Maybe the *New York Times* toward the end of the week."

There were about a dozen people waiting for Frank when he came out of the scoring area after the second round. A United States Golf Association media official told Frank that they would like him to talk to Fox, which would be televising the match-play rounds of the tournament, and then to Golf Channel for a minute, and then, finally, to about eight or nine print reporters who had requested to talk to him.

The Fox interviewer, Steve Flesch, who had once been an outstanding player on tour, only had a couple of quick questions for him. Then Frank was led to a raised platform with the Golf Channel logo directly behind it. He was introduced to Steve Burkowski, who, he knew from watching, was Golf Channel's leading expert on amateur golf.

Burkowski had a friendly smile on his face as he shook Frank's hand. "Nice playing today," he said to Frank. "This will only take a minute or two."

"No problem, Mr. Burkowski," Frank said.

"You can call me Steve," he said, and told Frank to just talk to him and not worry about the camera. Then he turned to his cameraman and asked if they were ready to go.

When the cameraman pointed at him and said, "Go,

Burko," Burkowski turned back to Frank and said, "Frank, six-under-par 65 today, low round of the championship so far—you made it look easy out there."

Remembering that Forman had told him to think funny and to call people by name whenever he could, Frank said, "Sure didn't feel easy out there, Steve," which drew a laugh from his interviewer. "I think making the eagle at number one relaxed me, and I was a lot less nervous than yesterday once that putt went in."

"Did you feel pressure coming in here, having reached the semifinals last year at sixteen, becoming the so-called Perryton Prodigy?"

"Absolutely. Last year when I got to Oakland Hills, just being there was a dream. Once I got through to match play, I was playing with house money. This year I know expectations are higher—mine and everyone else's."

"Last one," Burkowski said. "If the draw holds up, you'll face Rickie Southwick, the defending champion and the guy who knocked you out of the tournament in the second round. Have you given that any thought yet?"

Frank had no trouble being honest answering that one. "If I start thinking about Rickie now, I'm pretty sure my only contact with him this week will be watching him play Gil Beltke, because if I look past Gil even a little bit, he'll undoubtedly kick my butt."

That got another laugh.

Frank had done well. They shook hands, and he moved on to the print reporters.

The questions there were similar, and Frank was sort of enjoying himself when he saw, out of the corner of his eye, his father giving the USGA guy a *slash* sign indicating he should end the interview.

"We've got time for one more," the USGA guy said.

Frank was in no rush to leave. For some reason, his father apparently felt differently.

6

DURING MOST OF THE FLIGHT FROM LOGAN
Airport in Boston to LAX, Keith Forman was thinking he
might go to the golf course on arrival to pick up his credentials
and get the lay of the land, even though he'd been to Riviera
multiple times.

If Frank Baker had been playing in the late wave and he
could have gone out and watched him play the last few holes,
Keith would certainly have made the half-hour drive from the
airport to Riviera. But he knew Frank would be finished by
the time he landed shortly after one o'clock, and it would be at
least an hour—probably more—before he'd get to his rental
car, get out of the airport, and get to the golf course.

So he decided to go straight to his hotel, the Marriott
Marina del Rey, which was about fifteen minutes from the
airport and twenty minutes from Riviera. Because he had
an athletic VIP card from Marriott, he'd been able to get a
reasonable rate—for Los Angeles—and the location was about
as good as you were likely to get in the L.A. area.

As soon as he landed he wanted to check his phone to see how Frank had done that day. Slugger would be texting the minute they were done. As he was going through the nightmare that was security in Boston, it had occurred to him that he might be doing all this for nothing. Frank's opening-day 74 had put him in danger of failing to advance.

Keith took a deep breath and hoped for the best as he opened the message from his friend. He smiled when he saw that Frank had shot 65, knowing that would easily get him into match play. He was less happy when he saw the potential second-round matchup with Rickie Southwick. *Funny,* he thought. *I really don't know the kid well—at least not yet—and already I'm pulling for him.*

As he rode the shuttle bus to the rent-a-car lot—which felt as if it were somewhere in San Diego—he thought about a quote he had read once from the great *New York Times* columnist Dave Anderson, one of a handful of sportswriters to ever win a Pulitzer Prize: "First rule of sportswriting is, you're always allowed to root for yourself."

What Anderson meant was that it was okay to be biased in wanting to avoid extra holes so that you could make a deadline or catch a plane, or to root against extra innings or overtime. You were also allowed to pull for someone you had to interview at day's end so he'd be in a good mood—or, more important, not blow off the interview.

Keith remembered another sportswriter story, one involving Curtis Strange, the two-time U.S. Open champion, who was famous for his temper. A writer had been scheduled to interview

Strange over dinner at Jack Nicklaus's Memorial Tournament after the first round. The writer walked all eighteen holes with Strange that afternoon so he'd be able to discuss his round with him that night.

Strange played well until the last two holes, when he finished with back-to-back double-bogeys. The writer waited for Strange to sign his scorecard, as players are required to do at the end of a round, and then go to the range to hit some balls—no doubt to blow off steam.

As Strange walked off the range, the writer waited for him. Strange looked him right in the eye and kept walking.

Turning around, the writer said, "So should I assume we aren't having dinner tonight?"

Strange stopped, turned around, and said, "What was your first goddamn clue?"

Figuring he had nothing to lose, the writer answered, "The first goddamn double-bogey."

Strange couldn't stop himself from laughing. "I'll meet you in the hotel lobby at seven," he said, walking away.

Keith knew he had no story at all if Frank didn't make it to match play, and not much of a story if he didn't at least make the semifinals. Having spent his own money to get to L.A., he didn't want to go home empty-handed. But he also wanted to see the kid succeed for the simple reason that he liked him.

Of course he also knew that, for Frank, success on the golf course might lead to a lot of headaches off the golf course. That was why he was now handing his paperwork to the unsmiling guard at the rent-a-car gate: story or no story, Frank needed some outside help.

That's why Slugger had called him. It was also why Keith had given up a week at home going to see the Red Sox and Orioles play at Fenway to be in L.A. in the searing August heat. *Root for yourself, Keith,* he told himself.

And for the kid.

· · · · ·

Keith and Slugger had dinner that night at a Chinese restaurant in downtown L.A. It was expensive and not very good.

"Who told you about this place?" Keith asked, biting into a not-so-good egg roll. You could tell how good a Chinese restaurant was by the quality of the egg rolls. This was a C + at best.

"Sid Wilson," Slugger said.

Keith laughed. Sid Wilson had worked for the PGA Tour when he and Slugger were in college and while Keith was on the mini-tours. He showed up at occasional mini-tour events to scout potential future Tour players. He had once taken Keith, Slugger, and several others to a Chinese place in Florida that had been the worst Chinese Keith had ever had.

"Why in the world would you listen to Sid Wilson on the subject of Chinese food?" Keith asked.

Slugger shrugged. "I figured the odds were in his favor."

"Wrong."

As dinner moved on, Keith asked after Slugger's wife and two young kids, and then Slugger filled Keith in on Frank's first two days.

"I was really proud of him today, bouncing back the way he did after a tough round yesterday," Slugger said. "He handled himself like a thirty-five-year-old with the media until the old man stepped in and cut the interview short."

"What was that about?" Keith asked. "I figured he'd be lapping up the publicity."

"He thinks the only publicity that matters is TV and anything you get paid for."

"Earl again," Keith said, remembering Tiger's complete disdain for the print media.

"You got it," Slugger said.

"Plus, he's got that sleazebag Ron Lawrensen running around arranging interviews with *him*."

"Oh, jeez," Keith said. "He already thinks he's the star. Is Dad paying Lawrensen for this?"

Slugger laughed. "Just the opposite. Frank tells me if he makes it to the final, Double Eagle is going to put his dad on the payroll as a 'junior talent scout.'"

Keith shook his head. That was also straight from the Earl Woods playbook. He'd been on the payroll of IMG, the giant sports management firm, until Tiger turned pro and could legally have an agent. The joke in golf had been that Earl had earned his money by delivering the greatest junior in history.

"So how good is this guy Beltke?" Keith said, changing the subject to Frank's first-round opponent.

"Good," Slugger said. "All those Oklahoma State guys are good. Plus, he's twenty years old. This is a lot tougher draw than Frank had last year."

Keith nodded. "He might be a better player now than he was a year ago, but he might not go as far as he did then."

"He is a better player than last year for sure," Slugger said. "He's more consistent off the tee, and we've worked out some bugs with his putting. But you're right—that doesn't mean he gets to the semifinals again."

"Part of you thinking it might be better for him to *not* get that far—or a round farther?"

"Oh yeah," Slugger said. "Absolutely."

. . . . .

Keith was up at six the next morning, his body still adapting to the time change. He waded through some texts and emails, and then went for a run in the area surrounding the hotel. He was on the road to the golf course by seven-thirty. Frank didn't play until 10:48, but Keith wanted to make sure he had plenty of time to find the parking lot and the media tent—which would be different with the USGA in charge than they would be for a PGA Tour event.

He was also hoping to see Frank, if only for a couple of minutes, before he teed off.

Everything went off surprisingly smoothly, and Keith decided to wait inside the locker room for Frank and Slugger—who, he'd learned the night before, was caddying for

Frank—figuring that Frank's father wouldn't be able to get in there and he might get a moment or two to talk to Frank without the old man glaring at him.

He walked up the steep hill from the media tent to the clubhouse, gave a friendly wave to the security guard on the locker-room door, and stopped at the front desk area to ask the locker guys if they could point him to Frank Baker's locker.

"Third row on the right," one of them said, pointing a finger in the general direction of the two rows of lockers. "Don't think he's here yet," the guy added.

"Yeah, I know," Keith said. "Supposed to meet him."

He knew from experience that most locker-room guys and security people were suspicious of those wearing media credentials. Even though there was a poster outside the locker-room door that showed all the credentials that had access and one of them said in large block letters MEDIA, they often didn't believe that was true—or were stunned that it was true.

Keith remembered talking once to Jaime Diaz of *Golf Digest*, who told him that he'd sat in on a training session for USGA volunteers several years earlier.

"The guy threw up a slide with a photo of someone wearing a media badge," Diaz had recalled. "Then he said, 'These are the least trustworthy people you will encounter all week.' I remember thinking, *No wonder people always give us a hard time.*"

No one bothered Keith as he walked to the third row of lockers and found the one with BAKER, F., taped right over the name of the member to whom the locker normally belonged.

He saw a comfortable chair at the end of the row and sat down. He began looking at his phone, if only to appear busy while he waited.

He was reading a *New York Times* story on Rickie Southwick when he heard someone say his name.

He looked up and saw Frank Baker standing there with a grin on his face. Slugger was there, too—good news. At professional tournaments, caddies were generally let in the locker room only to carry a player's clubs inside. At the Amateur, where most of the caddies were coaches, relatives, or friends, they had locker-room access.

Slugger being there was good news. Thomas Baker and Ron Lawrensen were also right there. That was bad news and—when Keith read the credentials dangling from their necks—there was more bad news.

Lawrensen's credential said PLAYER REPRESENTATIVE. That wasn't a surprise, but his presence in the locker room was. Keith had figured that, at an event where all the players were supposed to be amateurs, agents wouldn't be allowed.

Apparently he'd been wrong about that.

Thomas Baker had two credentials dangling from his neck. One matched Lawrensen's and the other said PLAYER FAMILY. That player rep credential fit with what Slugger had said the night before about Baker being put on the Double Eagle payroll. It also meant that, combined with the PLAYER FAMILY badge, there was *no place* he couldn't go—other than inside the ropes or onto the driving range.

Keith realized he should have told Slugger his plan for the

morning. If he'd known that Baker and Lawrensen would show up in the locker room, he'd have avoided them. Now there was no way out.

Slugger tried to finesse things. "Thomas, I know you remember my old friend Keith Forman," he said. "Ron, I'm sure you and Keith have crossed paths on tour in the past."

"Sure we have," Lawrensen said, looking at Keith. "Since when do you cover the Amateur, Keith?"

His tone made his real question pretty clear: "What the blank are you doing here?"

Keith gave both men a phony smile and said, "Love Riviera, love L.A., and I'm always looking for the Next Ones in golf. You should know that, Ron. You're here doing the same thing."

Thomas Baker didn't bother to hide his anger at Keith's presence even a little bit.

"You may not be aware of this, Mr. Forman, but Frank's got a match to play in a little while."

"Totally aware," Keith said. "Just wanted to wish him luck. Beltke's a tough first-rounder."

"No kidding," Lawrensen said.

Keith glanced at Frank. He was white as a sheet. This had really been a bad idea. He decided it was time to cut his losses.

"Frank, all the best today," he said, stretching his hand out in Frank's direction. He was relieved when Frank took it and gave him a smile—his face still pale. "I hope I get a chance to talk to you after a win today."

"You can get in line with everyone else," Thomas Baker said.

Before Keith could decide whether to just swallow the obnoxious comment and bail out, Frank answered for him.

"I'm always glad to talk to you, Mr. Forman," he said. "You know that."

He gave Keith a friendly pat on the shoulder.

Keith returned it and then, without another word to anybody, pushed past Baker and Lawrensen and bolted for the door.

"Nice start, Keith," he murmured to himself as he walked back into the sunshine. It wasn't yet ten o'clock and he was already starting to sweat profusely.

7

"WHAT WAS THAT ABOUT?" SNAPPED THOMAS
Baker.

Frank could see in his father's eyes that he was really angry.
Clearly, Keith Forman's presence in the locker room had upset
him, and Frank's directing any warmth in the reporter's direction was some kind of violation of their father-son relationship.

Frank decided to play dumb.

"What was what about, Dad?"

It was the wrong play.

"That reporter is nothing but trouble, and you know it,"
his dad said. "He's just looking for some kind of story."

Before Frank could answer, his dad whirled on Slugger.
"You're the one who brought him to Perryton. What were you
thinking? And how did he get in the locker room here?"

He was shouting and Frank could see heads turning.
Embarrassed, he whispered, "Dad, keep it down."

Slugger looked stricken. Clearly, he didn't want to get into a fight of any kind with his star pupil's father—who also happened to be an important member at the club where he was employed.

"Thomas, the USGA decides who can come in the locker room," Slugger said, almost stammering. USGA had come out of his mouth as "U-U-S-G . . . A."

Frank could see he needed to be rescued. "Dad, this isn't the time to talk about any of this," he said. "I need to get to the range and warm up. And, for the record, I *asked* Slugger to contact Mr. Forman because I knew they went to college together and he knows a lot about the golf Tour."

His dad was taken aback by this—which wasn't surprising since it was a flat-out lie. Frank had barely known who Keith Forman was until Slugger had brought him up back in the spring.

But the lie worked—or perhaps mentioning that he needed to warm up worked.

His father shook his head, glared at Slugger for another second, and then said, "Okay, fine. We'll discuss this later." He looked at Lawrensen. "Come on, Ron, let's get something to drink in player family dining." He nodded at Slugger and Frank, then said, in a softer tone, "You go get ready."

Mercifully, he and the agent turned and left.

"Thanks for the bailout," Slugger said once they'd gone. "I wish Keith had told me he was going to look for you this morning. That was a bad idea."

Frank was now sitting on a bench in front of his locker, changing into his golf shoes.

"Probably," Frank said. "But I like him and I trust him—if only because I know you trust him." Then he changed the subject. "How come my dad thinks Ron Lawrensen is the be-all and end-all when it comes to golf?"

"He's smart," Slugger said as Frank stood up. "He keeps telling your dad what he wants to hear *and* he's paying him. If he tells your dad to fire me so he can bring in some big-name teacher who is one of his clients, your dad will probably do it."

"No, he won't," Frank said with a smile. "Not if he wants me to keep playing golf."

Slugger smiled.

"Think I'm kidding?" Frank asked. "See what happens if he tries."

He wasn't kidding. Not even a little bit.

. . . . .

Frank knew enough about Gil Beltke to understand that he was in for a long, tough day. Beltke made that crystal clear on the first hole of match play when he reached the green in two with what looked to Frank like a five-iron and then two-putted for birdie. Frank, a little unnerved by Beltke's drive—very long and very straight—missed the fairway left, hit his second shot into the left bunker, and then couldn't get up-and-down, missing about a 12-footer for birdie.

The match was less than ten minutes old and he was one-down.

It got worse before it got better. Frank bogeyed the

difficult second hole to go two holes down before Beltke birdied the third. He was three-down after three holes. Walking to the fourth tee, he saw Keith Forman waiting for him. Unlike his father and Ron Lawrensen, Forman was allowed to walk inside the ropes. Forman was smiling as Frank followed Beltke onto the tee.

"Hey, Frank," Forman said. "It's just golf. No one's going to die out here today. Take a deep breath and just play golf."

He turned and walked away before Frank could say anything. Frank glanced to the right of the tee where his father and Lawrensen were standing. Both had their heads down as if they were afraid to look at him at that moment. Slugger was standing to the right of the tee, his face impassive as always. If the slow start bothered him, he wasn't showing it. He had put the bag down and was wiping his face with a towel. It was closing in on noon, and the temperature was climbing quickly.

There weren't more than fifty people following the match—and more than half of them were wearing Oklahoma State orange and whooping it up for Gil Beltke. *With good reason,* Frank thought.

It occurred to him that Forman was right. It was just golf. He remembered something he had read once in a book about baseball: sometimes the key to success is to try *easier*. It talked about hitters gripping the bat too hard or pitchers gripping the ball too tightly.

Try easier, he thought. *Lighten up on your grip.*

The fourth was a 236-yard par-three, and the USGA had decided to play the hole from the back tee. Beltke took a three-iron, which seemed like a lot of club to Frank, especially with the mild breeze behind them. He was right. The ball landed in the middle of the green, took a hop, and rolled off the back edge. For the first time in the match, Frank had a small opening.

Slugger, having seen Beltke pull the three-iron, wanted Frank to hit four-iron. That made sense. Except Frank knew he was a little bit longer than Beltke and, with the breeze, thought four might be a little too much. Plus, he was more comfortable taking a hard swing with a mid-iron than trying to finesse it. He always seemed to lose the ball to the right when he tried to swing easy.

"I want to swing hard, not easy," he said to Slugger.

Knowing his propensity for losing the ball right when holding back, Slugger just nodded and handed him the five-iron.

Frank stuck his tee in the ground, stepped back, and took a practice swing and a deep breath. He made a point of gripping the club lightly, almost to the point where it felt as if it might fly out of his hands at impact. *Perfect,* he thought.

He got over the ball, relaxed his shoulders a bit, and took the club back in a smooth, graceful arc. His swing was hard but not strained. As soon as the ball came off the club, he knew he'd hit it perfectly. The question was, had he made the right club choice?

Slugger was thinking the same thing. "Be right!" he said as the ball soared in the direction of the green. That was golf-speak, meaning "be the right distance."

It was. The ball started at the center of the green, then faded just a little—Frank's best shot with an iron was a fade, and the flag was back-right. The ball hit near the front of the green, took a hop and then rolled straight at the pin. For a split second, Frank thought it was going in. But it pulled up somewhere very close to the hole—Frank couldn't tell how close standing on the tee—but the applause from near the green from the folks in orange told him it had to be very close.

"Great shot," Beltke said, walking briskly off the tee while Frank was still admiring his work.

As it turned out, the ball was about 18 inches from the hole.

Walking onto the green, Beltke turned and said, "Pick it up. Really nice shot."

Having conceded Frank's birdie putt from kick-in range, Beltke tried to hole out from behind the green with his wedge. He hit a good shot—it rolled about six feet past the hole—but not good enough.

Suddenly, Frank had life. He was now two-down with, as the saying went, a lot of golf left to play.

Try easier.

. . . . .

Whether it was his new mantra, Forman's "It's just golf" comment, or the soothing effect of his great tee shot on Number 4, Frank settled into a comfortable groove for the rest of the front nine.

The only problem was that Beltke, with two years of college experience under his belt, wasn't going to be unnerved by one great shot or one birdie.

Both played very solidly for the next five holes. Each made one mistake: Frank, perhaps a little cocky after what he'd done on Number 4, tried to attack a sucker pin on Number 6—it was tucked left front—but missed the green and short-sided himself, leading to a bogey.

"Lesson learned," Slugger said as they walked to the seventh tee. "They call it a sucker pin because only a sucker goes after it. Sometimes middle of the green is just fine."

Frank knew his coach was right. Once he missed the green, he had almost no shot since there was no way to stop the ball close to the hole with so little green between him and where his golf ball had landed.

Fortunately, Beltke gave him a hole back right away, finding a bunker on Number 7 and then leaving his third shot in the bunker. They both parred 8 and 9, and Frank walked to the Number 10 tee still two-down.

He found Forman, who had kept his distance for most of the morning, standing next to the rope, arms folded, eyes hidden by sunglasses.

"How d'you think you played those nine holes?" he said.

They had a moment to talk because the match ahead of them was still on the green and since the green was reachable, he and Beltke had to wait until it cleared.

"Other than the five-iron on four, no better than okay," Frank answered.

"Make any long putts?"

Frank was surprised by the question. Forman had been watching from the beginning. He knew the answer was no. He played along.

"Unless you consider the six-footer for par at eight a long putt, no," he answered.

Forman was nodding. "So you hit one truly good shot, didn't make a big putt, and you're two-down. What's that tell you?"

"That I can beat this guy?"

"Bingo," Forman said. "You probably should be three or four down. This guy's not a killer. Take advantage."

Frank nodded. The green was clearing. He was up.

. . . . .

The tenth at Riviera was one of the most famous short par-fours in golf. Not only was the green drivable, but many players could reach it with a three-wood. Frank fell into that category, and his tee shot on the hole the day before had given his round a huge boost, the same way the eagle at Number 1 had.

"What do you think?" he asked Slugger, unsure whether he should risk going for the green or lay up to a spot where he might have an easy pitch.

"More important, what do *you* think?" Slugger said. "What feels comfortable?"

Frank knew what Slugger was doing. He often played this

game with him when they were playing in the early morning. There was considerably more at stake now than a dozen donuts.

The pin was tucked front-right, meaning if he went for the green he'd almost certainly have a very long putt even if he hit a good shot because bouncing the ball through the narrow landing area would be difficult at best and there was no way to stop the ball at the front of the green—unless he got very lucky.

But a layup would have to be almost as precise because if he didn't get it onto the left side of the fairway—without reaching the rough—he'd have no angle to get close to the flag.

He was about to tell Slugger what he thought when the rules official who was refereeing the match said to him, "All due respect, Mr. Baker, but perhaps while we're still young?"

Frank actually laughed. "While we're still young" had been part of a USGA campaign to speed up pace-of-play, meaning when it's your turn to hit, don't take forever. Golfers from duffers to the pros hated having to wait on poky players ahead of them looking for a lost ball or contemplating their next shot.

Frank nodded, reached into his bag for his three-wood, and glanced at Slugger as if to say, *What do you think?*

Slugger shrugged. "If you like it, I like it."

Frank teed the ball up, stood behind it for a moment, and then took one practice swing. He wanted to start the ball left and fade it back toward the pin. He teed the ball higher than normal because he wanted to hit the ball as high as he could— landing it at a steep angle on the green and hope it stopped without rolling over the edge. It was a show-off shot—a risky one at that.

As soon as he made contact, Frank knew he'd done just what he wanted to do. The ball went so high into the sky that Frank lost sight of it for a moment in the sun. It started to the left and then, as it came down, began drifting right. It bounced on the front-left corner of the green, took a high hop, and began trickling toward the back. Over, Frank knew, was dead. He'd be lucky to make 4 from there, much less 3.

The ball rolled, slowed, and finally halted about two inches off the green on the fringe. He was probably 80 feet from the flag, but he had a putt.

"Some shot," Beltke said.

He'd had an iron in his hand, but when he saw where Frank's shot ended up, he went back to his bag for a three-wood. He tried the more standard shot, landing the ball short of the green and hoping it would run up. It did, but it went right through the green to the exact spot Frank had been hoping to avoid.

"Should have stuck with the iron," Frank heard Beltke say to his caddie. "I let the kid's shot intimidate me."

Frank smiled when he heard that comment. His gut told him that Forman had been right: Gil Beltke was a very good player. But he wasn't a killer.

8

EVEN THOUGH FRANK HADN'T PLAYED ESPE-
cially well on the front nine, it was apparent to Keith Forman
that the kid was the real deal. Slugger had been right.

He was clearly what the players called a shotmaker. He had
the ability to maneuver the ball in any direction, and his tee
shot at 10—launching the ball nine miles into the air and
getting it to land on the green at a steep angle to minimize
the bounce-and-roll effect and not go over the back—would
have been envied and admired by almost anyone playing
on the Tour.

The question, going forward, would be his putting. Slugger
had said he was a good putter, but more important, was he
an excellent *clutch* putter?

"Under the gun, he'll make almost anything he has to
make," Slugger had said.

So far, Keith hadn't seen any evidence of that. Then again,
so far he hadn't really seen him under the gun.

By the time Frank and Beltke reached the 12th tee, the

match was even. Beltke had been unable to get up-and-down from where he'd hit his tee shot on 10, and Frank had made a five-footer for birdie after hitting a good lag putt from 80 feet. Then he birdied the par-five 11th to get even for the first time since they'd walked off the first tee.

He did not, however, stay even for long. Beltke may not have been a killer, but he had a lot of match play experience and he could certainly putt. He made long birdie putts on 12 and 13 and was two-up again. Walking to the 14th tee, Keith was tempted to say something to Frank but decided not to—for two reasons.

First was the issue of what his role should—or should not—be in the kid's future. The whole thing might be moot if the father ordered the kid to stay away from Keith—and fired Slugger while he was at it. Keith knew both things were entirely possible. Stage fathers always wanted complete control, and anyone who threatened that control—whether from the inside or the outside—was usually thrown off the island.

If none of that happened, though, Keith had to ask himself: Was he here as a reporter working on a story? Or was he here at the request of his old college teammate to help out in a personal situation?

The problem was, the answer was *both*. He could feel his stomach churning with nerves because he wanted Frank to win and be successful. He had long ago given up on any notion that reporters were objective—*no one* was objective; everyone had biases. The key was recognizing your biases and always being fair to people whether you liked them or not.

But giving an athlete pep talks in the middle of a competition was clearly over the line. He'd known it the minute he'd done it on the fourth tee, yet he'd gone ahead and done it again on the tenth.

The other question was: When was enough, enough? It wasn't as if Frank had played 12 and 13 poorly; he'd just been the victim of an opponent with a hot putter. That was the toughest thing about golf: you couldn't play defense.

So Keith decided to keep his mouth shut, in part because he knew it was wrong to open it again and in part because he was pretty certain the only voice Frank needed to hear at this point in the match was Slugger's.

The players halved both the 14th and 15th, Beltke's lead holding at two-up. Keith was surprised by how difficult the setup of the golf course was for the day. Normally, in the first round of a match-play event, the hole locations weren't that hard. The officials tended to move the hole locations to make the greens more difficult with each passing day—except, he remembered with a smile, at the 2016 Ryder Cup—the tournament held every two years between teams from the United States and Europe—when the Americans, playing at home, had set the course up so easily on the last day that the Europeans actually complained about it.

"We're better putters than they are, so why wouldn't we put the pins in places where we're going to get a crack at making a lot of birdies?" Phil Mickelson had said. "It's called home-field advantage."

There was no home-field advantage here. Forman jotted a

note to himself in his notebook to ask about that later—if he was still around. If Frank, now two-down with three holes to play, lost, Keith would be on a red-eye to Boston that night.

. . . . .

The 16th was a short, 166-yard par-three. It occurred to Keith that this could be the last hole of the match if Beltke won it. That loomed as a serious possibility when Beltke hit a gorgeous pitching wedge with a lot of spin on the ball that landed behind the hole and spun back to about three feet for an almost-certain birdie.

Frank hit a reasonable shot to about 18 feet, but with Beltke close enough that under other circumstances Frank might have conceded the putt, Frank had what amounted to a must-make putt just to keep the match alive.

Well, Keith thought, *at least I don't have to worry about being too biased to write a story on the kid. If he doesn't make this putt, there will be no story.*

His hesitation on the tenth notwithstanding, Frank was a fast player—something Keith had happily noticed early in the match. That was Slugger's influence. If there was one thing in life he and Slugger agreed on, it was that slow play in golf was a pox. On the Tour, it got worse every year.

Frank didn't change his routine even for a do-or-die putt. He checked the line, said something briefly to Slugger, got over the putt, and took one practice stroke. A few seconds later, the putt was on its way.

It was one of those that you could tell was going in the hole almost as soon as it came off the putter. Even on the bouncy *Poa annua* grass, the ball went straight as a string on a line just left of the hole before dying just a little right a few feet from the hole and rolling in.

Center cut! as the TV guys loved to say when they saw a putt that perfect.

Keith felt himself take a deep breath. At least the match would go to the 17th hole, although Beltke would be two-up with two to play once he made his short birdie putt.

Keith was about to start walking in the direction of the tee, but he stopped because Beltke was taking forever to knock his putt in. He looked at it from both sides of the hole, marked his ball, placed it down, then marked it *again*.

"He's scared of it," Keith said under his breath.

Beltke finally got over the putt, for a very long time, and then pushed it to the right—it didn't even touch the hole. Suddenly, the match had gone from just about over to Beltke being only one-up. Watching Beltke walk off the green with a stunned look on his face, Keith was certain Frank was going to win.

The 17th was the longest hole on the golf course—576 yards from the back tee. The wind was into the players' faces, meaning going for the green in two would be virtually impossible. Frank's drive was down the middle. Beltke, clearly shaken, pulled his into the left rough—meaning he had to lay up a good 200 yards from the green, after his tricky lie in the long grass forced him to play a conservative second shot.

Frank and Slugger then had an animated conversation that Keith, standing by the ropes, couldn't hear. But when Frank pulled a wood, probably his three, he knew what the discussion had been about: Slugger wanted Frank to lay up, giving himself an easy chip shot to the green, knowing Beltke, from so far out, was unlikely to get his third shot close to the hole. Frank, being seventeen, wanted to go for the green.

It turned out Frank was right. His second shot was perfect, bouncing up the hill short of the green and rolling about 5 feet onto the putting surface, leaving him with 35 feet for an eagle 3.

Beltke appeared to be done. His third shot sailed right, into the front bunker. From there he skulled his fourth shot, flying it 40 feet past the pin. He was still away, and when his putt came up well short, meaning he could make no better than 6, he conceded the hole to Frank.

They were even. One hole to play.

Beltke managed to find his composure on the 18th tee, his tee shot splitting the fairway. Even so, he was 20 yards short of where the now pumped-up, out-of-his-mind Frank had hit his tee shot. Both players found the green with their second shots. Beltke hit a five-iron. (Keith knew because he saw Beltke's caddie signal five fingers to a TV gofer who was walking with the match—the gofer then whispered the info over his radio to the TV truck, which was why announcers always were able to tell viewers with absolute confidence what club was about to be used.)

It occurred to Keith that Fox Sports was now on-air

and—given the closeness of the match and the fact that the winner would face Rickie Southwick, who, according to the scoreboards, had already won his match easily—the matchup was probably being tracked pretty closely.

Frank hit a seven-iron. When Keith walked up the steep hill to the green, he could see that Beltke had about 25 feet for birdie; Frank about 20 feet.

Beltke again took forever stalking his putt, understandable because the green had a lot of slope to it and, if nothing else, he wanted to have a tap-in for par if he missed, not another tricky three- or four-footer. When he finally putted, he hit an excellent putt that looked, for a split second, like it might go in. But it swerved just left of the hole at the last second, leaving him with about a foot—a gimme putt Frank conceded right away.

Now, barring a three-putt, he would at the very least take the match to extra holes. For the moment, he had a 20-footer to win. Keith looked at his watch. It was remarkable that less than thirty minutes ago this kid had faced a putt he thought he had to make just to stay alive.

Knowing what was at stake, Frank took a little extra time reading the putt. Riviera's 18th green had ridges and slopes that made it complicated. Even from where he was standing behind the green, Keith could see that if Frank went after the putt too boldly, he could roll it well past the cup.

"Just get it close," he said softly, realizing he was now officially talking to himself.

Frank got over the ball and barely touched it.

At first Keith thought he'd left it well short. Then, as

the putt gathered some speed, he realized it was even more downhill than he'd thought. The ball was still traveling fast when it hit the hole, did a quick spin above the cup, and dropped in.

By now, the crowd had grown considerably and Keith heard a serious roar. It was only then that it occurred to him that Frank had *won*. He had gone birdie, eagle (on a conceded 35-foot putt), birdie to come from two-down with three to play to win. Slugger was hugging him, and Keith saw Thomas Baker approaching for a hug.

Frank seemed to see his father coming, but turned away and went to console his stunned opponent and his caddie. Only then did he accept a hug from his dad. Frank said something to his father, who nodded and walked back over to where Ron Lawrensen was standing.

Keith saw Pete Kowalski, the USGA's number-one PR guy, waiting for the hugs and handshakes to end. When he got to Frank, he pointed to a corner of the green where Holly Sonders, who did post-round interviews for Fox, was standing by with a camera crew.

Slugger walked off the back of the green, the bag slung over his shoulder and a huge grin on his face.

"I told you he was special," Slugger said as he reached Keith. "Do you believe me now?" He was flushed from the heat and the adrenaline.

"You know what, Slugger? I believe you," the reporter said.

And he did. The question now was whether the kid could make Rickie Southwick a believer the next day.

9

FRANK WAS A LITTLE SURPRISED BY THE post-match frenzy that surrounded his victory. He'd gotten a taste of media attention the year before, but he'd sneaked along pretty much unnoticed until he reached the semifinals, when people began to notice that a sixteen-year-old was in the final four along with three college players. Even then, it hadn't been quite like this.

Only later, when he had a chance to talk to Keith Forman for a few minutes on the telephone while his father, Ron Lawrensen, and Slugger were waiting for him in the hotel lobby to go to dinner, did he understand it.

"Part of it is that people remember who you are because of last year," Forman explained. "Another part is that you're playing Southwick next. And a third part is that the media, especially in L.A., likes a Hollywood ending. Two down with three to play and you go birdie-eagle-birdie, making a tough twenty-footer to win on eighteen? That's a Hollywood ending."

"Wasn't a real eagle, though," Frank said. He chose a green apple from the fruit basket that had been waiting for him in his room. His mom had sent it with a nice note wishing him luck.

"Not the point," Forman said, laughing.

Frank had gone from Holly Sonders, who was wearing the highest heels he had ever seen, to a gaggle of reporters gathered outside the scoring area, to several interviews with breathless local-TV types.

One had asked him if this was the greatest moment of his life. He was tempted to joke that meeting Holly Sonders was pretty great, but he passed on the thought. Then, finally, he had to be interviewed by someone from the USGA for the highlight film that was being made about the week.

Frank was so tired and drained from the match and the heat that he and Slugger had skipped their usual post-round session on the range.

"You need the rest more," Slugger said. "Your golf swing is just fine right now."

His tee time against Rickie Southwick was earlier than he'd expected. He knew that TV would want Southwick's match on the back nine during its window, which was 4:00 to 7:00 p.m.—*Eastern* time. Frank had sort of blanked on the time difference. On the West Coast, Fox would be coming on the air at 1:00 p.m., meaning they would want the Southwick-Baker match on the tenth hole no later than 1:30. And so their tee time was exactly the same time Frank had drawn on Wednesday: 10:48 a.m.

"That's perfect," Slugger had said. "Means we don't have to change our routine at all."

"Except it's probably a pretty good idea if Mr. Forman isn't waiting for us in the locker room again," Frank said.

Slugger laughed at that. "I'd tell you that I'll warn him, only I don't think I need to."

Frank probably would have spent a lot of time lying in bed that night trying to figure out how to deal with his father and Keith Forman—a relationship that was bound to be an issue if he kept winning. But his exhaustion and exhilaration, combined with the specter of Rickie Southwick in the day ahead, kept his mind on golf before he drifted off to sleep.

. . . . .

When Frank walked onto the range the next morning, the first person he encountered was Rickie Southwick, who was on his way off the range. Every golfer has a pre-round routine. Southwick apparently started his earlier than most.

"Hey, that was some win yesterday," Southwick said, stopping to shake hands as they crossed paths. "Birdie-eagle-birdie finish? Wow."

Frank was again tempted to explain the eagle hadn't *really* been an eagle, but decided Southwick didn't actually want to hear about it and was just being polite. Golfers almost *never* want to hear details about someone else's golf. Slugger had explained to him once that, on tour, if you told people you'd shot 79, half wouldn't care and the other half would wish it had been 80.

Southwick was about to become a pro, so Frank was pretty certain he wasn't looking for details on his win the day before. He was really only interested in kicking his butt starting in about an hour.

"Thanks, I finally got going when I had to," he said in response. "You sure made your own win look easy yesterday."

Southwick had won his match on the 14th hole. At this level of golf, a five-and-four win—winning by five holes with four holes to go—was roughly the equivalent of a 49–7 blowout in football.

"Kid was nervous starting out, and I got a quick lead," Southwick said. "See you on the first tee."

Frank thought about that for a second. *He'd* been nervous the day before and allowed Gil Beltke to jump to a quick lead. To some degree the difference was that he'd turned himself around with the tee shot at Number 4. But there was also something to the notion that Beltke didn't have that killer instinct, the extra gear a great player had when he had someone on the ropes.

Southwick had that gear. Frank had seen it firsthand the year before. He knew he'd get a close-up view of it again today.

The good news was that he didn't feel at all nervous. The day before, he'd been jumpy on the range, especially after the locker-room scene between his father and Keith Forman. Now he felt completely calm.

And why not? Forman and Slugger had both pointed out

to him that he was playing with house money. Rickie South-wick, as both the defending champion at the Amateur and the NCAA individual champion, was the dominant figure among the thirty-two players who were still alive.

Frank was no longer the darling he had been a year ago because he was now a known quantity, and seventeen was looked at as a lot older than sixteen. There were seventeen-year-olds who had made it through the PGA Tour's Qualifying School. It wasn't as if Frank was no longer a budding star—the omnipresence of Ron Lawrensen was proof of that—but he had a sense that he'd be on Fox today far more because of his opponent than because of anything he'd done, regardless of the way he had won his match a day earlier.

· · · · ·

The crowd on the first tee was considerably larger than it had been when he and Gil Beltke arrived the day before. Frank spotted his father and his shadow, Ron Lawrensen. His dad gave him a confident grin, which Frank returned. Yesterday, Keith Forman had been the only media member that Frank had seen standing inside the ropes at the start of the Beltke-Baker match. Now there were at least a dozen media members with the red ribbons on their credentials that allowed them to walk inside the ropes. There was also a Fox camera crew and Steve Flesch, who worked "on the ground," following matches for the network. Even though it would be another two hours before Fox went on-air, Flesch was there.

Flesch walked over and shook hands with Southwick, who greeted him like an old friend. Then he came over to say hello to Frank.

"Steve Flesch," he said, shaking hands. "We met Tuesday for a few seconds. Good luck today. If by some chance anyone on my crew gets in your way, or for that matter, if I do, don't hesitate to let us know."

Frank liked him instantly. He knew that he'd been a very good player on tour and was now playing on the over-fifty tour. He was always easily identifiable when he played because he was a lefty. There weren't that many of them out there.

Southwick, as the higher seed, had the honor.

After the starter had introduced him as "the reigning U.S. Amateur and NCAA champion, from Bend, Oregon," he tipped his cap to the crowd and stuck his tee in the ground.

"Let's have a good one, Frank," he said as he stepped back from his ball to go into his pre-shot routine.

"You got it, Rickie," Frank said, smiling because he'd caught himself just before he'd called him "Mr. Southwick."

Southwick hit a perfect tee shot, the ball bounding way down the wide fairway.

Frank didn't even watch it bounce. He was already putting his tee into the ground. "It's just golf," he said to himself, glancing at Forman, who had given him a small nod, nothing more, when he'd walked onto the tee.

"From Perryton, Connecticut, Frank Baker," the starter said.

Not quite as grand an introduction as Southwick had received. Then again, Frank didn't merit that sort of introduction.

He took the club back and swung. As with Southwick's shot, Frank didn't bother to watch it land. He knew it was perfect. He smiled for an instant and thought, *Okay, Rickie, you want a good one, let's have at it.*

And they did.

They both reached the first green in two and made two-putt birdies. Then, for the next fourteen holes, neither one of them was ever more than one-up. Frank bogeyed the fourth to go one-down, making a mental note that his pushed four-iron off the tee was the golf gods telling him that you don't almost ace a 236-yard par-four every day.

Southwick made a rare mistake when he three-putted the sixth for a bogey, and then Frank birdied the ninth to go one-up. As they walked to the tenth tee, he caught himself thinking, *I'm one-up on Rickie Southwick through nine. How about that?* Then he told himself: *Flush that thought. You're here to win.*

As had been the case the day before, they had to wait on the tenth tee. Southwick already had his three-wood out, letting Frank know he was going to go for the green.

Seeing Forman standing to the right of the tee, Frank walked over to him. Beyond that quick nod on the first tee, Forman hadn't said a word to him all day.

"So what d'you think?" Frank said.

"I think if you had any doubt at all that you can beat this guy, it should be gone by now," Forman said. "I also think you shouldn't pay any attention to that three-wood he's got out. He might be baiting you."

Frank hadn't thought about that. It was a good point. Why would Southwick take out a club without seeing where Frank's tee shot ended up? He was about to respond to Forman when he noticed his dad shouldering his way through people to get to the rope.

"Frank!" he whispered, his voice urgent but low because so many people were around. "What are you doing? Stay focused!"

"Easy, Baker. Maybe he needs to stay relaxed," Forman said, half turning to face Frank's dad.

"Maybe you need to stay out of my business!" Frank's dad said angrily.

"Your business?" Forman said. "Last I looked, Frank's the one playing, not you."

"Hey, hey, Dad, do me a favor and cool it," Frank said, seeing his father take a step in Forman's direction.

Forman had taken off his sunglasses as if to say, *Come and get me.*

Before his father could answer, he heard the voice of the match referee.

"Mr. Baker, the tee is yours."

Relieved, Frank turned and saw Slugger right behind him. He'd come over when the shouting match started. Now he put a hand on Frank's shoulder.

"I'm fine," Frank said. "Give me the three-wood."

Then he hit his tee shot about 25 yards left of the green.

He saw Southwick smile, put his three-wood back in the bag, and take out an iron. He laid up safely.

Frank had a virtually impossible shot from where he was because the green was so narrow. He tried to stop the ball but couldn't get under his wedge shot enough, so it rolled well off the far side of the green. When Southwick chipped to four feet from the pin and Frank could barely hold the green with his third shot, he picked up Southwick's ball and tossed it to him, conceding the hole.

The match was even.

As they walked to the 11th tee, Slugger stopped him.

"You need to calm down," he said. "Don't talk to Keith the rest of the way, and don't think about your dad. Just play."

"I'm calm," Frank insisted.

"No, you're not," Slugger said, putting a hand on his chest to keep him from continuing to walk. "Your tee shot was pure anger, and you shouldn't have given him the putt until you missed yours. You had twenty feet—what if you make and he misses and you steal a halve there? You need to clear your head."

Frank knew he was right. The tee shot had been awful, and not taking a crack at his par putt was a total mind block.

"Okay," he said finally.

"Sure?" Slugger said.

Frank nodded.

After that he settled back in, and the next five holes were halved. By the time they got to the 16th tee, it felt as if almost everyone on the property was following their match.

Southwick, who had been pretty chatty and friendly the first nine holes, had gone silent. About the only thing the players had said to each other since the 11th tee was "Nice shot."

Sixteen was the short par-three where Frank's birdie putt had turned the Beltke-Baker match around. Southwick still had the honor on the tee since no one had won a hole since the tenth. The pin was front left, tucked near a bunker. Southwick's tee shot looked perfect coming off the club, but it drifted just a little bit left. It took a funny hop and found the bunker.

"What the . . . ?" Southwick said, clearly stunned. It was the first time all day he had reacted to a shot.

"Middle of the dance floor," Slugger muttered to Frank, handing him the pitching wedge.

Frank knew it would be tough for Southwick to get up-and-down from that bunker. Par suddenly looked like a good score.

Frank did as instructed, landing the ball on the front-center and watching it stop about 15 feet from the hole.

"Perfect," Slugger said, handing him the putter.

It turned out he was right. Southwick's bunker shot flew 20 feet past the cup. His par putt stopped just short, and Frank conceded the bogey putt. He was waiting for Southwick to tell him to pick his ball up—he wasn't likely to three-putt from 15 feet—but Southwick said nothing.

He shrugged, looked the putt over, and cozied it to inside a foot. *Then* Southwick told him to pick it up. He was one-up with two holes to play.

The USGA had moved the tee up by about 30 yards on

17 to tempt players to go for the green in two, the hole playing only 545 yards.

Feeling confident, Frank crushed his tee shot 320 yards up the left side of the fairway. If he'd had one advantage over Southwick, it had been his length. Southwick clearly knew that Frank was going to have a chance to reach the green in two, because he tried to muscle up on his tee shot. When it flew left, Southwick let out an aggravated "Aaaaaaah!"

Frank practically skipped off the tee.

Again, Slugger stopped him.

"You have to think he's going to make birdie," he said. "Take your time getting to the ball—there's no rush. You need to forget what he's doing. You want to close out the match here, think about making three."

Frank knew his coach was right. He had read a book once about Tom Watson's famous duel with Jack Nicklaus at the British Open in 1977. Leading by one on the 18th hole, Watson had hit his third shot to 2 feet, while Nicklaus was 50 feet away.

"I knew," Watson said, "*knew* Jack was going to make that putt and I was going to have to make mine to win."

Sure enough, Nicklaus holed his putt, and Watson, hands shaking, made his two-footer.

"If I'd lost focus for a second, I'd have probably missed," Watson said.

Frank didn't think he was Tom Watson by any means, but he knew he had better figure that Southwick was Jack Nicklaus at that moment.

Southwick had to lay up out of the rough, leaving himself about 80 yards to the flag.

Frank's drive had rolled out so far that he only had 225 yards to the flag.

"Hybrid?" he said to Slugger. "Four-iron?"

"No, you're pumped up," Slugger said. "Five-iron is plenty."

Frank was surprised. He had never hit a five-iron uphill that far in his life. But no one knew his game better than Slugger.

Frank set up over the ball. He took a deep breath, made sure not to overswing, and watched the ball fly right at the green.

"Be right," he said.

Based on the roar up at the green, it was right. He couldn't tell how close he was, but he knew he'd hit a good shot.

As he walked up the fairway, Southwick shot him a thumbs-up. He returned it. Southwick was a class act.

Frank walked up the right side of the fairway while Southwick prepared to hit his third shot and saw why Southwick had acknowledged his effort. He only had about ten feet for eagle.

Southwick clearly wasn't ready to give up. He hit a gorgeous wedge, the ball settling about five feet from the flag. Nicklaus would have been proud.

As they walked onto the green, both players getting a huge round of applause from the gallery, Frank felt a chill go through him. A year ago, he'd played great just to stay close to Southwick. Now he had a putt to beat him.

Approaching the green, Frank took off his glove and put it in his back pocket. To get the right feel on the putter, real golfers almost never putted anything but bare-handed.

"I don't know about you," Slugger said as he handed Frank his putter, "but I'm really hungry. We've been out here forever. Do me a favor and make this."

Frank grinned. "You buying?" he asked.

"In a heartbeat," Slugger said.

Frank marked his ball—carefully swapping it for a buffalo nickel that his father had given him on his twelfth birthday. He handed the ball briefly to Slugger to clean and circled the putt to get a read. It was, he guessed, closer to 12 feet. But it was straight uphill, meaning he didn't have to worry about the speed.

He replaced the ball and picked up his coin, stood behind the ball for a moment to confirm his thought that the ball would die to the right as it approached the cup, took a deep breath, and got over it.

He glanced at the cup once, put his head down, and drew the putter back. For a moment, he thought he'd misread the putt and it was going to stay left of the cup. But his read had been correct. Two feet out, the ball began to fade right and, just before it went too far right, it hit the side of the cup . . . and dropped in.

Frank wasn't sure how to react. He kept his putter in the air for a moment and then saw Southwick walking in his direction, cap off, hand out.

"You're one hell of a player," Southwick said, pulling Frank close so he could whisper in his ear. "I'll see you on tour in a few years. Don't be in a rush."

All Frank could come up with in response was, "Thanks."

Slugger was waiting behind Southwick. He wrapped Frank in a hug and said, "Let's eat."

10

KEITH FORMAN SPENT MOST OF THE BACK
nine beating himself up for what had happened on the tenth tee.
He'd kept his distance from the kid on the front nine because
it had occurred to him driving to the golf course that morning
that he'd probably been lucky that after the Beltke-Baker match
Frank hadn't said something to the media like *Well, my friend
Keith Forman gave me a couple of pep talks that helped me out.*

He knew it wasn't his fault that Frank had walked over to
chat with him during the delay on the tenth tee, but he had
handled the situation with the father about as poorly as possible. At that moment, no matter what he was feeling, he had
to back off. He couldn't make himself part of the story. He'd
seen several other reporters talking to Thomas Baker as the
match went on, and he was convinced they were asking him
about the incident.

Fortunately, no one asked Keith himself about it, which
was a relief, although he'd worried they were going to come at

him if Frank lost, saying something like *The kid's father says you cost him the match.*

He knew now for certain that Thomas Baker was capable of that sort of thing. Frank had bailed him out by playing brilliantly after his tenth-hole meltdown, and he suspected Slugger deserved a good deal of the credit for that.

He stood a few yards away while Steve Flesch, whom he knew well from Flesch's days on the regular Tour, interviewed Frank about his remarkable win. Flesch was a smart guy and would steer clear of the ultimate cliché question in sports TV: *How does it feel to win?*

Keith winced whenever he heard that question. It seemed to him that was the first question asked to every single American who won an Olympic gold medal. How the hell did they think it felt? Great, beyond great! For crying out loud.

But Flesch's first question made Keith flinch.

"You had some trouble on the tenth tee there. What was happening and how'd you get straightened out?"

He saw Frank glance in his direction. "I just lost my concentration for a second," he said. "Instead of thinking about winning the match, I was thinking, *Wow, I'm one-up on Rickie Southwick.* You can't think like that. My swing coach, Slugger Johnston, who's also my caddie today, brought me back to earth walking to the eleventh tee."

Keith let out a big sigh of relief. The kid could have thrown him under the bus, but he hadn't. Even if he'd said the incident was his father's fault, he would have made Keith part of the story. That would have been bad—very bad.

He kept his distance as Frank was led through his media paces—which were quite lengthy, given the magnitude of the upset. He was walking in the direction of the locker room after Frank had finished with the print media—which had become something of a mob since this was going to be *the* story of the day—when he heard someone call his name.

He looked around and saw Rickie Southwick walking up behind him. Southwick was tall, probably about six-four, and had the sort of neatly groomed mini-beard that was very in with the twenty-something set. Keith had noticed that Southwick had graciously done all the post-match interviews he'd been asked to do, starting with Flesch—once Frank was finished—then print media, while they waited on Frank and, finally, a couple of local TVs. Keith was impressed.

Now the dethroned champion walked up, hand extended, and said, "Mr. Forman, I'm Rickie Southwick."

Keith smiled. He was always impressed when a young player didn't just assume that everyone knew who he was. "Please, call me Keith," he said. "Nice to meet you. Tough loss today, but I thought you handled yourself wonderfully with the media, for what it's worth."

Now Southwick smiled. "Losing is part of competing," he said. "That's what my mom always taught me. I've never bought that 'second place sucks' thing. I didn't play badly— the kid just outplayed me at the end." He shook his head. "Although I gotta admit, I still don't know how that ball ended up in the bunker at sixteen."

Keith understood. Luck—both good and bad—was very

much a part of golf, and Southwick had gotten the key piece of bad luck that probably decided the match. "Well, I guess that's why Greg Norman liked to say, 'There's a reason why golf's a four-letter word.'"

Southwick laughed. "He's got that right," he said. "Do you mind if I bend your ear for a minute?"

Before Keith could answer, he saw Sam Olson materialize. Olson worked for IMG, and it was well known that he was going to be Southwick's agent when he turned pro, which, Keith guessed, was pretty much right now.

Without so much as looking at Keith or apologizing for interrupting, Olson put a hand on Southwick's shoulder and said, "Rickie, you've done your media thing. You don't need to answer any more questions. We've got a dinner to get to tonight, remember? Traffic will be awful getting downtown."

Southwick turned and looked the agent in the eye. "Sam, I started this conversation," he said. "And I'm not finished yet. Do you know Keith Forman?"

Olson glanced at Keith. "Yep," he said. "I do. How's it going, Keith?"

"Fine," Keith said, accepting the weakly offered handshake. He was thinking of asking where they'd met since he knew they hadn't, but he was far more interested in what Southwick wanted to tell him.

"Try not to take too long, Rickie," Olson finally said, in a much less strident tone. Clearly he didn't want to upset his client-to-be. "I'll meet you in the locker room."

Southwick nodded and waited for Olson to walk away.

"Sorry," he said to Keith. "Sam can be rude sometimes."

"Sam's an agent—that's who they are and what they do," Keith said. "By the way, he and I have never met. He made that up."

Southwick shrugged. "Like you said, he's an agent. But that does lead me to what I wanted to say to you."

Keith waited. Southwick plowed on.

"I saw what happened on the tenth tee," he said. "I didn't hear the exchange, but I did see Baker walk over to you and the father charge over there."

"No big deal," Keith said.

Southwick put up his hand. "I know it's none of my business, but I think this kid's going to be a star and not just because he beat me. I could see it last year. You obviously see something in him, or you wouldn't be out here walking eighteen holes with him two days in a row."

Keith wondered how in the world Southwick knew he'd walked with Frank the day before when he'd been on the golf course.

Southwick read his mind. "Gil and I are good friends. We both read your stuff. You're one of the few guys covering the Tour who writes regularly about non-stars, and you aren't afraid to throw a punch." He took a breath, then continued. "So I'm going to tell you something you probably already know. That father is a problem. That's the word in the locker room already. And if you think Sam's bad news, wait until you get to know Ron Lawrensen. He tried to sign me when I was a sophomore. I won't even tell you what he offered, but let's put it this way: my dad told him never to even *speak* to us again."

Keith nodded, not wanting to interrupt.

"If you're working a story on Frank, that's good, but if you've got his ear at all—which I suspect you do since he went to you on ten—try to keep the dad and Lawrensen from ruining him. He seems like a really good kid."

Keith was floored that Southwick knew so much, even though golf tended to be both a running soap opera and a constant rumor mill. Beyond that, he was amazed that Southwick would *care* enough to stop him and talk to him. Golfers were generally pretty selfish athletes. They almost had to be, because if they weren't obsessed with their own success, then no one else—outside of family, their caddie, their agent, and their coach—was going to be.

Here, though, was Southwick, clearly concerned about the future of another player—even just a few minutes after that player had booted him from the U.S. Amateur in a stunning upset. Rickie Southwick, he decided, was a really good kid himself.

"I hear you," Keith said. "That's part of the reason I'm here. His swing coach, Slugger Johnston—"

"The guy caddying for him?"

"Right. We were college teammates. He called me to see if I could maybe get in the kid's ear a little. There may be a story here when all is said and done, but I'm out here because Slugger's got the same concerns that you do—and more."

"Good," Southwick said. "Clearly Frank likes you, so that's

a start. It looks like you're gonna have a battle ahead, though. And tell Frank if he ever wants to talk to someone who's dealt with a lot of what he's got ahead, he can always call me."

They exchanged cell phone numbers and shook hands again.

"Good luck," Keith said as Southwick started to walk away.

"Thanks, man," Southwick said. "I'll need it."

That was the last thing he said. It was also the first thing he'd said that Keith disagreed with. Rickie Southwick was only twenty-two, but he clearly had a pretty good handle on life in the spotlight already.

Keith could only hope the same would be true of Frank in five years. For now, though, he knew he had to focus on trying to help Slugger keep the kid on the right path for the next four days.

It would not be easy.

11

FOR THE SECOND STRAIGHT DAY, FRANK WAS too worn out to hit balls with Slugger once he finished with the media.

If he had thought he'd been asked to do a lot after the Beltke match, it was nothing compared to what he faced after beating the defending champion.

Most of the questions were easy—TV easy, he'd heard Keith Forman call them. There was the inevitable "How does it feel?" question. There was the ever-popular "Has it sunk in yet?" There was a question about Matthew Bryan, who would be his opponent the next day in the round of 16.

Frank almost said, "I've never heard of him"—which was true—but stopped himself, knowing that would come off as a putdown. Instead he said, "I've never played with him, but I've heard good things about his game."

He'd heard nothing about his game.

The only tricky moment came when Steve DiMeglio from *USA Today* asked a question during the scrum with the print media, after Frank had stepped off the podium. Forman had warned him that there were always writers who didn't want to ask an important question with the TV cameras rolling.

Sure enough, about a half dozen guys surrounded him as he came down the steps after a tournament PR guy had cut off the questions up there.

Ron Lawrensen was trying to push his way into the circle, saying, "Come on, fellas, he's done. He's got to play again tomorrow."

Before any of the writers could protest, Frank held up a hand. "I'm fine, Ron," he said, pointedly using his first name instead of calling him Mr. Lawrensen. "I'll meet you and Dad in the locker room in a few."

Lawrensen backed off.

Frank noticed his dad was nowhere in sight. Neither was Forman. It occurred to him that they might be somewhere having it out.

Gene Wang, from the *Washington Post*—Frank knew this because he could read the name on his credential—asked the question Frank had been surprised no one had asked him earlier: What had Southwick said to him when they'd embraced at the end of the match?

Frank explained how gracious Southwick had been and how he'd said, "I'll see you out on tour in a few years."

"Are you willing to wait a few years?" someone in the back asked. "There are rumors out there you might skip college and turn pro."

"I'm going to college," Frank said. "I'm just not sure where yet. I've still got another year of high school."

Then Steve DiMeglio—whom Frank recognized because he was a frequent Golf Channel guest—asked his question: "What happened on ten?"

Frank said he'd already talked about ten.

"No, not the tee shot," DiMeglio said. "The thing over by the ropes with your father and Keith Forman?"

Frank had wondered if he would get asked about that. But when no one asked him on the podium, he thought he was in the clear.

"Oh that," Frank said, stalling for time. "It was a misunderstanding, that's all."

"How so?" DiMeglio pressed.

"It was my fault," Frank said. "I went over just to say hello to Mr. Forman since we were waiting. My dad thought he had started the conversation and was concerned that might break my concentration. Keith—Mr. Forman—was trying to explain what had happened to my dad, and my dad got a little hot. He gets kind of tight when I'm playing."

DiMeglio dropped it at that point and, fortunately, no one followed up. A few minutes later, Frank escaped—more or less unscathed.

He suspected that dealing with his father and Lawrensen would not be as easy.

• • • • •

The locker room was almost empty when Frank walked inside, happy to finally feel some cool air. He had been dealing with the media for a solid forty-five minutes, meaning all the day's matches were over. All the losers had cleared out pretty quickly. Among the sixteen players still alive, most were either on the driving range or had gone back to their hotel rooms to rest.

The only other player Frank saw was Nathan Smith, who was on his way out. They'd played nine holes together on Sunday after running into each other on the tenth tee during a practice round. Smith was a "true" amateur in that he had a job and didn't play golf for a living. He had won the U.S. Mid-Amateur Championship four times. The Mid-Am was for players twenty-five and over. Slugger had explained that those who played in it had either failed as pros and regained their amateur status or had opted not to turn pro.

"A lot of them can really play," Slugger said. "Even if they don't do it full-time."

That was true of Smith. He'd shot 33 on the back nine Sunday and made it look easy.

"Hey, what a win!" Smith said, pumping Frank's hand when he walked in.

"Thanks," Frank said. Then, embarrassed that he didn't know the answer, he asked, "How'd you do?"

"Squeaked by, won on seventeen," Smith said. "I was a couple down at the turn but managed to get my act together in time."

When a player as good as Smith admitted he'd "gotten his

act together," it probably meant he'd blitzed the last eight holes of the match.

"Hey, if we both win twice more, we get to play each other," Smith added. "If we do, go easy on me, huh?"

Frank laughed. "Yeah, right."

He'd seen Smith's name in his half of the draw when he first looked at it but had completely forgotten about it because he'd been so focused on Southwick—and because the semifinals were *so* far down the road.

They shook hands again and wished each other luck the next day, and Smith took off. Frank walked to the row where his locker was, expecting to see Slugger, his dad, and Lawrensen waiting for him. They were. But there were three other men waiting there, too.

Frank pulled up short. He suspected Lawrensen had brought the surprise guests.

"Thought you'd never get here," Slugger said, giving him a guarded look. "Ron brought some guys who just wanted to say hello. They know you have to get out of here and get some rest."

The message was hardly subtle, but Frank was grateful.

Lawrensen introduced the three men: one was from Callaway, the club and golf-ball maker; one was from Nike, which didn't make golf equipment anymore but still had plenty of guys under contract to wear their swoosh; and the last was from ESPN. Since the sports network didn't televise golf anymore, that was a surprise.

All three gushed about how well he'd played that day.

They couldn't wait to get to know him better, but they knew now wasn't the time. He had a golf tournament to win in the next four days, didn't he?

Yammer, yammer.

Frank tried to keep his answers short and sweet, changing out of his golf shoes amid all the gushing. All he could think about was how starved he was—he hadn't eaten anything besides a couple of candy bars since he'd grabbed breakfast in the player dining area at nine-thirty that morning. He glanced at his watch. It was a few minutes after four.

The words of the three men were blending together as he picked a towel off the bench and wiped his face. Finally, he stood up and looked at his father as if his three new friends were invisible.

"Dad, I gotta pee," he said. "And I'm starving. Can we please get out of here?"

He could see that his father wasn't happy with the fact that his son was being borderline rude—at best—to these three nice men who apparently wanted to throw a lot of money in their direction at some point in the near future.

"Go ahead" was all he said.

As Frank walked away he could hear his father apologizing.

"I'm really sorry, fellas, he's just had a long day . . ."

That Frank could agree with. The best day he'd ever had on a golf course, and all he could think about was getting away from this place and stopping at a McDonald's. He would order a double hamburger and a large fries. No, make that two double hamburgers. Maybe a milkshake, too.

· · · · ·

Frank almost literally had to beg to get the Mickey-D's stop. Lawrensen had his own car, and the plan was for him to meet the Bakers and Slugger at six-thirty in the restaurant on the lower level of the JW Marriott where they were staying.

That sounded fine to Frank, but he didn't want to wait two more hours—minimum—to get something in his stomach.

"You don't need any junk food at this point," his dad said.

Slugger was driving, with Thomas Baker in the front seat and Frank stretched out in the back.

"Dad, I'm not a swimmer or a runner," Frank said. "I'm a golfer."

They were, not surprisingly, stuck in L.A. traffic heading downtown.

His father didn't answer. Instead, he started going off about how rude Frank had been to the three guys in the locker room.

"Cut him some slack, Thomas," Slugger said, surprising Frank, because Slugger almost never contradicted his dad in any way. At the club Slugger never addressed any members by first name until invited to do so. As far as he knew, his dad had never told Slugger to call him Thomas. Then again, they weren't at the club.

"Why?" his dad answered.

Frank saw Slugger shoot his father a look that said, *Are you kidding?*

"Because Frank just won the match of his life," Slugger finally said. "He won two draining matches in a little more than twenty-four hours. He did media for forty-five minutes—all of it in this god-awful heat. I told you before we even went in there that this probably wasn't the time for him to meet those guys. It's not as if he's turning pro tomorrow. There's plenty of time for all of this stuff later."

Frank knew his dad was about to lose it—he wasn't used to Slugger talking to him this way. "By the way, Dad," he interrupted, "what's with the guy from ESPN? They don't even cover golf anymore."

"They don't cover *tournament* golf," his dad answered. "Ron has pitched them the idea of a documentary covering your first year as a pro. They actually have a crew out here shooting some stuff for background just in case it happens."

Now it was Frank's turn to be steamed. "Hang on, Dad. Mr. Lawrensen is selling a documentary on me as a pro *now*? Bit premature, no?"

"Not necessarily," his father said. "You win here or make the finals and get to the Masters, we'll need to seriously consider our options after that."

"You think I should turn pro before I graduate from high school? Seriously?"

"You'll graduate two months after the Masters. Worst case,

we wait until the U.S. Open—since you'll also qualify for it if you win here."

Frank couldn't help but think about what Keith Forman had said to his dad back on the tenth tee when his dad had told the reporter to stay out of *his* business.

Your business? Last I looked, Frank's the one playing, not you.

Suddenly, Frank heard his father say, "McDonald's, next exit. Pull off, Slugger. Let's get the hero of the day a hamburger and some fries. He's earned it."

Frank, hearing sincerity in his father's voice, said, "Thanks, Dad. I appreciate it."

If he'd said anything beyond that it would have been along the lines of *That's the dad I grew up loving.*

Even so, he was pretty sure the incident on the tenth hole was going to come up before the night was over. He hoped he wouldn't lose his temper and start quoting Forman.

It's not just my business, he thought to himself. *It's my life.*

He hoped.

Meanwhile, his current version of Nirvana—the McDonald's drive-through window—loomed.

12

AFTER THE MATCH THAT DAY, KEITH FORMAN decided against even attempting to talk to Frank at the golf course. While Frank was still scrumming with a handful of guys, Keith saw Slugger, Frank's father, and the dirtbag agent walking into the locker room with three other men. He recognized one—the Callaway rep—but not the other two, although the large swoosh on one guy's shirt suggested he was from Nike. The third was anyone's guess.

Clearly, going into the locker room would only lead to another confrontation.

When Frank finished with the scrum, he was led away by a PR person and a couple of security guards. It had now come to that—the USGA had decided the kid needed security to escort him 50 yards to the locker room. Keith decided he'd call Frank later to catch up. He then had a completely paranoid thought: What if the old man insisted on looking at the kid's phone? At this point, anything was possible.

"Hey, Keith," a voice said. He looked up and saw Steve

DiMeglio coming in his direction. This couldn't be good. DiMeglio had covered golf for *USA Today* for years. He was out on tour more than just about anyone. He knew his way around campus, as the saying went.

"Steve, what's up?" he said, trying to sound casual.

"What was the deal with you and the kid's old man back on ten?"

"No deal, really," Keith said. "His swing coach is an old college teammate. He introduced me to the kid a few weeks ago, and we hit it off—I think. He walked over to say hello while they were waiting, and the father somehow thought I was trying to interview him during the match. Which, of course, was ridiculous."

"Looked pretty heated."

"Only for a second. It's all good."

DiMeglio looked at him. Clearly he was still suspicious.

"If you've already interviewed him, how come you haven't written anything about him? Are you writing today?"

Keith was flattered to be reminded that most of the golf media read his columns pretty regularly. He was also trapped.

"I'm working on a longer piece. I'm honestly not sure when I'll write. Of course if he wins here, I'll write something—I'm just not sure what."

"Well, you better be careful ESPN doesn't horn in and make some deal where the kid doesn't talk to anyone except them."

Keith had now gone from feeling trapped to being baffled.

"What the hell are you talking about?" he asked.

DiMeglio smiled. He seemed to like knowing something Keith didn't know.

"Didn't you see Arnie Pearlman out there today watching? Hell, he walked almost the entire way with the old man and that dirtbag Lawrensen. He was wearing an ESPN logo that was impossible to miss."

"I guess I was paying more attention to what was going on inside the ropes than outside," Keith said. "And, for the record, it's to your credit that you use the exact same word to describe Lawrensen that I do."

"He's about as bad as it gets. One of those guys who gets upset if you call him an agent."

"What in the world does he think he is?"

"A player representative."

"Oh God, one of those. But seriously, what are you talking about with ESPN?"

"I'm told Lawrensen and the old man are already negotiating a deal of some kind with ESPN. No idea what it's about, but they want in with the kid in some way, shape, or form."

Keith wondered why Slugger hadn't mentioned this to him. A potential TV deal struck him as being just the kind of incentive that could drive Frank's egomaniac dad to do something truly stupid—like make his son turn pro way too soon.

"Thanks, Steve," he said.

DiMeglio gave him a look. "You sure you aren't up to something?"

"Minute I am, you'll be the first one to know."

"Yeah, right," DiMeglio said. "I need to go smoke. It's been hours."

"Stuff'll kill you," Keith said.

"This job'll kill me first," said DiMeglio, who could find a cloud in every silver lining.

He walked off and Keith realized he was starving. He went down the hill to the media tent. But it was after four o'clock and there was no food to be found.

He settled for a cup of coffee, sat down with his laptop, and began to write. He had a lot he wanted to say about the day—to himself—before he had time to forget.

· · · · ·

In an hour he had written almost two thousand words on the events of the day. He walked to his car and decided that the ride back to his hotel—which would take a while during rush hour—was a good time to try to catch Frank. He was hoping the kid had gone back to his room to rest before dinner.

Before he started the car, he texted Frank. **Good time to talk?**

Just as he was wheeling out of the lot, his phone buzzed.

"Hey, Prodigy," Keith said, picking up the call. He'd gotten someone at the car rental place to sync his phone with the car's Bluetooth so he could be hands-free. "How you feeling?"

"Great . . . and not so great," Frank answered.

"Let me guess," Keith said. "You feel great about winning

the match—and you should—but not great about Lawrensen shoving those three losers down your throat in the locker room."

"How'd you know about that?"

"I'm a reporter, Frank. I know everything."

"You know, I really think it's this guy Lawrensen pushing Dad as much as anything," Frank said. "He's got Dad convinced that he's some kind of deal-making genius and the only thing keeping us from being instantly rich is me not turning pro."

"What was up with the ESPN guy?"

"Oh, man. Some crazy notion that they're going to follow me around for a year when I turn pro. Lawrensen and Dad want me to announce it after the Masters—if I get in—or, 'worst case,' as they put it, after Shinnecock."

Shinnecock Hills Golf Club, on Long Island, New York, was the site of next year's U.S. Open.

"What if you *don't* make Augusta?"

"They still want me to turn pro. Lawrensen apparently told Dad that getting to Augusta would be nice but that my win over Southwick will make me a hot property regardless. That's why he had those three guys in the locker room."

"Sounds pretty bad."

"Yeah, but I've got worse news."

"What's that?"

"Dad wants to fire Slugger."

"What?"

"He wants to wait until the Amateur is over and then fire him. Lawrensen is telling him he can get a big-name guy to take over, and Double Eagle will pay for it until the money starts to roll in."

"Does Slugger know?"

"No. Dad didn't bring it up until we were out of the car and Slugger had gone to his room. He made me promise not to say anything to him."

"Well, he didn't make *me* promise."

There was a long pause at the other end of the phone. Keith was pretty sure Frank was going to ask him to keep the secret at least until the end of the week.

"You're right," Frank finally said. "He didn't."

Keith told Frank he'd talk to him later; then he hung up, pulled over, and dialed Slugger. The hot shower and the room-service dinner he had been looking forward to were now out of the question.

Slugger picked up on the first ring. "About time," Slugger said.

"Forget about time," Forman said. "We need to talk."

"Okay, talk."

"Not on the phone. I'll be at your hotel in forty. I'll meet you in the bar."

He didn't wait for an answer. He cut the call and turned the car east, heading in the direction of the highway.

· · · · ·

Keith got to the JW Marriott at around six. He knew that most of the players and their families were staying at the plush upscale

Marriott because the USGA had been able to arrange a special rate for the week.

He didn't bother searching for self-park, just valeted the car and resigned himself to paying the forty-nine-dollar tab. Slugger was sitting at the far corner of the bar waiting for him.

"So what the hell is so important that you spent an hour in traffic to get here?" Slugger asked as Keith sat down.

"Hang on a sec," Keith said. "I haven't eaten anything since this morning."

"What?" Slugger said. "No free food in the media tent?"

"I'm sure there was, but I didn't get back in there until after four because I was *working* and it was long gone."

He got the bartender's attention, ordered a glass of wine, and asked for a menu.

"So?" Slugger said, clearly running out of patience.

"So the kid just gave me a heads-up about something. He said that after you guys got back here this afternoon and you went up to your room, his dad and Lawrensen were talking about firing you and bringing in some big-name teacher to take your place."

Slugger's eyes narrowed. He studied Keith's face for a moment. "You're serious, aren't you?" he finally said.

"Serious as a ball out-of-bounds."

Slugger took a long sip of the beer that was in front of him just as the bartender came back with Keith's glass of wine and a menu.

"When?" Slugger asked.

"Soon as the tournament's over for Frank. Could be to-morrow, could be Sunday."

Slugger took another sip of the beer, clearly trying to grasp what he'd just been told. "What do you think I should do?"

Keith had been thinking about that in the car. "First, you gotta tell Frank not to worry about it right now and that you and I have everything under control."

"We do?"

Keith shook his head. "Not at all. But we can't let the kid be distracted by this."

"Got it." Slugger was about to take his last swallow when he froze, the beer midway to his lips. He put the glass down.

"What?" Keith asked.

Slugger just nodded in the direction of the door. "We've got company," he said.

. . . . .

Thomas Baker and Ron Lawrensen headed straight to where Keith and Slugger were sitting. By the time Keith turned in his chair to see who Slugger had been staring at, the father and agent were almost on top of them.

"Forman, you can't keep away from us, can you?" was Baker's opening line.

"Slugger, whose side are you on?" Lawrensen said in a snarky tone.

"Are we choosing sides now?" Keith said. He had quickly

decided that the less Slugger got involved in this, the better. "I haven't done that since the sixth grade."

Baker was looking like he wanted to throw Lawrensen out of his way so he could get right up in Keith's face.

"You know exactly what we're talking about, Forman," Baker said. "My son might buy into your act, and you clearly have Slugger fooled, but Ron and I aren't seventeen and we aren't selling sweaters for a living either. So the sooner you get out of L.A., the better it'll be for you and"—he nodded in Slugger's direction—"for your old teammate."

Keith didn't back down. "You know something, Baker? How pathetic is it that a reporter and a golf pro are more interested in protecting your son than you are? You've thrown in with the worst of the worst with your chum here, and all the two of you care about is turning your kid into a human ATM."

He glared at Baker, who seemed to be thinking of an answer. But suddenly, instead of responding, he swung a wild right hook directed at Keith's jaw. Keith saw it coming at the last second, dodged the blow, and was only grazed. But as he stood up from the barstool, Lawrensen actually grabbed him from behind, holding his arms. Baker's next punch was to the stomach, and it buckled Keith's knees.

He was sliding to the floor when he saw Slugger grabbing Baker from behind, yelling, "Hey, stop, stop! What in the hell is wrong with you?"

Out of the corner of his eye, Keith glimpsed the bartender grabbing the phone. She was, no doubt, calling security. He had one thought: *I'm still not going to get anything to eat.*

13

HAVING FILLED UP ON MCDONALD'S, FRANK had excused himself from the dinner meeting and was drifting off to sleep watching the Dodgers and Mets when his cell phone rang. He saw Slugger's number and picked up.

"Houston, we've got a problem," Slugger said.

"Keith told you?" Frank said.

"Yeah, he told me, but we've got a more immediate problem than that."

He told Frank about the altercation in the bar and how security had tossed out all four participants. "My pal got punched in the stomach and never got to eat anything," he said, not able to resist a chuckle. "But that's not the worst of it."

"What's the worst of it?"

"Your dad fired me on the spot after I grabbed him to keep him from hitting Keith again."

Frank's first thought wasn't about Slugger but about himself. "So who's going to caddie for me tomorrow?"

After a pause, Slugger said, "Right now, your dad."

"I'll lose ten-and-eight."

The worst score a golfer could lose by in match play was ten-and-eight. It meant you lost ten straight holes to your opponent and didn't need to play the eight remaining because you couldn't make up the difference.

"No, you won't. You have to just stay focused on your match and not worry about any of this stuff."

"*How* can I not worry about any of this stuff?" Frank asked.

Slugger didn't have an answer to that.

Frank made a decision. "Where's my dad now?"

"The only thing I can tell you for sure is that he's not in the bar," Slugger said.

"I'll call you in a little while," Frank said.

He hung up and sat on the edge of the bed, feeling a sense of panic.

He tried to decide whether he should just go and knock on his father's door or call him first. He decided to go door-knocking. He pulled on a pair of sweats and walked from room 811 to room 819 and knocked.

No answer. He tried again. Nothing. He pulled out his phone, then had one more idea. His dad and Lawrensen had been intending to eat dinner. They would still have needed to eat even after they got tossed from the bar. So he took the elevator down to the lower level, where there was an upscale restaurant. Having failed at the bar, he figured there was a good chance his dad and Lawrensen had decided to go there.

He was right.

The two men were seated at a booth in the back of the room. The problem was the maître d'.

"Young man, I'm very sorry," he said in a polite but firm tone, "but we require appropriate attire."

Frank thought for a second about explaining to him that he had no intention of ordering a meal, that he just needed to talk to the two men in the back for a moment. He also thought about shouting to get his dad's attention. He decided against both. He wanted to sit down and have as calm a conversation as was possible.

"I'll be back in five," he said, not waiting for a response.

He went up to his room and changed into the one pair of long pants he'd brought on the trip and a collared shirt. Neither his dad nor Lawrensen was wearing a jacket, so he knew he didn't need one. He rode the elevator back down and presented himself again to the maître d'.

"I'm meeting those two men in the back booth," he said, pointing.

"Right this way," the host said, and walked Frank to the table.

Neither his father nor Lawrensen noticed him until he was standing in front of them. They were clearly engrossed in their conversation.

"Frank?" his father said. "I thought you said you weren't hungry."

"I'm not," Frank said.

Without waiting for an invitation, he more or less pushed Lawrensen into the booth so he could sit down next to him. He wanted to be able to look his father in the eye across the table.

"I know," his father said, now nodding. "Slugger called you."

"Did you think he wouldn't?" Frank asked. "He's only been my coach for three years. You fire him in the middle of the U.S. Amateur and you don't expect him to call me?"

He paused. He had a lot more to say, but he wanted to keep this as nonconfrontational as possible.

"I assume he told you what happened?" his father said.

Frank nodded.

"Then do you understand *why* I had to fire him?"

"Dad, think about it: Wouldn't you intervene in a two-on-one fight? Whatever you think of Mr. Forman, he and Slugger have been friends since college. Slugger didn't slug you, he just broke up the fight."

"He sided with the enemy," Lawrensen said, the first time he'd opened his mouth since Frank's arrival.

"Why is Mr. Forman the enemy?" Frank said, turning his head to look at the agent. "He came to Perryton as a favor to Slugger back in June because Slugger thought I could use a bit of unbiased advice on where I'm going next."

"That's not what you told me," his dad said. "You said it was your idea, not Slugger's, to talk to Forman. Advice is what you have me for."

Frank almost laughed out loud. "Dad, you think you're unbiased? You shouldn't be unbiased—you're my dad! Plus, do you honestly think you know anything about what it's really like on the PGA Tour?"

"Forman never came anywhere near playing in the PGA Tour," Lawrensen said.

"No, but he *lives* on the Tour," Frank said "He knows everyone and everything."

"He just sees you as a potential big story, nothing more," Frank's dad said.

"And what does *he* see me as, Dad?" Frank said, nodding at Lawrensen. "You think he's hanging around because I'm a charity case?"

"He's doing his job," Thomas Baker said.

"Exactly," Frank said, almost climbing out of his seat. "Mr. Forman first met me as a favor to a friend. He hasn't written a word about me—"

"Yet," Lawrensen put in.

"Okay, yet. But, believe me, Dad, I trust him a *lot* more than I trust your adviser here."

"You're completely wrong," his father said. "And watch your tone, son."

"Tell you what," Frank said. "Let's change the subject—at least for now. This actually isn't why I came down here."

• • • • •

Frank's father sat back in his chair just as a waiter showed up carrying two platters, each with a large steak. After filling the men's wineglasses, the waiter asked Frank if he wanted anything. Frank declined and the waiter left.

"Okay, Frank, what'd you come down here for if not to argue about Slugger?"

"Oh, I came down here to argue about Slugger," Frank said. "You just turned it into an argument about Mr. Forman."

"Fine, then. Go ahead."

"If either one of you really cares about me winning tomorrow, Slugger's got to be on the bag," Frank said. "We can discuss his future when this tournament's over. Not now."

"I know your game just as well as Slugger does," his dad said. "You'll be fine."

"A, no, you don't—not even close. And B—no, I won't. Not even close." He looked imploringly at his father. "Dad, can we have a few minutes alone, please?"

For a moment his father said nothing. Then he looked at Lawrensen. "Give us some space," he said.

Lawrensen clearly wasn't pleased. "I'll go to the bathroom," he said. "Back in five."

"Make it ten," Thomas Baker said.

The steaks would be getting cold by then, but Frank didn't care. He stood up to let Lawrensen out of the booth. For a second, Frank was tempted to eat Lawrensen's steak.

"Look, Frank, I know you're upset," his dad said when they were alone, in the soothing voice he always used when he was trying to calm Frank down.

"Dad, I'm not just upset about Slugger. I'm upset about

us—you and me. You used to be my best friend. Now this Lawrensen guy is your best friend and your first concern seems to be keeping him happy."

"That's not true," his father said, his voice rising. "You know you're my first concern—always."

"Then how could you fire Slugger—now or next week? You know how much he's helped me. We wouldn't be sitting here right now if not for him."

His father put down his knife and fork and sat back in the booth.

"Okay," he finally said. "Slugger stays. I'll explain it to Ron."

"Dad, you don't have to explain anything to Ron," Frank said. "But thanks. I love you."

"I love you, too, Frank. I hope you know that I only want what's best for you."

Lawrensen returned.

Frank stood up to go.

"You straighten him out?" Lawrensen said as he sat down.

"Not exactly," Thomas Baker said, looking at his son. "I think he straightened me out a little bit."

Frank was smiling as he left the room.

. . . . .

He was still in the elevator when a text popped up on his phone. It was from Slugger.

Don't know what you said or did, but it worked. I'm still your coach and your caddie at least for the rest of this week.

Frank called him after he'd gotten back to the room and flopped down on the bed. "Did he tell you what happened?"

"No. He just said he'd had a change of heart, at least as far as this week was concerned. You can tell me about it in the car tomorrow. We'll leave a little earlier and let your dad and Lawrensen ride together."

"Okay. Maybe we can grab a few minutes with Keith before they get there."

"Not sure that's a great idea. What if your dad and Lawrensen show up?"

"Don't care," Frank said. "Really don't care. Tell Keith to meet us in player dining at nine-thirty, all right?"

His match was scheduled to tee off at 11:36. Thirty minutes with Forman would still leave him his usual ninety to warm up.

"See you in the lobby at eight-thirty," Slugger said.

"I'll tell Dad we're leaving at nine," Frank said with a chuckle.

"Don't do that," Slugger said. "Let's not push our luck."

Frank's chuckle turned into a laugh. "Our luck is already sitting on a cliff."

"True enough," Slugger said. "Get some sleep."

14

KEITH FORMAN DID NOT GET A GOOD NIGHT'S sleep.

He knew he was caught in the middle of something he simply didn't belong in at all. He was a reporter, not an interventionist, and yet he'd intervened. He might have cost Slugger his job—not just as the kid's coach but also at the golf club if Thomas Baker decided to really make it ugly—and Keith now found himself in a full-scale brouhaha.

He had no problem being at odds with anyone if it had something to do with a story he'd written or was trying to write. But being in a fight with a newsmaker, one that involved punches being thrown, was a bad thing—regardless of circumstances. Putting Frank into a choose-sides situation, even if he had the best of intentions, was unfair to the kid and unprofessional on his part. Plus, his stomach was killing him.

Other than that, the week had gone well.

Before bed, he had gotten a text from Slugger telling him he would still be coaching Frank the next day. That, at least, was encouraging, although Slugger's future employment was clearly in doubt.

Still, he smiled when he read the rest of the text: **Frank wants 2 meet for breakfast in player dining at 9:30. We're going to leave hotel 30 mins b4 dad and his twin. Should give us some time.**

Keith considered that for a moment. He had a vision of the senior Baker and the omnipresent Ron Lawrensen bursting into the dining room but didn't really care that much anymore. And, if he did get thirty minutes with Frank, he could at least be a reporter during that time and try to get back to what he was really supposed to be doing.

He finally fell into a restless sleep sometime after midnight—he wasn't sure when—but the phone started ringing with his wake-up call about fifteen minutes later. Except it wasn't fifteen minutes later—it was seven o'clock, as he'd requested. He groaned, fell out of bed, and decided to skip his run. His brain was telling him he could use the endorphins, but his body was telling him to take a long, hot shower.

His body won the argument. He was in the car by eight-fifteen, wanting to be a few minutes early if there was no traffic, rather than late if there was. He pulled into the parking lot near the media tent a half hour later and walked up the hill to the clubhouse.

Player dining was down a long hallway and, arriving five minutes early, he nodded at the security guard and decided to grab some food from the buffet and find a table before Slugger and Frank arrived.

He was on his way inside the room when the security guard, who was actually a volunteer, not a rent-a-cop, stepped in front of him and said, "Sorry, sir, you're not allowed in here."

Keith sighed. He pointed at his credential and the lettering down the side. "What does PD mean?" he asked, pointing at the two letters.

"Player dining," the man said.

"And where exactly are we standing?"

"Yeah, but you have to be accompanied by a player."

"Where on this credential does it say that?" Keith asked. He was getting angry.

"This is what I was told," the guy said.

"No, you weren't," Keith said. "Not by anyone who knows what they're doing."

He was done. He took a step to his right to maneuver around the guy, who promptly grabbed his arm.

Keith lost it. "You had better get that hand off me right now or—"

"Or he'll probably kick your butt," Slugger's voice said over Keith's shoulder.

He and Frank had walked up during the argument. Both were grinning, especially Slugger, who had witnessed a number of Keith's run-ins with security types through the years.

The guard looked at Frank, recognized him, and began apologizing profusely. "If he'd just told me he was meeting you—"

"Sir, you have my deepest sympathy for having to deal with my hotheaded friend," Slugger said.

They all walked inside, leaving the guard sputtering, "Good luck, Mr. Baker," in Frank's direction.

"I wish you hadn't shown up," Keith said.

"Oh, I'm so glad we did," Slugger said. "I love seeing you get all wound up like that."

· · · · ·

They sat down to eat a few minutes later after going through the buffet. Frank and Slugger filled Keith in on the post-bar-fight events of the previous evening.

"Gutsy maneuver, Frank," Keith said. "What do you think the fallout will be?"

"Don't know," the kid said. "Won't know till we get home or at least till we're on the plane. He *does* want me to win. And, believe it or not, he does love me. That's why he backed down on Slugger."

"I'm sure you're right," Keith said. "And I think the smart thing to do right now is follow his example and not worry about anything except winning your match today. You think you can do that?"

"I can do it," Frank said. "If I lose, it'll be because the other guy's better. I'm good at focusing once I'm on the golf course, no matter what."

"Unless there's a good-looking girl out there," Slugger said.

"Yeah, I do sometimes get distracted if that happens," Frank said, smiling.

"I'll remember that just in case I ever need you to lose," Keith said.

They all laughed. It was a good sound to hear. It was clear to Keith that Slugger knew which buttons to push with the kid. All the more reason why it was important that he not get fired—no matter what happened the rest of this week.

. . . . .

Frank wasn't lying about his ability to focus once he teed it up. He birdied the first hole to go one-up on Matthew Bryan. From there, he never looked back. It seemed to Keith as if Bryan, who was a rising junior at Duke, felt like reaching the round of 16 was all he could possibly expect. Playing the young phenom who had beaten the defending champion, he looked intimidated early, falling behind four-down at the turn.

Bryan played better on the back nine and actually pulled within two-down after birdieing 15. But Frank birdied his favorite hole on the golf course—16—to win the match three-and-two. Keith could tell by the look on his face as he shook hands with his opponent that he was disappointed that he'd allowed Bryan to hang around until the 16th hole.

As the carts pulled up to ferry the players back to the clubhouse, Keith had a few seconds with Frank. He knew that Baker and Lawrensen were already on a clubhouse-bound cart.

"You want to ride on the back?" Frank asked.

"No need. Pulling up to the clubhouse and having your dad and Lawrensen see me on the back of your cart would be like waving red in front of the proverbial bull."

Frank nodded. Slugger was already on a four-seater cart with Bryan's caddie. Bryan was in another cart.

"Didn't play so well on the back nine today, did I?" Frank said.

Keith knew that's what he was focusing on.

"Ever hear of Dean Smith?" he said.

"The basketball coach?"

"Yeah. He used to say all the time that a one-point win was fine with him, regardless, because it meant you won. You had an easy win—you were always in control. Enjoy it."

"Tell that to my dad, will ya?" Frank said.

"Good idea," Keith said. "I'm sure he's dying to hear what I think right about now."

They both laughed. Frank climbed onto the cart.

"Remember," Keith said. "You're in the quarterfinals. That was your goal for today. Period."

The cart pulled away and Frank waved as it headed toward the clubhouse. Keith started on foot in that direction. The weather was cooler than it had been, so he didn't mind a little extra walking.

"Hey, Forman," someone said, coming up next to him, hand extended. "Mind if I walk with you?"

The guy was short and was sweating profusely, even though it wasn't all that hot. Keith had never seen him before.

But he had seen the logo on both his shirt and cap. They were identical and each had four letters: ESPN.

"Arnie Pearlman," the guy said, giving him a phony smile. "I work for ESPN."

"No kidding," Keith said, and gritted his teeth at what he knew was soon to come.

15

BY NOW, FRANK HAD GROWN ACCUSTOMED TO the media swarm that awaited him at the end of each match— although it did seem to grow every day.

As he rode in the cart back to the clubhouse, Pete Kowalski, the USGA public relations boss, told Frank that he hadn't done a green-side interview because he was going to be taken straight to the 18th hole tower to talk to Joe Buck and the Fox TV analysts. Once that was over, he'd go through his paces with the print media, Golf Channel, and local TV and radio.

Frank thought the idea of sitting in the tower with Joe Buck, Paul Azinger, and Brad Faxon sounded pretty cool. As the cart drove up, Frank could see that his father and Lawrensen were already there. Frank guessed they had been told what the USGA's plans were and had asked to be driven to the tower.

But when the cart stopped at the bottom of the steps leading to the tower, Frank noticed that there seemed to be a problem. As Frank started to get out of the cart, he saw his father and Lawrensen in what looked like a heated conversation with someone he recognized as Mike Davis, the executive director of the USGA. He recognized Davis from having seen him on TV repeatedly during U.S. Opens.

Davis always came off on TV as outgoing and friendly. He was talking as Frank exited the cart, but it was clear right away the conversation wasn't friendly.

"Mr. Lawrensen, Mr. Baker, I'm going to try to explain this one last time," he said. "The USGA does not pay golfers to do interviews. In fact, in the case of an amateur, his college eligibility could be jeopardized if we *did* do it, which, again, we do not. The same is true of Fox. If you don't believe me, I can connect you to Mark Loomis, who is their executive producer, and he'll confirm that.

"Now, Frank isn't required to go up in the tower at all. Most players—especially young ones who already have an 'adviser' "—he nodded at Lawrensen, his voice dripping with sarcasm—"think the publicity is a good thing. But obviously, it's your call."

Frank and Pete Kowalski had both frozen in their tracks, listening to Davis.

Kowalski turned to Frank and said very quietly, "Do you want to do the interview?"

"Of course I do."

"Then don't look over there, and follow me."

He turned in the direction of the steps leading up into the tower that were to their right. The argument was several yards away to the left. Frank followed.

When they reached the steps, a guard took down a rope to allow them to pass. "No one not wearing a USGA credential comes up these steps until I come back down," Kowalski said. "Understand? No one."

The guard nodded.

At that moment, Frank heard Lawrensen's voice. "Hey, where are you going, Frank? Stop!"

"Keep walking," Kowalski said, and Frank did as he was instructed.

Lawrensen was still yelling as they ascended the steps. Frank didn't look back. He remembered something he'd read once: "Sometimes it's better to ask for forgiveness than permission."

He'd ask for forgiveness later. Or perhaps not. What did he care what Lawrensen thought? His dad, though, was another story.

Fox was in a commercial break when they walked onto the set. There was an empty seat between Joe Buck and Paul Azinger that was apparently for Frank.

"You're right there," a young woman wearing a headset said, pointing at the empty spot. "We're back in two minutes. Thanks for coming."

"It was nothing," Frank said, winking at Kowalski.

Buck, Azinger, and Faxon all shook his hand and congratulated him as a technician attached a microphone to the front of his golf shirt.

"That your home club?" Buck asked, nodding at the Perryton Country Club logo.

"Yes, sir," Frank said.

Buck smiled. "No sirs up here, okay, Frank? I'm Joe, he's Paul, and he's Brad. Just relax and enjoy this."

"Thank you, sir," Frank said, adding, "Sorry," as everyone smiled.

"Thirty seconds!" someone shouted.

The thirty seconds felt like an hour.

Buck welcomed everyone back to the "Sweet Sixteen of the U.S. Amateur." Then he lavishly introduced Frank as "the sensation of this event to date, the teenager who beat defending champion Rickie Southwick in a fabulous match yesterday and made it look easy today against a very good player, Matthew Bryan."

He turned to Frank and said, "Having fun yet?"

"Yes, sir," Frank said, then reddened. "I mean, Joe. But I can tell you for a fact that it *wasn't* easy today. Matthew's a very good player, and even when I got him down, he kept coming at me."

Azinger jumped in, saying, "Rickie Southwick was gracious enough to talk to us yesterday even after you beat him, and he told us he thought he played well—but you were just better than he was. He also said if you weren't seventeen, you'd be ready for the Tour. What do you think?"

"I think I'm seventeen," Frank joked, starting to feel a little more at ease. "I'm lucky enough to have a teacher, Slugger Johnston, who was a very good college player and understands there's a lot more to the Tour than what happens inside the ropes. I'm looking forward to playing college golf."

They showed some highlights and asked Frank to talk over the shots—which he was glad to do.

They came back on camera—Frank could tell because the woman who had directed him to his seat was pointing at the camera they were supposed to look at while they talked.

"One last question, Frank," Buck said.

Frank assumed the question would be about playing Jerry Gallagher the next day in the quarterfinals. "Sure," he said.

"A lot of people have noticed Ron Lawrensen, a very well-known agent, walking around with your dad all week. Now, we know it's perfectly legal for an amateur to have an adviser like Lawrensen, but is there something more to it than that?"

Frank was caught off guard by the question. He felt himself go red again.

"Mr. Lawrensen is not my adviser. He's talking to my dad about things that may happen down the road," he finally said. "It'll be a while before I need an agent."

That was good enough. They thanked him and Buck said, "Let's throw it back to Steve Flesch on seventeen."

"Clear," the headset woman said.

"Didn't mean to trip you up with the last question," Buck said. "My producer wanted me to ask you because I guess a lot of people have noticed."

"I'm sure they have," Frank said. "I'm sure they have."

He shook hands, thanked everyone, and followed Kowalski back down the steps, dreading the sight of his dad and Lawrensen waiting for him.

But Frank saw no sign of the two. Confused, he said to Kowalski, "You think you can find out where my dad went?"

Kowalski nodded and pulled a radio from his belt as they got back into the cart, both sitting in the back. The PR boss told the driver to take them back to the media flash area—where the print reporters would be waiting—and put the radio to his mouth.

"Mike Davis," he said.

"Here, Pete," a voice came back instantly.

"Mike, can you go to eighteen, please?" Kowalski asked.

"Got it."

Kowalski turned the little dial on the radio, jumping it from the number 4 to the number 12.

"Eighteen is our code for channel twelve, which is more private," Kowalski explained. "Only a few of us know to use it."

"Here, Mike," he said.

"Go," Davis answered.

"Frank Baker and I are on a cart headed to the flash area," he said. "Frank's wondering if you have a twenty on his dad."

"Yes, I do," Davis said. "He'll be waiting for him in player dining once he's done at the flash. I'll meet you there to explain."

"Copy," Kowalski said, and turned the dial back to 4.

"Something must have happened after we went upstairs," Frank said.

"Probably," Kowalski said. "Mike will fill you in when we get there."

. . . . .

It took about five minutes to get to the flash area, which looked slightly chaotic. There were cameras everywhere, and Mike Davis was waiting in a roped-off area just behind the podium where Frank would be going.

"I'll just take a sec," Davis said. "Pete, do me a favor and go up there and tell them Frank needs a moment so they don't all go nuts."

Kowalski nodded and headed to the podium.

"First, Frank, congratulations on the win," Davis said. "I didn't get a chance to say that."

"You were a little busy," Frank said.

Davis laughed uncomfortably and shook his head.

"I'm guessing you heard the conversation," he said. "Unfortunately, when you and Pete went up the steps, your dad tried to follow."

"I heard Lawrensen yelling," Frank said.

Davis nodded. "Well, I'm glad you kept going. But once you were onstage, your dad and Lawrensen got a little out of control. They tried to push past the guard, and it . . . got physical. Mostly it was Lawrensen. I felt like your dad was just going along with Lawrensen. Not quite an innocent bystander, but not the main agitator."

Frank was, sadly, not at all surprised.

"No one got hurt, but we had to bring in a couple of security guards to settle them down. Both were profane and kept threatening to sue the USGA."

"Oh man, I'm so sorry," Frank said. He felt sick to his stomach.

"Don't be sorry, Frank. You did nothing wrong. But our head of security wanted them removed from the grounds. We finally compromised that they'd be taken to the player dining area and stay there until you're finished. Then we'll have all of you escorted to the parking lot."

Frank sighed.

And now Pete Kowalski was back. "They're getting restless," he said.

"There's one more thing, Frank," Davis said. "I have to warn you. I'm not sure how, but my top lieutenant, who is actually running the tournament, tells me the media's gotten ahold of this. I'm pretty certain you'll be asked about it when you get up there."

"What do I say?" Frank asked.

"I have no idea," Davis said. "Only advice I'd give you is that if you don't tell the truth, it'll probably come out at some point anyway."

Frank nodded. Gingerly, he walked up the steps. People were shouting questions as if he were the president getting into a limo.

"Frank," said someone, his voice somehow cutting through all the other noise. "What happened with your father and Fox?"

There was a pause while everyone waited to see if Frank would answer.

Frank sighed again and remembered what Mike Davis had just said.

"I honestly don't know," he said, skirting the truth. "When I pulled up, my dad was talking to Mr. Davis. I guess it was heated, but you'd have to ask them about that. Mr. Kowalski took me straight to the set, and when I came back down, my dad and Mr. Davis were both gone."

He decided bringing Lawrensen up was a bad idea. Everything he had said was true. He'd just left a lot out.

"Where's your dad now?" someone asked.

"Player dining, waiting for me to wrap this up," Frank said.

"Can you speculate on what the argument was about?" someone asked.

"I probably could, but I'd prefer not to," Frank said. He realized he sounded like a politician.

"Frank, there's a report that your dad had an altercation in a bar last night with a journalist. Can you tell us anything about *that*?"

"Wasn't there," Frank answered, another non-lie.

"Two more," Kowalski said, stepping into his PR role. "Anyone got one about golf?"

There was silence. Dead silence.

16

KEITH HAD GONE INTO THE LOCKER ROOM TO
use the bathroom and was on his way out when he saw Slugger
standing outside the door, phone pressed to his ear.

"I'll go try to talk to him," he heard Slugger say. "But he's
not in much of a mood to listen to me."

He hung up, looked at Keith, and said, "I swear to God,
you can't make this stuff up."

"What now?" Keith asked.

"That was Mark Loomis, the Fox producer. We're friends
because I've played with him down at Winged Foot a half
dozen or so times. Good player."

"Yeah and . . . ?"

"Fox wanted Frank to sit on their main set with Buck and
Azinger and Faxon," Slugger said. "The father and that idiot
Lawrensen wanted to be paid—either by Fox or the USGA or
both."

"You're joking," Keith said, knowing full well that Slugger
wasn't. "So what happened?"

"I'm not a hundred percent sure, but, bottom line, Frank went up on the set and the father and Lawrensen tried to get up there to stop him. They were taken away by security."

"Arrested?"

Slugger shook his head. "No, but they took them back to player dining and they're holding them there until Frank finishes with the print media. Then they're going to escort them out. No charges—this time."

"Anyone else know?"

"I'm guessing yes," Slugger said as his phone buzzed. He held it up for Keith to see. The name *Steve DiMeglio* was on the screen. "That's the fourth call in the last fifteen minutes. I haven't picked any of them up . . . Loomis suggested I go in there and try to calm the father down, explain to him how this works."

"What about Lawrensen?" Keith asked. "*He's* the one who should be able to explain to Baker the world doesn't work this way."

"Apparently, it was Lawrensen's idea to ask for the money," Slugger said. "At least that's what Mark says. He says Lawrensen contacted him directly. Said it was time to change tradition."

"He's at least half the problem, isn't he?" Keith said.

"At least," Slugger said. "A good agent, even a semi-good agent, is supposed to be the one who explains to the client what's possible and what's not possible."

"And keep him out of fights," Keith added.

"Yeah, that too. What do you think I should do?"

Keith had a thought—a bad one, probably. But he made a decision on the spot. It was time to go all-in on this or all-out.

"You go back to the flash area," he said to Slugger. "Monitor what happens and make sure you're there with Frank. Don't let him scrum for too long if you can avoid it. When he's done, tell Pete Kowalski you want him to go straight to the car."

"But what about the old man and Lawrensen?"

"They've got their own car, remember? As soon as Frank's off the grounds, security'll escort them out."

"But?"

Keith held up a hand. "I'm not going to say 'trust me,' because what I've got in mind doesn't merit trust. But . . . play along with me. We've got just about nothing to lose at this juncture."

Slugger nodded. "On that point, I do trust you— completely," he said.

They shook hands—for some reason—and Slugger walked in the direction of the flash area. Keith turned and started walking to the clubhouse entrance—and the player dining room.

. . . . .

This time, there was no problem getting past the security guard standing at the door to the player dining area. The guard barely looked up when Keith walked by, perhaps because it was late, or perhaps because the room was almost empty.

A couple of players sat with friends or family, but the food was all gone and so was the incentive to spend much time in there.

Thomas Baker and Ron Lawrensen were seated in the back of the room at the table farthest from the door. Two yellow-jacketed rent-a-cops sat a couple of tables away, giving them space but making it clear that the two men were not free to get up and leave until they received word to the contrary.

Keith walked to the side of the room so that he could approach the table without going past the guards. Lawrensen was facing him, and his face took on a look of disgust as Keith walked up. By the time Baker turned to see what Lawrensen was looking at, Keith had grabbed a chair and taken a seat between the two of them.

"You have to be kidding," Baker said.

Keith held up a hand. "Mr. Baker, let me talk for about two minutes. When I'm finished, if you want me to leave, I won't say another word."

At that instant, Keith felt a hand on his shoulder. He looked up and saw one of the yellow-jackets.

"Sir, you have a pass to be in here?" he asked.

Keith showed him the pass, pointing to the PD lettering.

"That's only if invited," the guard said, and Keith was getting ready to tell the guard he didn't know the damn rules when, much to his surprise, Baker said, "It's okay. He's with us."

The guard looked surprised, too, but nodded and retreated.

Keith started to thank Baker, but the father simply shook his head and said, "I have to admit I'm curious what you could possibly have to say to us that you'd think we'd want to hear. So say it, then get lost."

Shortest truce in history, Keith thought. *Ten seconds? No, closer to five.*

"You got it," he said. "Look, I know you've viewed me as an interloper and probably a troublemaker since we first met back in June at Perryton . . ."

"Probably?" Lawrensen said.

"Hang on, Ron," Baker said.

"I get that because you don't know me and so, like a lot of people who haven't dealt with the media much, you automatically view me with suspicion. And I have no doubt you've been egged on by your shadow here. Just like today with Fox."

He paused for a second, wondering if this was a good or a bad time to inject a little humor. He decided he had nothing to lose.

"Viewing the media as the enemy is what some folks believe will 'Make America Great Again.'"

Baker was trying not to smile. "I can't argue with that," he said.

Baby steps, Keith thought.

"Slugger and I are old friends—I think you know that's why he called me in the first place. *All* he wants is what's best for Frank. He's got no financial stake in any of this other than what you're paying him. He has no desire to become one of those master teachers on TV or charge a thousand bucks an hour for a lesson. He likes what he does. More important, he really likes Frank and cares about him. I know you know that. And, even though I don't know him one-tenth as well as Slugger does, I really like Frank, too. Mr. Baker, he's a special kid—and I'm not talking about his golf. He reminds me of Jordan Spieth. When I close my eyes, I think I'm talking to a thirty-year-old."

This time, Baker did smile. "Thank you," he said. "I've honestly tried to teach him right from wrong."

He looked away for a moment, and Keith could swear he saw his eyes misting just a bit.

"Sometimes, maybe I forget that."

Keith decided to chance more humor. "When you meet someone who's perfect," he said, "let me know. Because *that* will be a story."

Another smile. He was on a roll.

As if to bring him back to earth, Baker said, "So what's your point, Keith? Your two minutes are about up."

It was the first time Baker had used his first name. He decided to plow on.

"Here's what I'm saying: With all due respect to Ron, who I know is very good at his job, why are you in such a rush? If Frank's going to be as good as you expect him to be, there will be *plenty* of time for him to get rich. The only real risk, as I see it, is if he's pushed too hard, too fast, and goes down the same rabbit hole as Ty Tryon."

Keith knew he didn't have to explain who William Augustus "Ty" Tryon IV was to either man: Ty was the kid who had made it through the PGA Tour's Qualifying School at seventeen, had bypassed college and gone pro, and had become a has-been by the time he was twenty-five.

"Frank's different from Ty Tryon."

"Really? How do you know that? I played mini-tour events that Ty was in during my very brief pro career. He was a terrific kid: smart, good guy. He was just pushed too hard, too fast, and couldn't handle it. Most kids, no matter how mature, aren't ready for *life* on the Tour as teenagers. Even Earl Woods let Tiger go to Stanford for two years."

"Earl Woods is not my role model," Baker said, getting riled again. "But whatever he did, it worked out pretty well for his kid, didn't it?"

"I don't know. Did it?" Keith said. "Do you want Frank to grow up to be Tiger Woods *off* the golf course?"

Baker didn't answer that one for a moment. Lawrensen started to say something, but Baker stopped him with a look.

"Last chance," he said, turning back to Keith. "What's your point?"

"My point is that you should give him some space. Let's say you'd gotten ten grand today for him to talk to Fox. If he's as good as you think, that'll be latte money a few years from now. Let him become a star and make you all rich when he's ready. Mature as he is, he's not ready for this now. He needs to go to prom, not make sponsor appearances. The best news is, he doesn't have to be ready. Let him *play* golf, not work at golf. Let him be a kid for a few more years, because he *is* a kid. You aren't broke, and you don't have to get rich in the next fifteen minutes. Trust Slugger—he's good at what he does, and he cares about your son."

"So you're saying he shouldn't trust me?" Lawrensen broke in, clearly nervous that Baker might be listening to what Keith was saying.

"I never said that, Ron," Keith said.

"You did between the lines," Baker said.

"Let me say this, then, as my closing line: Ron's good at what he does. But his job isn't to worry about what's best for Frank. His job is to make as much money as possible for Double Eagle. *Your* job is to do what's best for Frank."

He stood up and put out his hand. Thomas Baker shook it. Neither of them said another word.

. . . . .

Keith called Slugger as soon as he walked back outdoors. No answer. He saw Steve DiMeglio walking in his direction.

"Where's the kid?" Keith asked.

"Just left under armed guard," DiMeglio said. "Where were you when he was talking?"

"I had someone there taking notes for me," Keith answered.

"I don't doubt it," DiMeglio said. "I gotta go smoke."

Keith wondered if he should go back to the media center or get to his car and try Slugger again. His phone buzzed and he saw Slugger's name come up.

"Sorry, we were getting into the car when you called with security guys pushing the media back," he said. "Quite a scene."

"That's fine. We need to talk."

"So, talk."

"In person, with Frank."

"He wants to stop at an In-and-Out Burger. He's never been to one, but he's heard Mickelson loves them, so he wants to try it. There's one two exits down once you're on the 405. Why don't you meet us there? Apparently Dad and Lawrensen are still in player dining and haven't been released yet."

"Yeah, I know," Keith said. "I'll explain when I get there."

Not surprisingly, traffic was awful. It took Keith twenty minutes to navigate two miles on the interstate to the exit. Then it was three backed-up lights to the In-and-Out.

It was late afternoon and he was starving—again. The schedule made it pretty impossible to eat lunch if you were following a match, and there had been chaos of some kind every day he'd been out here.

Frank and Slugger were carrying food toward a table when he walked in. He waved at them and got in line—which, fortunately, wasn't that long since it was only five o'clock. Keith ordered a double hamburger and French fries and then threw in a vanilla milkshake. He'd walked a solid four miles each of the last three days. He was entitled.

He walked over, congratulated Frank on his win, and sat down.

"I just got a text from my dad," Frank said. "He said you and he had a talk and that some of what you said made sense. Tell me about it."

Keith nodded, put a few fries in his mouth, and began to explain.

17

NEITHER FRANK NOR SLUGGER INTERRUPTED
once while Keith told his story. When he finished, Frank took
a long sip of his milkshake and simply said, "Wow."

Slugger nodded. "That was a risky move," he said. "You
could have gotten punched or arrested or both."

Keith laughed. "Already been punched," he said. "Worst-
case scenario, I might have gotten tossed out of there. I don't
think I was going to get arrested by rent-a-cops, especially for
going into a room I was clearly credentialed for."

Frank's mind was racing. He wondered how his father
thinking that "some" of what Keith had said made sense
would actually manifest itself. At the very least, he didn't think
he had to worry about Slugger getting fired—at least not this
week. That alone was a relief.

"I would advise you not to look online tonight or read the
newspaper in the morning," Keith said. "This is now officially
a tabloid story the media can blow up into more than it is."

"Except a lot of this drama isn't made up," Slugger said.

Keith nodded. "True. Which is all the more reason to go back to the room and, if you're hungry before you go to bed, order something lighter than this"—he nodded at Frank's tray—"and just worry about Jerry Gallagher."

Frank had already been thinking about Gallagher. He knew he was, like Nathan Smith, a true amateur and that he'd finished second in the Amateur twelve years ago, meaning he'd played in the Masters. Playing in a quarterfinal match in the Amateur wasn't likely to intimidate him.

"Already thinking about him," Frank said. "I know he's a good player and, you're right, a good night's sleep is exactly what I need." He paused. "Now tell me what you think my dad will do next. Do you think there's any chance he'll fire Lawrensen?"

Keith shook his head. "No, no way," he said. "Remember, your dad is on the Double Eagle payroll now. Plus, I promise you by tomorrow morning—if not sooner—Lawrensen will have him convinced that everything I said was in his plan from the start." Keith paused for a moment to let Frank take that in. "The good news is, you should have a reprieve for the rest of this week. After that, all bets are off. A lot of what happens in the next few months will depend on what happens in the next three days."

"Or one day," Frank said.

Keith smiled. "I'm being optimistic, and the way you're playing—in spite of all this—gives me confidence that it'll be three days. I like your approach, though. Worry about tomorrow before you think any farther down the road. Don't even think about Saturday yet."

They were all quiet for a minute, finishing their food.

Frank was so hungry he was tempted to go back for more. He decided against it.

Slugger stood up. "I think I'm going to have a cup of coffee," he said. "You guys want anything else?"

"You know, I wouldn't mind coffee either, now that you bring it up," Keith said.

"Me too," Frank said.

"Be right back," Slugger said.

"You drink coffee?" Keith said.

Frank shrugged. "I'm up by six every morning, spring, summer, and fall to play golf or work in the pro shop," he said. "I started to drink coffee when I was thirteen. Usually I only drink in the morning, but if you guys are having one, I'll have one, too."

"I was the same way," Keith said. "I get it."

Frank leaned forward in his seat so he could lower his voice, although he wasn't certain why he was doing so. "I gotta ask you a question," he said.

"Shoot."

"I really appreciate everything you've done and are trying to do," he said. "I wasn't so sure about Slugger asking you to come talk to me back in June, but I'm really glad he did."

"But . . . ?"

"But I'm wondering: What's in this for you? You haven't written anything about me or all that's gone on this week. So . . ."

"You'd like to know what I'm doing here," Keith said.

"More like, why have you put yourself out there for me the way you have?"

Keith just smiled.

"Did I say something funny?" Frank asked.

"No, not at all," Keith said. "I'm smiling at how quickly you pick up on things."

It was now Frank's turn to smile. "Well, my dad is a stock broker, but somehow he doesn't get a lot of this golf-business stuff, so I guess I have to," he said. He paused. "Then again, maybe you opened his eyes a little."

Slugger, returning with the coffees, heard the last comment. "Guess we'll find out tomorrow," he said.

Frank and Keith didn't respond. They didn't have to.

. . . . .

The answer turned out to be yes—sort of.

The morning routine didn't change at all: after Slugger drove Frank to the golf course, they had breakfast and went to warm up, Frank working his way through a bucket of balls at the range, hitting his shorter irons first and then moving to the bigger clubs as he loosened up.

Frank's dad arrived at the range with Lawrensen right by his side. Frank waved at his dad, who waved back.

"You think Lawrensen convinced him that everything Keith said yesterday was really his idea?" Frank murmured to Slugger, continuing his routine as he spoke.

"No doubt," Slugger said. "But let's not focus on that now. Let's focus on Jerry Gallagher."

As it turned out, there wasn't that much to worry about. Gallagher had one of those days that even good players have on occasion. His first tee shot went way left and found deep rough. With Frank in the fairway, holding an iron in his hands for his second shot, Gallagher tried to gouge his ball out of the rough with a hybrid, knowing Frank was likely to reach the green in two.

The ball barely moved. He tried again. And again. By the time he got the ball onto the fairway, he was lying five and it was still his turn.

"Let's not waste time here," Gallagher said to Frank. He picked up his own ball, nodded at Frank, and said, "That's good. Nice two."

Frank laughed. "My first double-eagle," he said to Slugger as they crossed the fairway to get to the second tee.

"Don't get carried away by it," Slugger said. "It's one hole."

The second hole was better for Gallagher; he made a par, but Frank rolled in a long birdie putt on one of the toughest holes on the golf course to go two-up.

"I'm four under," Frank said. "Maybe I'll shoot twenty-nine on the front nine and close him out on ten."

He didn't shoot 29, but he came close to closing Gallagher out in 10. Gallagher bogeyed the next three holes to go five-down and was reciting his concession speech after they both made par on the sixth.

"At least now I won't lose ten-and-eight," he said as they walked up the hill behind the green to the seventh tee. He lost, instead, eight-and-seven. Frank birdied the ninth to go six-up, then watched Gallagher take his driver at Number 10 and hit it so far over the green that he had no chance to get his second shot on the putting surface. He barely got his third shot onto the green, missed for par from 30 feet, and conceded Frank's 15-foot birdie putt.

"I'd have made you putt just in case you three-putted," Slugger said as they walked to the 11th tee.

"I think he just wants to get this over with," Frank answered.

It was over on 11. Gallagher hit his second shot into the creek fronting the green and then somehow found the bunker hitting a wedge with his fourth shot. He blasted out to 20 feet and then took his cap off and shook hands. Frank was on the fringe with about a 35-footer for eagle. In theory, he could four-putt and Gallagher could hole his bogey putt to halve the hole and keep the match alive. But not likely.

Clearly, Gallagher wanted no part of it.

"I'm really sorry," he said as they shook hands. "Quarter-finals of the U.S. Amateur, you deserved to play someone who could at least give you a decent match."

Frank wasn't sure how to respond. He understood what Gallagher was saying; he knew he was embarrassed and he felt bad for him. "Everyone has an off day," he said finally.

"I picked a hell of a time to have one, didn't I?" Gallagher said, forcing a smile. "Good luck on the weekend. I hope you win the whole thing."

He then shook hands with Slugger while Frank shook hands with his opponent's caddie.

Frank's dad popped out of the crowd of onlookers to give him a hug and a backslap before the officials arrived to escort the players to the media area. Although Frank couldn't see him, he knew Lawrensen was somewhere behind the ropes, but he was glad the agent didn't come over to ruin the moment.

"I promise you one thing," Slugger said as they rode the cart back to the clubhouse and the waiting media. "Tomorrow will be a lot tougher than this was, no matter who you play."

Frank's opponent would either be Nathan Smith or Edward Anderson III. He'd never met "Edward Anderson the third," but he knew he was the son of some very rich CEO type who was a member at Augusta. Someone had told him that in the locker room earlier in the week.

He hoped he would be playing Nathan Smith. Win or lose, the day would probably be a lot more pleasant that way.

Frank was now two wins away from being the U.S. Amateur champion. He knew if he won, he'd be the youngest U.S. Am champion in history, eight months younger than Byeong Hun An had been in 2009 when he'd won a month shy of his eighteenth birthday. He was also one win away from making it to the Masters, which he knew was what his father and Lawrensen cared most about.

As he got off the cart where the media awaited, he had two thoughts. The first one was important: at this moment, more than at any other time in his life, he needed to focus on just one match. He couldn't worry about what might happen in the final on Sunday, he couldn't worry or care about who he played, and he couldn't worry about what anyone else might have in mind if he made the Masters or if he somehow won the tournament.

All of that was for later.

The other thought was far less important: even though his was the first match to finish, Fox hadn't asked him to come up to the booth today.

He wasn't surprised.

. . . . .

After Frank finished with the reporters, he headed back to the locker room to take a shower. It had been the most humid day of the week, and he was dripping. His father had texted to say that he and Lawrensen were on their way to the hotel for a meeting and they would see him at dinner. The final line of the text had nothing to do with plans: **I haven't said this all week and I should have: I'm really proud of you.**

Hmm, Frank thought. Maybe his dad *had* heard some of what Keith Forman had said.

Frank was fine with his dad and Lawrensen having post-match plans. He really didn't care what sort of meeting they were going to or who was meeting with them. He decided he wouldn't even ask when he got to dinner.

Keith Forman, whom he'd only seen from a distance all

day, was waiting for him just inside the locker-room door with Slugger, watching the other matches on a television that was behind the counter where the locker-room guys worked.

"Hate to be the bearer of bad news, but you're playing Edward Anderson tomorrow," Keith said.

"Nice to see you, too, and, yes, that was a nice win today, wasn't it?" Frank said lightly.

Keith laughed. "Sorry, the Anderson-Smith match ended ten minutes ago on seventeen. And I'd tell you nice win, except even I could have beaten that poor guy today."

Frank nodded. "I can't argue with that. He just couldn't get it together. And I am sorry I'm not playing Nathan. He seems like a very good guy."

"Don't know him that well, but I promise you he's a better guy than Anderson. The dad has quite a reputation, and so does the kid. Classic born-on-third-base guy who thinks he tripled. He's already transferred colleges once or twice, apparently because nobody can stand him, even though he's a really good player."

Frank nodded. "I hear his dad's a big Trump supporter."

"Not many members at Augusta who aren't," Keith answered.

"Spoken like a true Commie," said Slugger, getting a laugh.

They had walked back to Frank's locker as they talked. Frank was taking off his shoes when Nathan Smith walked in, still sopping with sweat.

"Condolences, Nathan," Frank said.

"Thanks, man," Smith said.

"Didn't they make you talk to the media?" Keith asked.

Smith nodded. "Yeah, but I told them I needed a few minutes to cool off first. Literally and figuratively."

"Don't blame you," Frank said.

"Yeah, but that's not really why I came in here," Smith said. "I wanted to be sure I caught you before you left. Frank, we need to talk."

"About what?"

"About Edward Anderson the blanking third."

18

THE FOUR OF THEM WALKED TO THE BACK OF the locker room, where there was a card room that had been empty most of the week. There was no one in there, although the television was on. As they walked in, Frank could see his next opponent on the screen, sitting on the Fox set with Joe Buck.

It occurred to Keith Forman that Edward Anderson III's father probably hadn't asked Fox for money in return for the interview. Then again, ten grand was *already* latte money for him.

Keith knew Nathan Smith because he'd done a story on him a few years earlier when he had played in the Masters. The Mid-Amateur champion received an automatic invitation to the Masters, so Smith had played there four times.

Smith had agreed when Frank asked if Keith could join them in the meeting on the condition that he wouldn't be quoted on anything unless Keith circled back to him first to ask permission. Keith honestly didn't think Smith was going to say anything he'd want to quote, but as long as he had the option to go back if something became important, he was fine with that condition.

The sound was down on the TV, so they left it that way. They sat at a round table, and Keith, Frank, and Slugger looked at Smith expectantly.

"Here's the deal," Smith said. "There are a lot of rumors about Anderson in amateur golf circles. Mainly, that he's a cheat. The main reason he transferred out of Stanford and Alabama is that his teammates couldn't stand him and there'd been complaints from opponents that he colored outside the lines when it came to the rules. It was never anything blatant enough for him to get disqualified or in any kind of serious trouble. It was stuff that's impossible to prove unless you've got a camera on the guy, and college golf isn't on television except for the NCAAs."

"What kind of stuff?" Frank asked.

"Re-marking balls a little closer to the hole, improving lies in the rough just a little by tapping the ground behind the ball with a club during his pre-shot routine—"

"Hardly 'little stuff,'" Slugger said.

"Yeah, but tough to prove."

Keith shook his head. "Hard to believe no one from either school ever said anything publicly about why such a good player would transfer."

"Good point," Smith said. "But remember who his dad is; being the son of an Augusta member makes you just about untouchable in golf. No one wants to mess with Augusta."

Keith knew that was true. He knew enough people who

worked at CBS, ESPN, and Golf Channel to know that even the all-powerful TV networks lived in fear of upsetting the Augusta membership, who had their own way of doing everything.

"So you're saying I need to keep an eye on him tomorrow," Frank said.

"Yep," Smith said. "Especially on the front nine. You won't be on TV until the back nine. That's what happened today. He and I almost got into it on the fourth hole—before TV coverage came on the air. The kid isn't stupid by any means."

"What happened?" Frank asked.

"He hit his tee shot way right—not where it was going to be lost, but where he might have tree trouble. He and his caddie walked over there, and I wandered in that direction, too. When he got to where the ball was, I was standing about twenty yards away.

"So he called over the rules official and made a big deal of showing him some twigs and small branches that were loose—all of which he was allowed to move. The official told him it was fine to move them, then came over and explained to me what was going on.

"I said fine, but then I walked over a little closer. Anderson was moving stuff, and then I saw him reach very carefully for what I thought was a twig. Suddenly he pulled his hand back really fast—the way you do when you've made a mistake and maybe caused your ball to move.

"He looked up at me, then went back to moving stuff like

nothing had happened. I said to him, 'Ed, what just happened there?'

"He said, 'Nothing, just moving these loose twigs.'

"I said, 'Why'd you jerk your hand back like that?' By now, I'd walked over to him and his face was bright red. I had no doubt the ball had moved. So I just asked him point-blank.

"He goes, 'No, absolutely not!' the way you deny something when you're flat-out lying.

"I called the rules official back over. I told him what had happened and that I thought the ball had moved—though I couldn't absolutely prove it, since I hadn't seen his lie.

"The official was David Fay, who, remember, was once executive director of the USGA. He's here this week with Fox as their rules expert, but he volunteered to referee one match a day through the quarters. He looked at me and said, 'You really want to do this?'

"I said, 'You bet I do.'

"He asked Anderson the question again about whether the ball moved. Anderson said, 'The ball didn't move. If it did, I'd have called it on myself.' Then he looked at me and said, 'I really resent you calling me a cheat.' I looked at him and said, 'Ed, I haven't called you anything. I just asked you a question.'

"At that point, Fay walks over to the ball and crouches down next to it. He looks at it and says, 'Mr. Anderson, I have to tell you, the ball appears to be lying differently than when you called me over.'

"Anderson says, 'Are *you* calling me a cheat?'

"Fay is very cool. 'I'm expressing my opinion,' he says. 'I can't penalize you, because I didn't witness an infraction and, unfortunately for all of us, we don't have TV replay available. So it's up to you and your conscience to decide what the right thing is to do here.'

"Anderson's glaring at both of us. Finally, he says: 'I know what I did and I know the rules, Mr. Fay. I grew up playing at Augusta. I don't need you or anyone trying to guilt me into penalizing myself for something I didn't do.'"

"Very subtle with the Augusta reference," Keith said.

"Yeah, no kidding. Fay and I just walked away. He apologized to me."

"What'd he say?" Keith asked.

"That he should have stayed there and observed. He probably should have, but who expects someone to do something like that?"

They were all quiet for a moment.

"So what should I do?" Frank said.

"On the first tee, you take whoever is refereeing aside and you ask him to please keep an eye on your opponent. You don't have to explain anything—my guess is, he'll know what you're talking about."

Keith was concerned that Frank might spend too much time worrying about his opponent cheating. Slugger read his mind.

"That's exactly the right thing to do," Slugger said. "Except

I'll be the one to talk to the referee, and I'll keep an eye on Anderson, too. *You*, Frank, just worry about playing golf."

Smith nodded. "I agree. Honestly, I wish now I hadn't even watched him. I was so angry I think I was distracted the rest of the day."

"What happened on the hole?" Frank asked, a second before the words came out of Keith's mouth.

Smith smiled sadly. "He hit his second shot onto the fringe and then holed out from there for par to halve the hole. He's a cheat, but he can play."

Keith found that especially unfortunate. The only thing worse than a cheat, he thought, was a cheat who was good enough to also win playing by the rules.

. . . . .

After the meeting broke up and Frank headed to the shower, Keith decided to try to find David Fay. He had his cell number in his phone, so he walked outside and punched it in.

Fay was in the TV tower, on call in case he was needed to explain a ruling while the last two matches were wrapping up. One was on 17, the other on 16, the first one all-square, the second dormie—one player two-up with two to play.

"Can I meet you when we're off the air?" Fay said.

Keith said he'd be at the bottom of the steps as soon as the last two matches were completed.

Good to his word, Fay was waiting for him when he arrived.

"Once both players were on the eighteenth green," he said, referencing the only match that had gone to the 18th, "they didn't need me anymore. What's up?"

Keith didn't know Fay that well. He had retired as executive director of the USGA at the end of 2010, but his reputation was nothing short of sterling. He had brought a liberal conscience to the organization: taking the U.S. Open to a true public golf course—Bethpage Black—for the first time in 2002. He had also done the seemingly impossible when he had convinced the executive board to allow caddies to wear shorts, which was only slightly more miraculous than the taking down of the Berlin Wall.

He looked younger than his age and wore wire-rimmed glasses and a friendly smile.

"I wanted to talk to you about the Smith-Anderson match that you reffed today," Keith said.

Fay's smile disappeared. "What about it?" he said.

"The fourth hole."

For a moment, Fay said nothing. Then he half smiled and said, "You want an answer for the record?"

"I want an answer that's the truth."

Fay sighed. "We have to at least go on background, then, not on the record. You can't use my name or quote me directly, or I might never set foot inside Augusta National again." His smile came back for a moment. "Actually, I'd be okay with that. Once you've seen twenty-nine Masters, you've seen 'em all. But I still have friends who'd like to play there someday."

"Okay, background, then," Keith said, pulling a pen and notebook from his pocket.

"Would I be correct in guessing you've spoken to Nathan Smith?" Fay asked.

"You'd be correct."

Fay shrugged. "The kid, Edward Anderson, made a big show of asking me for a ruling on some loose impediments around his ball. Obviously, he had the right to move anything as long as it didn't affect his lie. I told him that. I noticed Smith walking over to watch."

Fay went on to verify all the details Keith and the others had heard from Nathan.

"There was nothing I could do. No video evidence, no witness—Smith wasn't close enough to be sure, and it was up to the kid to call it on himself. I told him that, and that's when he started into the speech about growing up at Augusta."

Keith knew he had a juicy story on his hands. Even if Fay didn't go on the record, Smith certainly would and he could back it up with Fay as a "USGA source"—since he was working for the USGA that day as an official.

"If I write this and put it up online now, based on what Nathan said, with your backup as an unnamed source, is there anything the USGA can do to remedy the situation?"

Fay shook his head. "Absolutely not. Only thing that can change the outcome would be Anderson having an attack of conscience and saying he failed to penalize himself and withdraw. The result of the match can't be changed, though."

"So what would happen if Anderson withdrew?"

"His semifinal opponent would get a walkover win into the final."

"And into the Masters," Keith said.

"That too," Fay said. "But that kid isn't fessing up. You write it, he'll catch some flak, but you'll catch more."

Keith knew Fay was right. He'd hold his fire on Edward Anderson the blanking third.

For now.

19

FRANK HAD TROUBLE LOOKING HIS OPPONENT in the eye when they shook hands on the first tee at noon the next day. They were the second semifinal match. The first one, between Allen Barton and John Caccese, the NCAA runner-up, had gone off fifteen minutes earlier.

"Let's have a good time out there today," Edward Anderson said with a big smile.

Frank bit his tongue, resisting the urge to add, *And let's try not to cheat.*

Slugger was standing near the ropes, shaking hands with the match referee, a big smile on his face as if they were old friends. The referee's name was Tom Meeks. Slugger had never met him.

Just before the starter introduced the two players, Slugger wandered back to Frank. "All under control," he said quietly.

"Really?"

"Before I finished my first sentence, Mr. Meeks said, 'Don't worry, I've already been warned.'"

The first six holes were uneventful. Feeling nerves, Frank pushed his tee shot on Number 1, had to lay up, and made par. Anderson hit a perfect drive, found the middle of the green with his second shot, and two-putted for birdie. Not an encouraging start.

But Frank got back to even when Anderson three-putted the fourth hole—*Karma*, Frank thought—for bogey. They matched pars for the next two holes.

The seventh was a par-four, playing 408 yards. Frank knew if he hit a good drive, he'd have a wedge in his hands for his second shot. If you missed the fairway, especially right, there was all sorts of trouble. Frank had already figured out that he was longer than Anderson off the tee, so he felt comfortable taking a three-wood, knowing that accuracy was more important than distance. He hit it perfectly, drawing the ball just as he had hoped. The ball started off over the right rough, drew back to the fairway, and rolled to a stop on the left side of the fairway—giving Frank a perfect angle into a back-right pin.

"Good one," Anderson said, walking onto the tee.

That had been the tone so far—very little talk—other than walking off the second tee when Frank had asked Anderson where he planned to go to college in the fall. That had been a mystery since his departure in the spring from Alabama.

"I'm not going back to school," Anderson had answered. "No reason to, really. If I beat you and get in the Masters, I'll play the Am circuit and practice until April, then turn pro after that. If you beat me, I'll turn pro right away. I've already got a bunch of sponsors' exemptions lined up for the fall events."

That had been the only time there had been any conversation beyond "Nice shot." If Anderson was curious in any way about Frank, he never expressed it.

Having seen how far Frank's three-wood had gone, Anderson tried to crank his driver up a notch and ended up opening his club face as he came through the ball. The shot flew wide right, so far right that it flew toward the thick kikuyu grass well off the fairway. Anderson said nothing, just started walking off the tee, handing his driver to his caddie as he went.

Frank knew that Anderson was in a lot of trouble. Kikuyu was a grass only found on the West Coast. It was thick and gnarly stuff, and if you found the wrong spot, your ball might very well be lost. If you found the right spot, you might *still* have to declare an unplayable lie and lose a stroke to give yourself a better one.

Frank followed a few yards behind Anderson as he picked his way through the crowd in the direction of his ball. Tom Meeks had walked in that direction, too. A couple of marshals were already searching for the ball. Apparently, they hadn't seen exactly where it landed.

Almost as if he knew where he was going, Anderson walked into the kikuyu and began plowing his way through, presumably in the direction of the ball. The ref followed until the kikuyu got thick and Frank stopped next to him.

"I have this covered, son," Meeks said, looking surprised that Frank had come over rather than walk to his own ball.

"I know," Frank said.

He didn't move. Meeks said nothing. Anderson and his caddie were now walking with their heads down, peering into the kikuyu as if hoping for a miracle.

A Fox cameraman stood a few yards away, not wanting to get too deep in the kikuyu but following Anderson as he searched.

"Do me a favor, pal," Anderson said, waving his hand. "Give me some space here."

The cameraman said nothing, just took a small step backward.

"Mr. Anderson, you've got five minutes," Meeks told him. "I've started the clock."

"I know the rules," Anderson said, shooting a look at Meeks.

"I assume you do, son, but it's my job to be sure you're aware."

Frank was reminded of a famous incident during the PGA Championship years earlier when Dustin Johnson, with a one-shot lead on the final hole, had hit his drive so far right he was outside the gallery ropes. His ball landed in a sandy area that people had walked through all week, which had garbage in it and was never raked. Nevertheless, for some reason, the PGA had put in a "local rule"—one that was specific to that golf course as opposed to being in the rules of golf—designating *all* sandy areas as bunkers. That meant Johnson wasn't allowed to ground his club, since touching the sand pre-shot with his club was not allowed in any bunker.

In the heat of the moment, Johnson completely forgot the rule and grounded his club. He was penalized two shots and finished two shots out of a playoff because his bogey on the hole became a triple-bogey. The walking rules official never reminded him of the local rule, which would have saved him.

Meeks obviously wanted to be sure that Anderson understood that time was an issue.

Frank was daydreaming a little, thinking maybe he should walk back to his own ball as Meeks had suggested, when he heard Anderson's caddie say, "Got it!"

He was leaning down into the kikuyu to identify the ball. Anderson and Meeks both walked over to where the caddie was standing. Anderson leaned down to look at the ball. Every player puts a unique mark on his ball with a Sharpie before putting it into play so it will be easy to identify. As was custom, the two players had shown each other how they marked their balls before the match had started.

Frank's mark was a red circle around the number on the ball. He chose that marking for luck, since you put a circle around a birdie on your scorecard, and because it was easy to do. At that moment, he was playing a Titleist 2.

Anderson's mark was much more distinctive. Above the brand name was the Augusta National logo—a U.S. map with a flagstick and hole marking Augusta—with a little green star drawn next to it.

"This is it," Anderson said as Meeks looked down at the ball. "You can see my mark."

"Ball's in play," Meeks said, nodding. "Play away when you're ready."

Frank had followed Meeks, if for no other reason than his surprise at how quickly the caddie had spotted the ball in the thick kikuyu. He knew that sometimes you got lucky like that, but Nathan Smith's message was still in the back of his mind: "Keep an eye on him."

"Satisfied?" Anderson asked as Frank peered over Meeks's shoulder.

"Of course," Frank said.

The lie, he thought, was remarkably good given the thickness of the grass around it. Frank walked back to his ball, still feeling as if he was missing something, although he had no clue what it might be.

Anderson took plenty of time before hitting his second shot, walking up about 100 yards and over to the edge of the fairway to get a yardage. He came back and took several practice swings, cutting through the kikuyu near the ball. Frank glanced at Meeks, still standing close to where Anderson was to see if there was any chance he'd think Anderson was improving his lie. Meeks said nothing.

Then, Anderson hit a screaming low line drive that bounced up the fairway and rolled all the way to the front fringe of the green. The crowd howled its approval. It was, no doubt, a wonderful shot, and looked even more impressive if you were on the far side of the fairway and couldn't see that the lie had been as good as it was.

Slugger was talking to Frank, who realized he'd zoned out again, still trying to figure out what had just happened. Was he being paranoid?

"Hey, earth to Baker," Slugger said. "Where's your mind at?"

"Sorry," Frank said. "Got a little distracted."

"Well, tell me about it later," Slugger said. "Meanwhile, let's play golf. You've got a hundred and eighteen front and one twenty-three flag."

That meant Frank was 118 yards from the front of the green and 123 yards from the flag, which was five paces—five yards—from the front of the green.

"What do you think?" Frank asked.

"The wind's helping," Slugger said. "I think it's a full sand wedge or an easy pitching wedge. Depends how hard you want to swing right now."

Frank could feel adrenaline pumping through him. He wasn't sure why, but he could feel it. "I like the sand wedge," he said.

Slugger was already pulling the club even before he finished the sentence.

Frank made a smooth pass at the ball, and it took off like a rocket. He was surprised by how explosive the shot was and by its relatively low trajectory.

"Whoa!" Slugger said, clearly surprised, too.

The ball landed on the middle of the green, took one big hop, and went over the green and down the hill behind it.

Frank looked at Slugger. "How'd that happen?"

"You're too pumped up," Slugger said. "It's the seventh hole—calm down."

Frank was still away. He was in gnarly grass and had to try to pop his third shot high in the air and get it to land just on the fringe and roll toward the pin. He couldn't do it. The ball landed on the green and rolled 15 feet past the hole.

Seeing a surprising opening, Anderson decided to putt. He missed making birdie by inches. Frank conceded the putt. Then he missed his own par putt, the ball swerving left at the last second.

Suddenly, the momentum on the hole—and in the match—had completely turned around. Anderson said nothing, just turned and strutted to the eighth tee.

Frank knew he had to get his mind off what had happened in the kikuyu grass or he was going to be in trouble. There was no margin for error here.

"Let's go," Slugger said. "Let's get it back. This isn't a big deal, okay?"

"Got it," Frank said, trying to convince himself that Slugger was right.

He walked off the green and saw Keith Forman standing there, along with the rest of the media walking inside the ropes. Forman gave him a slight head nod, indicating he should walk in his direction.

Frank picked up the signal and Forman fell into step with him.

"What happened over there in the kikuyu that freaked you out?" he asked.

"I honestly don't know," Frank said. "It was just weird."

"I get it," Keith said. "The chances of finding a ball in that stuff are normally close to zero."

"And in about the only semi-decent spot was right where he found it," Frank said.

They were almost at the tee. Keith put a hand on Frank's shoulder.

"You worry about playing golf," he said. "Let me work on what happened over there."

Frank nodded. He felt better. If something *had* happened, he believed Forman was the person who could figure it out.

20

KEITH FORMAN KNEW EXACTLY WHERE HE needed to go and whom he needed to talk to after witnessing what had happened on the seventh hole. Since there was no place to walk on the right side of the fairway, he had been walking along the ropes a good 50 yards across the fairway and away from the kikuyu where Anderson's ball had landed.

He was fairly convinced something fishy had gone on—no doubt influenced by Nathan Smith, but also by Frank's body language.

The reporter made his way back to the media center, walking up Numbers 8 and 9 to get there, and found PR honcho Pete Kowalski. "Where's the TV compound?" he asked.

If Kowalski found the question strange coming from a print reporter, he didn't show it. "It's down the first fairway from here," he said. "Five-minute walk, tops."

At that moment five minutes sounded like five miles. Keith had half walked, half run up the eighth and ninth holes.

Kowalski seemed to sense that. "If you want, I can get one

of our volunteers to cart you over there," he said. "You look worn out. You okay?"

"Just worn out by the heat. A ride would be great," Keith said. He knew there wouldn't be much going on in the media tent until the two matches finished, so Kowalski had plenty of volunteers available at the moment.

A few minutes later, he was dropped off amid the various trailers and trucks that made up the TV compound. He saw a young woman wearing a U.S. AMATEUR logo on her shirt walking past him.

"Can you point me to the truck?" he asked.

"Fox or Golf Channel?" she asked.

He'd forgotten that even though Fox had the TV rights to the tournament, Golf Channel was still broadcasting from here both pre- and post-play each day.

"Fox," he said.

She pointed him past two trucks and a trailer. The good news was that the TV compound was one of the few places on the grounds at a golf tournament where there was no security. Since it was almost always in the middle of nowhere, no one who didn't need to be there was likely to think about trying to find it.

He pulled open the heavy door slowly and walked into the back of a room filled with TV monitors, computers, and lots of people.

A kid who looked to be about sixteen spotted him and walked over. "Can I help you?" he asked.

"Yeah, I need to talk to Mark Loomis," Keith said.

"He's a little busy right now. We're on the air live."

Keith smiled. He was guessing the kid's job was to make sure everyone in the truck had plenty to drink, but, naturally, he said "we" as if he himself were producing or directing the show.

"Can you just do me a favor? Tap him on the shoulder and point at me. We're old friends, and it's important."

The kid looked skeptical but nodded. He walked down to the front row, where Loomis sat surrounded by all the people working for him as Fox's executive producer of golf. He was wearing a headset and talking into it even as he turned in Keith's direction when the kid tapped him and pointed.

When Loomis saw him, he looked surprised, but he nodded and put up a finger to indicate he needed a minute or two. He put his hand over the microphone attached to his headset and said something to the kid.

The kid walked back to Keith. "He said he'll meet you outside in five minutes. Next break."

"Thanks."

Keith walked outside to wait. The sun was now very hot, and he sat on the steps leading to the truck because there was no place else to sit.

He had met Mark Loomis shortly after he'd started to write, and they sometimes played together at Winged Foot, Loomis's club in Westchester County, north of New York City.

"This better be really important." Loomis was standing behind him on the steps, a bottle of water in his hands.

"It is," Keith said.

The two men shook hands and then walked in the direction of a nearby tree to find some shade.

"So what's up?" Loomis asked. "I've got about three minutes."

"Come on, Mark, you've got four players on the golf course. One of your guys can bring you back from break if need be."

"Okay, five minutes," Loomis said. "Talk."

Keith rattled through what he had witnessed and voiced his suspicions. He knew he could trust Loomis, who would want to be sure that the integrity of the event hadn't been damaged.

"We were on Anderson the whole time," Loomis said. "We had a camera so close to him that he asked our guy to back off."

Keith nodded. "But you had your other cameras rolling so you could switch shots quickly, right?"

"Sure, but no one told me they saw anything funny."

"But you record everything? Just in case something happens off-camera that you want to go back to later?"

"Of course," Loomis said.

"Can I get a look at what's on those other cameras?"

Loomis looked at Keith as if he had just asked him to leave him everything he owned in his will.

"Now?" he asked.

"Now," Keith repeated. "Look, Mark, you know Nathan Smith. He doesn't make stuff up. If nothing happened, I should let the Baker kid know, because he's convinced it did. But if something did happen, Anderson needs to be nailed."

"I've played with Smith," Loomis said. "Completely honorable guy and not a sour-grapes loser."

Someone came out of the truck and hollered for Loomis. "We're almost back, boss!"

"Tell Steve to handle it," Loomis shouted back.

After the guy went back inside, Loomis was silent for a moment. "Tell you what," he said to Keith. "I'll get one of my associate producers to take you over to our backup truck. He can pull all that video, and you can take a look."

"You got an AP we can trust with this?" Keith said.

"Yeah, absolutely," Loomis said, pulling his phone off his belt. "Give me a minute."

He hit what was clearly a speed-dial button. "Tom, I need you here outside the truck right now," he said.

Within a minute, Loomis was introducing him to Tom Goldman.

"Keith will explain what he needs," Loomis said. "Take him to the number two truck and show him everything he wants to see."

Goldman nodded. "Follow me," he said.

Loomis was already walking back to the truck. "Let me know what you find," he said. "Or don't find."

. . . . .

It took the AP about ten minutes to figure out what Keith needed to see. There had been three other cameras in addition to the handheld working on the seventh hole: one behind the green, one behind the tee, and one mounted on a crane that could take in several holes.

"The crane-mount was on a wide-shot while that was going on," Goldman said. "It won't help."

They went through what was on the other two cameras almost frame by frame. Only the one shooting back from the green had the caddie in the frame, but the shot was too long to show anything other than him bending down and checking the ball when he found it.

"Nothing," Goldman said. "Sorry."

Keith sat back in his chair. The number 2 truck was much smaller than the main truck, with only a few monitors and computers and only four chairs. He was a little bit surprised and, he had to admit, disappointed. He'd been convinced that all the modern technology available would show them what had happened. It was, however, possible that nothing had happened.

Goldman was starting to stand up when Keith had one last thought.

"What about the blimp?" he asked, referring to the MetLife blimp that was buzzing above the tournament, adding aerial shots to the coverage.

Goldman blinked in surprise for a moment and then said, "Never thought about that. Give me a minute."

He turned back to the monitor and began pressing buttons. About a minute later, the shot the blimp had been recording came up on the screen. Keith could clearly see all four participants in the search: Edward Anderson, the caddie several yards away, and Tom Meeks and Frank observing.

"Can you get a closer shot?" he asked.

"I can enlarge it," Goldman said, pressing one button repeatedly. The four men came into sharper focus and, when Goldman began to roll the video, Keith could see Anderson turning to say something to Meeks.

Just as he did, Keith saw the caddie pick up his left leg slightly and shake it.

"Hang on!" he shouted. "Go back."

Goldman did.

"Look at that!" Keith said, watching the caddie again as he shook his leg. This time, the video kept rolling and, sure enough, Keith saw something that looked white and round drop out of the bottom of the caddie's pant leg.

"Oh my God!" Goldman shouted.

Without another word, he rewound the video and then slowed it down at the right moment. There wasn't any doubt about it: the caddie had dropped a ball from inside his pant leg to the ground. He then bent over as if examining something he'd just found before waving to the others that he'd found the ball.

"The old hole-in-the-pocket trick," Keith said. He'd seen guys pull it in junior golf but never anywhere else.

"Having the caddie do it is smart," Goldman said. "People are more likely to be watching the player."

"Notice he did it while Anderson was talking to Meeks,"

Keith said. "I'll bet they planned it that way. Anderson was the decoy. Everyone's looking at him because he's talking while the caddie does the deed."

"What do we do now?"

"First, we get Mark in here to look at this. Fox is now going to be part of the story."

Goldman nodded and said, "Stay here. I'll be right back."

While the AP ran back to the truck, Keith pulled out his phone and checked the status of the match. They had just finished the ninth hole, and Frank was two-down.

A minute or two later, Loomis burst into the truck, looking a little bit pale.

"True?" he asked as Goldman followed him in.

Keith stood up to give Loomis his chair. "See for yourself," he said, nodding at Goldman, who retook his seat.

Goldman replayed the relevant sequence, slowing it down so Loomis could clearly see what had happened. As he watched, Loomis murmured profanities, his voice rising as it became more apparent to him that the U.S. Amateur was about to become a soap opera.

Finally, he turned to Keith and said, "Well, I guess I'm never getting invited to join Augusta National."

"It's very possible that neither one of us will ever set foot on the grounds there again," Keith said. *Gallows humor,* he thought.

They both laughed.

Loomis turned to Goldman. "Email me the segment from

the video file so I can show it on my phone. Then get over to the truck and tell Steve he's in charge for a while," he said. "You take over his chair in the meantime."

Goldman nodded as Loomis got up from his seat.

"Let's go," Loomis said. "We have to make the USGA aware of this as soon as possible. Your guy is about to bogey ten and go three-down. This can't wait."

Keith followed Loomis out the door, and they walked to the far side of the compound. There were a number of carts lined up there. One said LOOMIS.

They both jumped in and Loomis pulled away, gravel and dirt kicking up as he floored the accelerator.

"Where are we going?" Keith asked.

"We gotta find Thomas Pagel," Loomis said. "He's the senior director in charge of rules. He'll have to decide what to do next."

What to do next, in Keith's mind, was easy: walk out on the golf course, disqualify Edward Anderson and declare Frank Baker the winner. However, he knew it wouldn't be that simple.

Golf was never that simple.

21

FRANK WAS MARKING HIS BALL ON THE 11TH green, looking at a 25-foot eagle putt. He was in excellent position to close the gap back to one-down. He'd made a long par putt at the tenth to halve the hole, and Anderson had hit his tee shot at 11 in the rough, laid up, and then hit a really poor wedge shot that left him with a putt for 4 just as long as the one Frank was looking at for 3. Frank could feel the momentum he had lost on the seventh hole turning back in his direction.

Then he looked down the fairway and saw three carts coming toward the green. It was the first time all week he had seen a cart in a fairway, and he couldn't imagine what was going on. He didn't recognize the two USGA guys in the first one, but, as they drew closer, he could see that Keith Forman was in the passenger seat of the second. There were two more men in the third cart he didn't recognize, but they were both wearing shirts that said FOX SPORTS.

Clearly, Keith had kept his word and figured something out.

Anderson stopped looking his putt over when the three carts braked to a halt in front of the green. Frank heard him mutter, "What the hell?"

The two men in the front cart walked quickly onto the green.

Keith and his driver and the two Fox guys in the third cart trailed them. The entire thing felt surreal to Frank.

"Gentlemen, a word please," said the man who had been driving the first cart. He was tall, with short dark hair under a red cap, one that said USGA. He didn't appear to be very old, no more than forty, Frank guessed. The other man looked to be even younger. He was shorter, but dressed identically.

They walked to the middle of the green, indicating they wanted the two players and presumably their caddies to meet them there. There were no handshakes, greetings, or small talk. Clearly, the middle of a U.S. Amateur semifinal wasn't a place for any of that.

"Gentlemen, I'm Thomas Pagel," the taller man said. "I'm the USGA's senior director of rules and amateur status." He nodded at his cart passenger. "This is Ben Kimball, the director of this tournament." He then paused as if deciding what to do next. "Mr. Anderson, I'm here to inform you that we have video evidence of a gross violation of the rules that took place on the seventh hole."

Frank felt his heart starting to race. He looked at Keith, who simply put a finger to his lips.

"What in the world are you talking about?" Anderson said.

The confident smirk that had been in place most of the day was gone.

"We're talking about the search for your ball to the right of the fairway following your tee shot on number seven," Mr. Pagel said.

He turned to Anderson's caddie. "What is your name, sir?"

"Jared Hopkins," the caddie said. "But—"

Pagel put a hand up to stop him. He turned to one of the men who had been in the third cart. The man was holding a phone.

"On this phone is a video file taken from the camera in the blimp that shows you, Mr. Hopkins, dropping a golf ball from your pants pocket—specifically the left pocket—and then declaring that you had found Mr. Anderson's tee shot."

"No way!" Hopkins said.

Anderson put his hand on his caddie's shirt to quiet him. "Mr. Pagel, I can't believe anything like that happened. But even if it somehow did, I didn't know anything about it."

"Mr. Anderson, I know you're fully aware of the rules of golf, one of which is that a player is responsible for his caddie at all times. Your caddie blatantly broke the rules by dropping that ball. Whether you were aware of it or not, you are responsible for that action."

Frank could see Anderson and Hopkins looking at each other as if deciding what to do. Hopkins started to speak, but Anderson held up a hand.

"Okay, so *if* you can prove this, it's just loss of hole, right?

Also, I have a right to look at the video before you penalize me, don't I? Or do we wait till the end of the match and somehow figure it out then?"

Frank wanted to jump in. This was match play. How could they possibly play on not knowing who had won the seventh hole?

Pagel, though, was shaking his head quite firmly in response to Anderson.

"This isn't a loss-of-hole offense, Mr. Anderson," he said. "This is a blatant violation of the first two rules in the USGA's handbook. Rule 1-1 describes how the game is to be played, from tee to green, which you violated by dropping a ball. Rule 1-2 says a player may not exert influence on the movement of a ball or alter physical conditions. Changing golf balls, without informing anyone and not declaring the penalty involved, is clearly a violation of that rule. Given that we believe the violation to be intentional, you are disqualified."

Frank felt his knees go weak. Slugger, clearly just as shocked, put a hand on Frank's shoulder to steady himself. Keith was grinning and nodding. Frank could see that all color had drained from Anderson's face under his green cap.

"You *can't* do that!" Anderson yelled, lifting his chin. "Right here in the middle of the match! *No way!* It didn't happen."

"You're welcome to look at the video, but I guarantee it won't change anything. We looked at it quite carefully before we came out here because, honestly, none of us wanted to believe it. In the meantime, just to remove any doubt you might have, Mr. Anderson, let's ask your caddie about it. Mr. Hopkins, do you mind showing us your left pocket?"

Hopkins took a step back. "Yes, I do mind. It's my pocket."

"Even if there's a hole it doesn't prove anything," Anderson insisted.

"No, it just backs up what we already know," Pagel said. "It's your call. But I'm not obligated to show you the video; I'm only willing to show it to you as a courtesy. If you want the chance to protest the decision after seeing the video, I'm going to insist on seeing the pocket."

By now, the crowd was getting antsy. Some were booing, others were clapping rhythmically. There were some cries of "Let's play golf!"

Frank looked over and saw that his father and Ron Lawrensen had stepped under the ropes and were walking in their direction. Another man, whom he didn't recognize, was doing the same. Frank put up a hand to indicate to his father and Lawrensen not to come closer.

Frank saw Anderson glance in the direction of the other man. He guessed it was his father—the Augusta National member. He wondered how *this* would play down there.

"Show him the pocket," Anderson finally said to Hopkins. "Either way, it proves nothing." He turned back to Pagel. "You give me your word I can see the video?"

"Absolutely," Pagel said.

Hopkins reached into his right pocket. Several tees fell out. There was no hole in the pocket.

Pagel smiled. "I asked to see your *left* pocket, Mr. Hopkins."

Hopkins sighed. He pulled out the left pocket. The hole was clear to see.

"Unbelievable," Frank heard Slugger say.

"Not really," Frank muttered.

Frank saw Ben Kimball pull a radio off his belt. "We need extra carts out here on eleven green ASAP," he said. "Security, too."

"Roger that," a voice came back.

Pagel turned in the direction of what was now an extremely restless crowd.

"Ladies and gentlemen, I regret to inform you that we have had a disqualification in this match due to a rules violation. Mr. Baker is the winner and will play in tomorrow's final."

He said nothing more. No details—although they would, of course, come out shortly. Frank could see several carts racing up the 11th fairway.

He wasn't sure what to do next.

"Should I shake his hand?" he said to Slugger.

"I think not," Slugger said.

The man who Frank assumed was Edward Anderson's father was now confronting Pagel.

"What do you think you're doing?" he yelled. "What is this about? You can't possibly have grounds to disqualify my son! Even if the caddie dropped a ball, there is nothing in either Rule 1-1 or 1-2 that says anything about disqualification."

"Unfortunately, Mr. Anderson, we have more than enough

grounds," Pagel answered. "If you look, Rule 33-7 says the committee has the right to disqualify a player at any time for what it considers a gross breach of the rules and etiquette of the game. This is clearly both."

Anderson the elder was pointing a finger in Pagel's face. "This isn't over!" he screamed. "Where is Mike Davis? We'll sue the USGA if we have to!"

Frank had met Mike Davis at the bottom of the Fox tower two days earlier. He wondered exactly where he was and if he knew what was going on. He got an answer quickly.

"I contacted Mike before I came out here," Mr. Pagel said. "I explained the situation to him, and he was completely in agreement that disqualification was our only option. I'm truly sorry this happened."

"You'll be even sorrier before I'm through!" Anderson replied, stalking over to put an arm around his son.

It looked to Frank like the younger Anderson was nearly crying.

Keith was now standing next to Frank, offering a hand. "Not the way you wanted to win, I'm sure, but the guy's a flat-out cheat," he said.

"You think he knew?" Frank asked.

"What do you think?" Keith answered.

"Slugger?" Frank said.

"One hundred percent. It isn't like the kid didn't have a reputation. He just pushed it too far. My bet is that caddie worked every round with a hole in that pocket just in case."

By now, all decorum around the green had evaporated.

Pagel and Kimball had security people surrounding them because a number of fans were shouting at them, demanding an explanation.

There were two security guards lurking near Frank, just in case. His father and Ron Lawrensen came up, both with wide smiles.

"So what happened on seven?" Frank's dad said. "The guy dropped a ball over there in the kikuyu?"

"The caddie did," Frank said.

"That's why he was showing them his pockets?" Lawrensen asked. "He had a hole in one of them?"

Frank nodded.

"How'd they figure it out?" his dad asked.

Frank nodded at Keith, who briefly explained.

By now, in addition to the fans who were flooding the green, all the members of the media who had been walking with the match were there, too, trying to figure out the situation.

Almost by magic, Pete Kowalski had appeared.

"Media members, please listen up," he said. "In fifteen minutes, the USGA will hold a press conference in the media tent to explain what happened."

"What about the players?" someone yelled.

"We will ask both to come in after Mr. Pagel and Mr. Kimball are finished," Kowalski answered.

Kowalski walked over to where Frank and his entourage were standing.

"You okay with that?" he asked Frank.

Frank shrugged. "Sure, why not?"

"We'll have some time first, right?" Lawrensen said. "This is a very delicate situation."

Frank looked at Lawrensen and at his father. "When did he become 'we'?" he asked.

"Easy, Frank, not now," Slugger said.

Frank realized his coach was right.

"You've probably got at least thirty minutes," Kowalski said in answer to the question.

They began walking in the direction of the carts. Slugger had to go over and retrieve Frank's bag, which was sitting by the side of the green. The Andersons had somehow disappeared.

"Where did those guys go?" Frank asked Keith.

"My bet is, if they aren't in the parking lot yet, they will be momentarily," Keith said. "They aren't going to answer any questions."

Frank's dad walked up behind them. "I guess we owe you a thank-you," he said to Keith.

"Just trying to do the right thing, is all," Keith said.

Thomas Baker then put his arm around Frank and smiled broadly. "Son," he said, "you're going to the Masters!"

That thought had not yet crossed Frank's mind. Now it did. But it didn't make him smile. Not even a little bit.

PART II

22

"MR. BAKER, WELCOME TO AUGUSTA NATIONAL.
Please follow me."

Frank just nodded at the middle-aged man in a blue sports coat who had come around the counter just inside the entrance to the locker room. Frank's head had been on a swivel from the second they had pulled through the gate that took them down Magnolia Lane to the players' parking lot.

As Frank, Slugger, and Frank's dad had gotten out of their courtesy car, they had seen Rory McIlroy, the Irish superstar, getting out of *his* courtesy car. Every player arriving in Augusta was met at the airport by someone from the club who handed them the keys to their courtesy car—this year, a Cadillac Escalade. Except for the color—McIlroy's was blue, Frank's white—the two SUVs were identical.

But Frank wasn't behind the wheel of his. Even though he had a driver's license, the tournament organizers had asked him not to drive because he was still legally a minor, and their insurance wouldn't cover him.

McIlroy had smiled when he saw Frank. It was Sunday morning, four days before the Masters actually started, and the players' lot was less than half full.

"Frank Baker, the Perryton Prodigy himself," McIlroy said, walking over to where the three of them stood, hand extended. "Rory McIlroy. It's a pleasure to meet you."

As they shook hands, Frank was totally stumped for a response. Rory McIlroy was introducing himself to *him* as opposed to the other way around?

He finally came up with, "Mr. McIlroy, it's an honor." Then he introduced his dad and Slugger. There, he'd done it. Words had come out of his mouth. He'd never been more proud.

"It's Rory," the twenty-something star said to Frank as he shook hands with the others. "I'm not *that* old."

That broke the ice.

Slugger was pulling Frank's clubs out of the back. McIlroy had no clubs and there was no sign of a caddie. He seemed to read the confusion on Frank's face.

"I've been here since Friday," McIlroy said. "Decided to go with the get-in-early approach this year." He smiled. "Figured I might as well try something different. Nothing else has worked in the past."

McIlroy was trying to wrap up a career Grand Slam. He'd won the PGA Championship twice, the U.S. Open, and the British Open. All that was left was the Masters.

"Are you headed for the locker room?" Slugger had asked, no doubt hoping for some direction.

McIlroy shook his head. "No, I don't go in there much. Harry just meets me at the little hut next to the range and we get to work. But if you go in the front door, the locker room is straight ahead on the right. They'll set you up in there. Then you go next door to register."

"Thanks, Rory," Frank said, trying out the use of his first name.

McIlroy gave them a friendly wave and veered off in the direction of the range—or, as Frank knew it was technically called, the tournament practice area. Augusta National had a language all its own. There were no fans—there were patrons. There were no grandstands—there were observation stands. And, even though one of the tournament's oldest sayings was "The Masters doesn't begin until the back nine on Sunday," there *was* no back nine, according to the membership. There was a first nine and a second nine.

Frank had studied all of this in his preparation for the tournament. He had lost the 36-hole U.S. Amateur final to John Caccese, a fifth-year senior at Oregon, three-and-two. He hadn't played poorly at all; Caccese had just made every single important putt he looked at all day.

Being honest, even though he had given the match everything he had, Frank simply didn't have much left emotionally after the insanity of his semifinal match with Edward Anderson.

Not surprisingly, Anderson hadn't spoken to anybody in the media that afternoon after being thrown out of the tournament. As Keith Forman had predicted, he had gone straight to the parking lot as soon as the match had been declared over and had driven off in a cloud of dust with TV cameras recording his lightning-fast departure. His father had stuck around to declare that he would fight the DQ, "to the Supreme Court if need be," before also storming off.

Frank had been left to say that he was stunned and disappointed by the way the match had ended. "I wanted to beat him fair and square," he was quoted most often as saying, "but he took away my chance to do that."

Forman had become something of a celebrity when both Thomas Pagel and Mark Loomis made the point that he had been the one who had asked to see several camera angles on what had gone on at the seventh hole. "It was nothing more than a gut feeling," he said. "Something funny was going on over there. I could tell by Frank Baker's face that he thought so, too."

The only good thing that had happened on the day of the final had been Oregon coach Casey Martin making a point of telling Frank how much he admired the way he had handled the whole incident and the way he'd played all week.

"If you decide you want to play college golf on the West Coast, I'd be happy to offer you a scholarship right now," he said. "You're an impressive young man."

It had taken a while, after returning home, for Frank to figure out that losing the final was probably a lucky break—even if it was one he hadn't sought. If he had won the match and been the U.S. Amateur champion at seventeen, the pressure from his father and Ron Lawrensen to start quietly making deals would have been huge. As it was, Frank knew Lawrensen was lining up corporate deals and his father still wanted him to turn pro after the Masters.

"What have you got left to do as an amateur?" he kept saying whenever the subject came up.

"Play in college?" Frank answered.

"You can go to college anytime you want," his dad had said repeatedly. "The money Ron will make us from all the corporations, especially if you play well in the Masters, will never be greater. Corporate America loves youth."

Slugger and Forman were Frank's voices of reason during this period. Frank was being recruited by every major golf school in the country—and some not-so-major golf schools that were pretty good schools academically, notably Harvard and Yale, which were practically in his backyard. Slugger took Frank on a number of recruiting visits. His father allowed them to go on the visits in large part because Lawrensen had told him that the possibility that Frank might go to college would put him in a stronger negotiating position. As in: "If you can't pay him X, then he just might go to college and keep his amateur status."

Frank wanted to go to college, and he wanted another crack at the U.S. Amateur—especially since it would be played the following year at Pebble Beach, arguably the most famous golf course in the country—other than Augusta National.

Even though he hadn't won the Am, the seventeen-year-old was getting a lot of attention as Masters week approached.

Golf Channel sent Rich Lerner, its main anchor, to interview him and put together a lengthy feature that would air during Masters week.

Forman had stayed in touch regularly, but more in his role as unofficial under-the-radar adviser than as a reporter. They had talked about Keith "writing something when this is all over," but neither of them knew what "something" meant or, for that matter, when "this" would be over.

"We'll know," Keith had said. "We won't have to figure it out."

They had decided to travel to Augusta on Saturday the week before the tournament and play the golf course for the first time on Sunday morning. Frank had been asked to appear early in the afternoon to meet the finalists in Augusta's annual Drive, Chip & Putt Championship.

Augusta National and the PGA of America had launched DC&P five years earlier to encourage more kids to play golf. The carrot was this day—the Sunday before the Masters—when the finalists, ages seven to fifteen, got a close-up glimpse at Augusta National.

The competition wasn't actually golf, just a golf skills contest. The only part of the famous golf course the kids actually got to play was Number 18—the putting part of the contest took place on the green there.

Because the DC&P finals took place at Augusta National and were televised by Golf Channel, they received a good deal of publicity. Frank hadn't ever entered when he'd been eligible because he was interested in winning real golf tournaments, not a hyped contest. His goal was to actually play the whole golf course, not just putt on the 18th green.

Now he'd achieved that—even if the way it had happened still haunted him a little.

The plan for today was to walk on the first tee and see who was there. If the tee was empty, he'd play by himself, which was fine with him. Slugger was again caddying for him; his coach and his father had been getting along better since the blowup in Los Angeles and Forman's subsequent talk with his father.

There was still, however, plenty of tension in the group. Frank and Slugger's plan was for Frank to make a final decision on where to go to college when the Masters was over. He still had one more trip left: to North Carolina to see Duke, UNC, and Wake Forest.

Frank knew his dad was hoping he'd play well enough during the coming week that the corporate offers would skyrocket to the point where it would be impossible to say no. Frank's feeling was that no number was high enough: he wasn't ready. Slugger felt that way, and so did Forman.

There was likely going to be a big battle in the not-so-distant future. For now, though, Frank had decided to push it out of his mind—or at least to the back of his mind. He had two goals for the week: enjoy every minute and try to make the 36-hole cut after Friday's round so he could play on the weekend. Anything beyond that was pure gravy.

• • • • •

The engraved invitation with the Augusta crest on it, which he'd been sent in February formally inviting him to play in the Masters, got them inside the building that housed the locker room. Frank showed the invitation to another guard standing in the doorway, and then he was shown to his locker by the gentleman in the blue jacket.

A few minutes later, having decided to tee it up, play right away, and worry afterward about time on the range—whoops, "the tournament practice area"—he walked out the clubhouse door with Slugger. They passed under the famous oak tree, planted in the 1850s, and made their way outside the ropes to the first tee. The public wouldn't be allowed on the grounds until Monday, so Frank could see the panorama of the golf course clearly.

"Wow, this is really something," he said to Slugger.

Some of the DC&P kids were down on the 18th green with a coterie of their families around the edge.

He walked onto the first tee, where two players were getting ready to tee off.

"Hey, you want to join us?" the first guy said. "I'm Jordan Spieth."

Frank managed to remember his own name as he introduced himself and shook hands.

The second player came up behind Spieth. "Justin Thomas. First time here, right?"

"Um, yeah," Frank answered.

"Well then, come on," Spieth said. "We'll try to give you

some of the secrets about where to hit it and where not to hit it."

"Sure," Frank sputtered. He caught Slugger's eye and they exchanged a can-you-believe-this? look.

"We've already hit," Spieth said. "You're up, rook."

Frank nodded and found a tee in his pocket. Slugger handed him his driver and a golf ball.

He got the ball and the tee in the ground and heard Spieth say, "Just pretend the whole world is watching you, because that's how it's going to feel on Thursday when they call your name."

"No pressure," Thomas added. "No pressure at all."

Frank looked at the two major champions. They were grinning from ear to ear.

Welcome to the Masters, he thought, and looked down at the ball. There was nothing left to do but swing the club.

23

KEITH FORMAN'S ORIGINAL PLAN HAD BEEN TO arrive in Augusta on Sunday night so he'd be at the golf course on Monday morning. But when Frank told him the Augusta National people had asked him to come down on Sunday to glad-hand with the Drive, Chip & Putt kids, he changed his plans. He wanted to witness as much of Frank's experience as he possibly could. He still wasn't sure what form it would take, but he knew he was going to write something on everything that had happened.

The most interesting thing that had happened since the U.S. Amateur had little to do with Frank—except that it did.

Early in March, an online golf newsletter called *Morning Read* had reported that Edward Anderson II, the father of Frank's disgraced U.S. Amateur opponent, had "resigned" his membership at Augusta National. Since the club never commented on membership, the newsletter quoted several club sources as saying that Anderson had been told he would not be receiving a dues statement for the following year and had been offered the chance to resign before the statements went out. The club never told a member directly he'd been bounced; it just didn't send a bill for the next year's dues.

After screaming from the highest hilltop that he would sue the USGA blind following his son's disqualification, Edward Anderson II had gotten very quiet upon seeing the video showing Jared Hopkins clearly shaking the ball out of his pants pocket. He then fired Hopkins, who was Anderson II's driver in real life, almost on the spot.

That had turned out to be a huge mistake, because Hopkins had instantly gone public, saying that both he and Anderson III had holes in their pockets and that the senior Anderson knew exactly what was going on as well.

After *Morning Read* broke the story, Keith decided to see if he could get either of the Andersons to talk. Augusta members—except for the chairman—never talked to the media on the record, but Anderson was no longer a member.

Through a member Keith had known long before the member had been invited to join the club, Forman was able to get the elder Anderson's cell phone number. Much to his surprise, Anderson answered on the second ring.

"Mr. Anderson, this is Keith Forman. I work for *Golf Digest*—"

"I know exactly who you are," Anderson broke in. "How did you get this number? Who do you think you are, calling me?"

"I think I'm someone who would like to give you a chance to tell your side of the story on your resignation from Augusta."

"I will tell that story when I feel it is appropriate," Anderson said, unintentionally confirming that the newsletter had the story right. "But it certainly won't be to the muckraker who started this whole thing!"

In the back of his mind, Keith heard a little voice saying, *Never argue with a source.* But he couldn't resist. "With all due respect, sir, your son and his caddie started the whole thing by cheating. He was a good enough player—"

"Call this number again and I will file harassment charges against you," Anderson said, and cut the call.

On the one hand, the little voice had been right. On the other hand, Keith suspected if he had done everything by the book, he wouldn't have gotten anything more from his source. At least, he told himself, he'd confirmed Anderson's resignation.

He wrote a brief story for his website confirming that Edward Anderson II had resigned from Augusta, quoting the conversation verbatim. After that, Anderson was nothing more than a memory. Time to move on.

· · · · ·

Keith always had mixed emotions when he arrived at Augusta National. There was no denying the beauty of the place. The golf course, designed in the 1930s by Bobby Jones (the most successful amateur golfer of all time) and Alister MacKenzie (the famous British golf-course architect), had been lengthened and tweaked constantly, but the basic aesthetics had never changed.

For anyone who played golf or loved golf, seeing it for the first time was almost a religious experience.

But there was also no denying the club's troubling history. No African American had played in the Masters before Lee Elder in 1975, and that came only after the rules had been changed to make any PGA Tour winner an automatic invitee. Several other very good African American players had been denied invitations to the tournament throughout the 1960s and early '70s, prior to Elder's victory at the 1974 Monsanto Open.

It wasn't until 1990 that Augusta National first invited an African American to join the club—and that came only after the embarrassment at Shoal Creek, in Alabama, had almost caused the PGA Championship to be moved or canceled that year. Hall Thompson, Shoal Creek's founder—who happened to be an Augusta member—had been asked by a local reporter in Birmingham what the reaction would be at the club if an African American applied for membership.

"That would never happen in Birmingham," he had said, going on to add, "We don't discriminate in every other area except when it comes to blacks."

The comments set off a national firestorm, and when it finally died down, Shoal Creek had an African American member and the U.S. Golf Association and the PGA Tour had declared they would no longer hold tournaments at clubs that discriminated against anyone, whether by race, religion, or sex.

Augusta National was exempt from this rule because the Masters was technically not a PGA Tour event. It was a very small loophole, but Augusta had continued to crawl through it for another twenty-two years: although it did admit its first African American member shortly after the scandal at Shoal Creek, it only admitted its first female members in 2012— after years of controversy surrounding their absence.

Forman also found the club's arrogance overbearing. TV "partners" lived in fear of violating any of Augusta's various rules and traditions. God forbid an announcer should call the fans anything but "patrons," or refer to a "front nine" or "back nine" instead of the "first nine" and "second nine," or imply that anyone played in the Masters for anything but the hope of an iconic Augusta National green sports jacket and their name inscribed on the trophy at the clubhouse. Money? Never mind the two-million-dollar first prize—we don't talk about money at Augusta.

That was no doubt because the membership was so overwhelmingly wealthy that it could do just about anything it wanted. Need a new driving range? Sure, let's just get rid of the main parking lot, buy up all the land across the street, and move all the parking there. Build a new tee on the 13th hole? No problem—we'll purchase land from Augusta Country Club next door at an outrageous price and build it. Want to move the media from a press building next to the first hole to use that space for corporate partners? Why don't we build a Taj Mahal–like press center at the far end of the grounds and dig up Berckmans Road to create parking space?

Doing his job as a reporter was harder for Keith at Augusta than at any other golf tournament. The media had less access at the Masters than at any major: no range access, no inside-the-ropes badges. Access to the nonchampions locker room, yes; champions locker room, no. Most reporters didn't mind. The parking was great, the food was excellent, and they could cover the tournament without ever leaving the Taj Mahal if they wanted. Many didn't leave, except to buy souvenirs.

Forman knew he was privileged to cover the Masters and he was in a place any golf fan would kill to be, but the atmosphere of the place—the entitlement of it all—made him feel a bit squeamish.

This year, though, was different. He wasn't here looking for general stories. He'd explained to the editors at *Digest* that he was working on a project involving Frank Baker and wanted to devote the entire week to him. They were intrigued enough to go along.

And so, after collecting his credentials in the press center, complete with the usual warnings about the instant expulsion—if not death—that would occur if you used your cell phone anywhere but at the Taj or the media parking lot, he set out in search of Frank.

He had sent him a text before getting out of his car because he knew that carrying his phone in the direction of the golf course and the locker room was a risk not worth taking. Just before he left the Taj, Keith saw a text from Frank: **About to go play a few holes. See you out there?**

Keith sighed. He'd made a mistake. Media had been

allowed on the grounds on Sunday at Augusta National only since the launch of Drive, Chip & Putt. But it wasn't until Monday that there was access to the golf course or the locker room. Until then, you were allowed in the three places where the DC&P competition was taking place: the so-called tournament practice area, the putting green, and the 18th green. You were also allowed under the famous tree outside the clubhouse entrance, where most of the golf world would gather to make deals, gossip, and be able to say, "I was talking to Tom Watson under the tree today and . . ."

On Sunday, Tom Watson would be nowhere in sight, nor would most of the players, unless you got lucky and caught one en route from the locker room to the golf course or vice versa. Keith knew that Frank would show up under the tree at some point to greet the DC&P kids along with defending champion Sergio García and a couple of other name players that Augusta National had "asked" to come and meet the kids. In the golf world an ask from Augusta National carried the same power as a presidential executive order. They asked; you did what they wanted.

It would be more than two hours before the kids' tournament was over. Keith was trapped with nothing to do until then. He went into the restaurant, grabbed some chicken from the buffet, and sat down by himself. There weren't a lot of media members on campus on Sunday. DC&P was covered extensively by Golf Channel—another "ask" from Augusta National—but the only reporters who covered it were those who had a local player participating or those like Keith who showed up claiming they were there to cover it but who were actually hoping to grab some time with a player or players. There were probably about thirty guys already in town. The rest would arrive the next morning.

"Hey, Keith, you here looking to interview a ten-year-old?"

Keith looked up and was pleasantly surprised to see Larry Dorman walking in his direction, tray in hand. Dorman had retired several years ago as the golf writer at the *New York Times*. He was not only one of the best golf writers of his generation but also the kind of guy who went out of his way to help and advise young writers—Keith had been one of those who had benefited from that.

Keith stood to greet Dorman, then shook his head as they sat down.

"I'm stalking Frank Baker," he said. "Doing a lousy job of it right now. Why are you here?"

Dorman now wrote the annual *Masters Journal*, the official tournament book that chronicled the entire week.

"The club asked me to be here today so I can include some of the DC&P kids and highlights in the program," he said. "Not exactly Woodward and Bernstein stuff, but they asked . . ."

"So you do." Keith finished the sentence with a laugh.

Dorman nodded, digging into a salad. Even in his mid-sixties, Dorman still looked like the dogged reporter he'd been—slender, with dark hair and a trimmed beard with just enough gray in it to make it clear he was no longer young. His current assignment didn't require doggedness. Keith suspected he missed that.

"So what's up with Baker?" Dorman asked.

"I've been dealing with him and his family since the Amateur," Keith said. "The answer is, I have no idea what's up with him. He's got the classic pushy father who smells big bucks, the sleazy agent hanging around ready to cash in. But he's a nice kid who just wants to play golf and go to college."

"Let me guess: the old man and the agent want him to turn pro when this is over."

Keith nodded. "When his last putt hits the cup at eighteen, whether on Friday or Sunday, corporate America will be backing a Brinks truck up to the garage of the Baker house."

"Any good guys in this?" Dorman asked. "Besides you?"

"His teacher at the home club in Connecticut," Keith said. "Guy named Slugger Johnston. Old college teammate of mine. But we're both pretty helpless to do much."

"That reminds me—what ever happened to the Anderson kid you caught cheating out at Riviera?" Dorman asked.

"The USGA suspended him from their events for a year," Keith said. "Didn't matter, though. He turned pro anyway. He made it through Q-School for the Web.com Tour last fall and has had a couple of top tens already this year."

"So he can actually play a little."

"Yeah, that's kind of the shame of it. If he's ever good enough to be in contention somewhere, the cheating thing will be in the first paragraph of every story."

"And the old man resigned from Augusta?"

"Yeah, apparently he was asked to."

Dorman laughed. "We all know how that turns out, don't we?"

"Every time," Keith answered. "Every time."

For a moment his mind drifted. He wondered where Edward Anderson II would be spending the week.

24

FRANK FELT AS IF HE WERE DREAMING AS HE, Jordan Spieth, and Justin Thomas made their way around the front nine. The beauty of the place was everything he had expected—and more.

Spieth and Thomas could not have been nicer, which didn't surprise him, given their reputations. Still, they went well out of their way on every hole to warn him where not to hit it, which side of the green to play to, and to tell him what to expect as the week went on.

"Watch where we're putting to on each hole," Spieth urged. "Those are the places where the holes are likely to be starting Thursday. They've got 'em all in the middle of the greens today, but there's no chance you'll find a flag there once the tournament begins."

"And don't pay any attention to the speeds," Thomas added. "These greens are probably rolling about eleven and a half or twelve right now. I promise you, on Thursday morning they'll be fourteen."

"At least," Spieth added.

Frank knew that Augusta was notorious for its green speeds—and the club's secrecy about them. Green speeds were measured by a very simple device known as a Stimpmeter, so called because a man named Edward Stimpson had invented it.

A Stimpmeter was an angled, three-foot-long track made of aluminum. You rolled a ball down it and measured the number of feet the ball rolled once it hit the green. Then you did the same test from where the ball stopped in the opposite direction. You added the two measurements together and divided by 2 to get the green speed. If the speed was five feet, you said the greens were rolling at 5; ten feet meant 10, and so on. The ideal green speed for championship golf was usually between 12 and 14. Some players insisted the greens at Augusta were as fast as 16 at times.

No one knew for sure, only that they were very fast once the tournament began. "You gotta figure they'll be at least two or three feet faster on Thursday than on Wednesday," Spieth said.

Even though they paused to try chips and putts from different spots on each green, they played quickly. Augusta had a one-ball rule, meaning players were not supposed to play more than one ball at a time in a practice round. Most places, players would routinely try a second or a third shot from the tee or from specific places. At Augusta, when you did it, you looked around first to make sure no one wearing green was watching.

"Better enjoy this," Spieth said as they walked onto the

seventh green. "By tomorrow, when everyone's here, if you want to play eighteen holes it'll take you five or six hours."

"Easily," Thomas added. "That's why we get here early, so we can play nine holes the next three days and still feel like we know the golf course."

"Helps to have played here before," Spieth said.

Helps, Frank thought, *to be a great player.*

Jordan Spieth was already a three-time major champion at the age of twenty-four, and his first three finishes at the Masters had been 2-1-2. Justin Thomas, who was three months older, had won his first major, the PGA Championship, the previous August.

Thomas was almost blindingly long off the tee. Augusta's fairways were wide enough that the players didn't mess around with three-woods or irons off the tee—especially in a practice round. They just blasted. Thomas was no more than five foot ten, and if he weighed 150 pounds it was a lot. But his clubhead speed was amazing. Spieth was supposed to be not long, but he was plenty long enough. Frank, who considered himself long, found himself muscling up on a couple of occasions to keep up and, as a result, he sprayed a few drivers.

"Long helps, but isn't required around here," Spieth said. "Look at me, Zach Johnson, Mike Weir. None of us is that long, and we've all won. Finding fairways in the right spots is critical."

Frank felt like he was in a PhD program for playing Augusta National. Which was why he felt a wave of disappointment when the three of them walked up the steep hill to the ninth green and saw three Augusta members wearing the club's signature green jackets waiting for them.

"Perfect timing, gentlemen," one green-jacket said, waiting near the back of the green as the three players walked off after putting out. "We'd be very grateful if you'd come and join us and meet some of the young people we've gathered here. Sergio's already up there."

He was smiling and his tone was light, but Frank knew this wasn't a request.

One of the other green-jackets looked Jordan up and down. "Mr. Spieth, I know you'll need a minute to go upstairs and grab your jacket."

"Absolutely," Spieth said. "Be down in a moment."

"Do we need jackets, too?" Frank whispered to Thomas.

Thomas laughed. "Not unless one of us has won the Masters," he said softly.

Frank got it. Spieth was going up to the champions locker room to get the green jacket he'd won in 2015. He knew that only the current champion—in this case, García—was allowed to take his green jacket off the club grounds. The other past champions had a green jacket waiting in their lockers when they came back each year. During tournament week, they were expected to wear their jackets for any non-golf public appearance.

"Justin, Frank, if you come with us, there are some youngsters who are very excited to say hello," said the third green-jacket.

Spieth was literally running in the direction of the locker

room. "Can't he just send someone to get the jacket?" Frank asked Thomas. "Why's he running like that?"

Two security guards had fallen into step with them, just in case someone stopped them for an autograph or a stray reporter showed up on the walk from the ninth green to the tree, where they could see a knot of people and a number of cameras. In truth, there weren't many people around. The only folks allowed inside the gates were the families of the DC&P kids, the media, and, of course, members and their families. The security escort seemed unneeded to Frank, but he knew his was not to question why.

"No one can go in the champions locker room unless escorted by a champion," Thomas said. "And Jordan just likes to run. Walking's not his thing."

When they got to the tree, the kids were lined up to meet them. It occurred to Frank that the oldest ones were only a couple of years younger than he was. Yet here he was going down the line behind Thomas, signing autographs, posing for selfies, asking kids their names, and congratulating those who were introduced to him as age-group champions.

One of the older girls was at least six feet tall and had a beautiful smile. "It's an honor to meet you, Mr. Baker," she said in a southern drawl.

"Uh, call me Frank," he said, his cheeks burning.

He was relieved when his green-jacket escort gently nudged him to keep moving. He'd used up all his clever lines with "Uh, call me Frank," so he didn't object.

Suddenly he heard a loud cheer. He turned and saw Spieth

walking over in his green jacket. The kids were golfers. They knew who Thomas was, and they had a vague notion that Frank was one of the amateurs who had qualified for the tournament. But Spieth was a superstar: he and Rory McIlroy had become the two biggest names in the game when Tiger Woods's problems had sidelined him.

McIlroy had won four majors, and Spieth had won three. Plus, they were both young and cool and friendly. Frank had seen that up close already today.

Spieth was clearly comfortable in this role. He took his time, working his way down the line, shaking hands, hugging some of the kids, kneeling to get down to eye level with the younger ones. Frank and Thomas had reached the end of the line so they stood and waited for Spieth.

Spieth made sure he left every kid with a smile on his or her face. When he reached Frank and Thomas, Frank noticed that another man in a green jacket had come up behind them to greet Spieth. This one he recognized: it was Jonathan Tucker, the new chairman of Augusta National.

He was tall and *looked* like a golfer—which he had been; he'd won the U.S. Amateur in the 1970s and had been a very good college golfer.

Tucker had a wide smile on his face as Spieth approached. "Jordan, great to see you again," he said. "Thanks so much for doing this."

"Happy to do it, Mr. Chairman," Spieth said.

Tucker turned to Frank and Thomas.

"And thanks to both of you, too," he said, shaking hands

with them. "Justin, haven't seen you since the PGA. Belated congratulations. That was great playing."

"Thank you, Mr. Chairman."

"And Frank, it's a pleasure to finally meet you," Tucker continued. "Having played in the Masters as an amateur, I'm always thrilled to meet the amateurs who've qualified to play here."

"Thank you, Mr. Chairman," Frank said, having picked up from Spieth and Thomas that this was how you addressed the guy.

"Are you all ready to say a few words to the kids?" Tucker asked.

They nodded. Frank had been briefed on this via an email prior to making the trip south. He had decided against writing anything out. That was Forman's advice. "You write it, you'll sound stilted and nervous," he'd said. "They're just kids and won't be listening anyway. Just tell 'em how you feel and get off the stage. They'll all be waiting for Jordan and Sergio anyway."

García had apparently spoken earlier, when he had helped present the DC&P trophies, and already exited. That had unofficially become one of the defending champion's jobs during tournament week.

Now, Tucker took a step forward and held his hands up for quiet—which he got almost immediately.

"Kids, I know you've heard enough from me already when I introduced Sergio," he said. "But, as you know, we've got three more participants here who would all like to say a few words. First, let me introduce one of the six amateurs playing in this year's Masters. He's a high school senior from Connecticut, and he was runner-up in last year's U.S. Amateur. So please welcome Frank Baker!"

The audience gave Frank a nice round of applause as he stepped forward. Tucker handed him the microphone he'd been holding.

"Thanks, Mr. Chairman," Frank said, pausing to take a deep breath. At least he'd gotten that part right. "I just want to say what an honor it is to be here and to talk to all of you. I know how proud your families are and how awesome it is to get to be at Augusta."

He noticed a Golf Channel camera not too far from him and felt himself beginning to sweat. He heard Forman's voice in his head: "Tell 'em how you feel and get off the stage." The last part sounded pretty good right now.

"So I hope you had fun today, and it was great to meet you all."

He handed the microphone back to Tucker and stepped back to polite applause.

Thomas and Spieth were—not surprisingly—far more polished than he was. Spieth finished by saying, "My younger brother, who I can't stand because he's five inches taller than I am"—pause for laughter—"played college basketball at Brown. Every year, Brown played at Penn, in Philadelphia, which plays its games in the Palestra, one of college basketball's most famous buildings. There's a small plaque in the lobby of the Palestra. It says, *To win the game is great . . . To play the game is greater . . . But to love the game is the greatest of all.*"

Another well-timed pause. The kids were silent.

"I feel that way about golf," Spieth continued. "Winning is great, playing is great, but *loving* to play and respecting the game you love is the greatest of all. Always try to remember that, every day you get a chance to play this great game."

The kids were mesmerized for a moment. Then they broke into wild cheers. Tucker stepped forward and hugged Spieth—green jacket to green jacket. Frank heard him say, "That was perfect, Jordan, just perfect."

Frank didn't disagree.

25

KEITH FORMAN FINALLY FOUND SLUGGER IN the shade under the enormous limbs of the big oak tree while Frank, Jordan Spieth, and Justin Thomas were meeting and greeting the DC&P kids.

"Even you have to admit that this is a cool thing for the kids," Slugger said.

"I don't doubt that it's cool for them," Keith said. "But I don't see a lot of inner-city kids in that group, do you? Not many kids of color. Lotta white one-percenters."

Slugger shook his head. "There you go again, Commie," he said. "You don't know that to be true."

"My best friend growing up has a nephew who made it here last year," Keith said. "His dad is—surprise—a money manager who belongs to five different golf clubs. He told me most of the kids who make it are like that."

"Yeah, fine," Slugger said. "I still say it's cool."

"I'm not saying it's *not* cool," Keith said. "But let's not pretend it's more than it is."

Slugger laughed. "Look around you," he said. "What about this place is real?"

Keith couldn't argue with that one.

The best description he'd ever read of Augusta National had been in a story describing the contrast between what was outside the gates on Washington Road: honky-tonks, tourist traps, lots of fast food, and a place called The Master's Gift Shop—the apostrophe being quite intentional and "The Master" in question not being a golfer but *the* Master—as in Jesus Christ.

The story described walking through the gates of Augusta National as akin to landing, like Dorothy's house, in Oz. Clearly, you were no longer in Kansas—or on Washington Road—anymore. Everything was green, perfectly manicured, and beautiful.

Keith heard Jonathan Tucker's voice on the microphone, and he and Slugger moved closer to the rope that would separate the public from the privileged the next day to listen to Frank.

"The shorter the sweeter," Keith said to Slugger.

"You got that right," Slugger said.

Frank did fine, Thomas did better, and Spieth—not surprisingly—knocked it out of the park.

"Boy, that kid's good," Slugger said.

"Your guy's only seventeen," Keith said. "Give him time. By the way, where are the Bobbsey twins?"

The Bobbsey twins were cute little kids from a hundred-year-old mystery series who were known for always sticking together. Keith had applied the nickname to Thomas Baker and Ron Lawrensen since they never seemed to be apart.

"Upstairs on the veranda, watching from there," Slugger said, turning in the direction of the clubhouse, where a number of people were seated at outdoor tables looking down on what was going on.

Keith spotted them, seated at a table with an excellent view.

The three players were approaching now, Spieth and Thomas signing some more autographs as they walked. Frank wasn't in as much demand, although he had a security guard trailing him. Spotting Slugger and Keith, he walked over.

Keith shook hands and said, "Well done."

"I got through it," Frank said with a sigh.

"So, what'd you think of the front nine?" Keith said, smiling.

The guard interrupted. "Mr. Baker, your media obligations are over. You don't need to answer any more questions today."

Keith was about to say something, but Frank beat him to it. "This gentleman is a friend," he said. "I'm fine. Thanks."

The guard didn't seem too pleased with that answer, but said nothing.

"The front nine—I mean, the *first* nine—was great," Frank said, looking around as if he was afraid someone might have heard him use the non-Augusta term. "Jordan and Justin gave me all sorts of tips. I want to get out here as early as possible tomorrow and play the back—I mean, the second."

They all laughed.

"I assume those guys warned you about pace-of-play starting tomorrow," Keith said.

"Oh, yeah, they did. That's why I want to be here at seven. Tuesday I have to play a little later because I'm playing with Rory and Jason."

That would be Rory McIlroy and the Australian star Jason Day, Keith knew. Slugger had been able to contact their reps to see if Frank could play with them one day, and they'd each said yes and agreed on Tuesday at 9 a.m. Apparently neither was an early riser except when he had to be.

"I met Rory walking in," Frank said.

The teenager's eyes were shining with excitement. Keith was happy to see he was enjoying himself. He deserved it.

"Slugger mentioned it," Keith said. "I told you he was a great guy."

"Couldn't have been nicer," Frank said. "I really think this is going to be a great week."

"As long as all you have to do is play golf and enjoy yourself," Keith said.

"He'll do that," Slugger said. He glanced up at the veranda for a moment. "I promise."

Keith hoped that was a promise his old friend could keep.

· · · · ·

Everything changed on Monday, as Keith had known it would.

Sunday, he had breezed down Washington Road to the press parking lot beside the Taj Mahal.

Monday morning, it took him twenty-five minutes to go the last two miles of his trip. Almost everyone with practice-round tickets did *not* have tickets to the actual tournament. Those were locked in every year, and the Monday-Tuesday-Wednesday tickets were sold through a lottery. For most golf fans, the chance to walk inside the gates of Augusta was a trip to golf mecca. They arrived early to drink in every minute and buy as many souvenirs as possible, since Augusta remained one of the few places on the planet that didn't sell its logoed merchandise online. You had to get *in* to Augusta to bring something *out* of Augusta.

Keith knew that Frank would already be on the golf course. His plan was to grab breakfast, make a quick tour of the locker room to see if he could find any players willing to talk on or off the record about the Baker-Anderson match at the U.S. Am, and then meet Frank on the tenth tee. Slugger had told him they would probably get there at about nine o'clock.

Most players didn't spend a lot of time in the locker room. It was a place to occasionally grab a shower or, more likely, a quick meal.

Keith walked in, said hello to the locker-room guys, and circled the almost-empty rows of lockers, figuring he wouldn't see anyone noteworthy. Much to his surprise, he found Rory McIlroy sitting in front of his locker signing some yellow Masters pin-flags, the kind you could buy in the souvenir tent.

Seeing Keith, McIlroy grinned sheepishly. "Not sure why anyone would want my signature on these," he said. "It's not like I've ever won here."

They shook hands, and Keith sat down on a chair that someone had left at the next locker. They made small talk for a couple of minutes, and then Keith asked how McIlroy was feeling about his game this week.

"I think it's close," Rory said, and smiled. "Never heard a golfer say that before, I'll bet."

They both laughed. "It's close" was the mantra of almost every golfer on the eve of a major championship.

"Gotta ask you about something," Keith said finally. "And it might be something you know nothing about."

"Jeez, by your tone, I hope that's the case," McIlroy said.

Keith grinned and tried to sound less ominous with his question. "You know about what happened in the semis at the U.S. Amateur last August?"

He asked vaguely on purpose because he didn't want to lead his witness in any way.

"You mean the cheating thing?" McIlroy said.

At the very least he'd heard about it.

"Yeah, that," Keith answered.

McIlroy nodded. "I was in Northern Ireland when it happened, so I didn't see it live," he said. "But I saw the video later and read about it. I honestly can't believe someone tried to pull a stunt like that. It was awful."

McIlroy never said "off the record" or asked if a reporter would be quoting him. That wasn't his way. You asked him a question, he answered it, and if someone didn't like his answer, that was fine with him.

"I'm writing about Baker, not sure what, but something," Keith said.

"Met him yesterday," McIlroy said. "Playing with him tomorrow. Seems like a nice kid."

"He's one of the good ones. He can't wait to play with you and Jason."

"And Phil," McIlroy said. "I got Phil as the fourth. I figured a little heckling would help prep him for Thursday."

Phil Mickelson was world-renowned for giving people a hard time during Tuesday money matches. Problem was, Keith knew that Frank didn't have any money.

McIlroy read Keith's mind. "Don't worry—I'll front him," he said. "He'll be my partner. Playing for my money will put so much pressure on him that Thursday will feel like a walk in the park."

Keith laughed. "Do you feel bad for Frank getting in here because of a DQ?"

"I feel bad for him that people are going to bring it up like it's his fault. From what I read, the reason Anderson cheated was because he was beginning to feel like he couldn't beat Frank. The pressure on him to get in here must have been unbearable, especially with his father being a member."

"You know the father resigned from the club," Keith said.

McIlroy looked around and lowered his voice when he answered. "I heard they told him not to show up this week, but he said they couldn't stop him. He's still got tickets, apparently."

"Won't they spot him if he shows?"

McIlroy shrugged. "And do what? Make a scene having him taken out? I doubt it."

"I just hope he doesn't harass Frank in some way, especially if you don't think they'll stop him."

McIlroy's face darkened a little. "I hope not, too. But very rich people don't take being embarrassed very well."

"I guess you'd know," Keith said, unable to resist.

McIlroy punched his shoulder lightly. "Watch it," he said. "I'm sure I can find a club rule you've violated pretty quickly if I want to."

"No doubt."

"I gotta go practice," McIlroy said, signing his last flag with a flourish and standing up. "I'm close, you know. Real close."

· · · · ·

Keith followed McIlroy out of the locker room. At the door, the golfer turned left to go in the direction of the range; the reporter turned right to walk past the throngs standing around the tree and then through more throngs en route to the tenth tee. He had to wait for a moment because there was a group on the first tee and, even on a practice day, when someone was on the tee, the marshals acted as if it were Sunday afternoon and stopped all foot traffic.

He finally walked behind the tenth tee just in time to see Frank and Slugger along with Kevin Streelman and his caddie, Frank Williams, walking through the ropes to the box.

Keith knew Streelman pretty well. He'd been on tour for about ten years and had won twice, including four years earlier in Hartford, when he had birdied the last seven holes to win by a shot. Streelman was a perfect guy for Frank to play with on Monday: friendly and easy to talk to, not likely to draw a massive gallery the way Jordan Spieth and Justin Thomas would if he had played with them today instead of Sunday.

Both players walked over to say hello when they saw Keith standing behind the tee. He wasn't inside the ropes, because that was strictly verboten at Augusta, even on practice days.

"Frank tells me you've been stalking him since last summer," Streelman said with a smile. "I can see why. Boy, can he play."

Frank was grinning from ear to ear.

Slugger, a step behind, was not. "Bobbsey twins at nine o'clock," he said softly.

Keith looked to his left and saw Thomas Baker and Ron Lawrensen approaching. His relationship with them had thawed briefly after his involvement in exposing the Andersons in Los Angeles, but with big money perhaps on the horizon, father and agent were back to seeing him as the enemy again.

"Eighty-nine players in this field, and you choose these two to follow for a few holes?" Lawrensen said in his usual half-joking-but-not-really-joking-at-all way.

"Of all the tees in all the towns in all the world, you two walk into mine," Keith said.

To his credit, Thomas Baker got the *Casablanca* reference. "Here's *not* looking at you, Forman," he said. He actually smiled when he said it.

He and Lawrensen headed down the right side of the fairway while Frank and Streelman waited for the fairway to clear. A group had teed off ahead of them on number ten, normally a violation of etiquette.

"I hope they'll let us through," Streelman said as they waited. "They're four, we're two. We flew the first nine holes. Your boy here shot thirty-four playing his first ball."

"I love this course," Frank said. "I mean, I haven't seen the back nine yet. Can't wait."

"That's second nine," Keith reminded him. "When you play with the big boys tomorrow, the media's going to want to talk to you when you're done. Do *not* say 'back nine,' especially on camera."

"He can say it," Streelman joked, "but only if he doesn't mind not being allowed to play on Thursday."

The fairway had cleared. Keith could see the Bobbsey twins trudging down the hill in the direction of the landing area.

He sighed. It was going to be a long week.

26

FRANK ACTUALLY ENJOYED THE BACK NINE more than he had the front.

There was a lot more variety to the holes. The flag was dead center on the tiny, treacherous 12th and, as they walked on the tee, Streelman said, "You see where the flag is? *That's* where you aim, no matter where the hole is on any given day. Hit it in the middle, make three, and get out of here."

Frank knew enough about the history of the golf course to know all about the famous meltdowns that had occurred at the 12th, most recently Jordan Spieth's 8 on Sunday in 2016 when he walked onto the tee with a three-shot lead and walked off the green trailing by three—since Danny Willett, the eventual winner, was birdieing 15 at the same moment.

He also knew all about 13 and 15, the famous par-four-and-a-halfs. Both were reachable par-fives fraught with danger—and plenty of water. One could make 3 on either hole, or 7. The 15th was especially daunting, with water both in front of the narrow green and behind it.

The 18th tee was about as scary a tee shot as Frank had ever seen—there were trees pushing up against the fairway on both sides, making it look as if you were trying to fit the ball down a bowling alley. The hole was long and uphill. If you hit a draw and couldn't fly the fairway bunker, you had trouble. If you hit a fade and pushed the shot even a little, you had tree trouble.

Streelman, who would be playing his sixth Masters, reminded Frank on several occasions to not believe what he was seeing and sensing on the greens today—just as Spieth and Thomas had done. He showed him where he thought the first day's hole locations would be, but told him he'd be feeling his way—like everyone else—on Thursday.

Even though Frank understood that playing the golf course well on Monday was a bit of a mirage, he was still fired up when he rolled in a six-foot putt for par on 18 to shoot 68. If nothing else, he could always tell people he'd shot 68 at Augusta National, practice round or not.

His father and Lawrensen were waiting for him when he and Slugger walked from the 18th green to the clubhouse inside the ropes that separated the public from those with special passes. Lawrensen was, comically, wearing a credential that said ANDREA SASAKI. That was Frank's mother's name, now that she'd remarried, so clearly his dad had applied for a badge for her even though she had no intention of coming.

Since Augusta National always limited the number of credentials it would give to agents—and to media outlets—it was routine for agents to use extra family badges. It was also routine for everyone to look the other way.

"You played great!" his father said, beaming. "Second time on the golf course, and you shot four under par!"

"This wasn't the golf course I'll be playing Thursday," Frank said, although he was pretty excited by how he'd played, too. "The greens will be completely different then." Now he was just parroting Streelman, Spieth, and Thomas.

"True, but you showed you can handle the length of the course," Lawrensen said. "That's important."

Frank didn't disagree. He was looking around for Forman, who was nowhere in sight.

"Let's go eat," his father said.

"Dad, Slugger says the best food in the place is in the caddie barn," he said. "A lot of the players eat there. I think I'll go eat there with him, if that's okay. We'll have dinner tonight at the Double Eagle house."

Like a lot of the big-time agencies, Double Eagle Inc. had rented a big house not far from the golf course. They brought in a chef for the week and invited all their important clients to dinner every night. It was a way to get a good meal in relative privacy and not hassle with getting a reservation at a restaurant when the town was bursting at the seams with people.

Frank's dad hesitated. "Can the media eat in there?" he said. He was clearly thinking about Forman.

"Nope," Slugger answered. "Just players and caddies."

"Fine, then. You going to hit any balls after lunch?"

"Don't think so," Frank said. "It's getting hot, and this is not an easy golf course to walk. I want to eat, get back to the Marriott, and get off my feet."

His dad nodded. "Perfect. Let's meet in the lobby at six to go to dinner. I hear you have an early tee time tomorrow."

Rory McIlroy had texted Frank that morning—they'd exchanged cell phone numbers—to say he and Jason Day wanted to play early because the planned nine o'clock tee time would mean a six-hour round.

"They told me we'd tee it up about seven-thirty. Rory and Jason say that's the only way to play eighteen holes and not lose your mind. So I want to be here by seven to warm up."

"I'm going to store the clubs and get out of the jumpsuit," Slugger said. "I'll meet you in the eating area."

Slugger was wearing the white-and-green jumpsuit that all Masters caddies were required to wear, even during practice rounds. The jumpsuit had the name BAKER on the back and the number 36 on the front. Frank knew that meant he had been the 35th player to register for the tournament. The number 1 always went to the defending champion. The rest of the numbers were given out in the order in which players arrived.

Frank and Slugger walked down the hill to the area roped off for the caddies. As they started to walk in the direction of the club storage area, a guard stopped them.

"Sorry, young man," the guard said, nodding at Frank. "Caddies and players only in this area."

"He's a player," Slugger said.

The guard laughed. "Sure he is—I bet he's the next Tiger Woods."

Slugger reached into his bag, where he had stored Frank's wallet, watch, and player ID while they were playing. He shoved the ID in the guard's direction. The guard took it, looked closely at the photo and then at Frank, and finally handed it back to Slugger.

"How old are you, young man?" he asked.

"Seventeen," Frank answered.

"Well, good luck to you, then," he said. "Maybe you *are* the next Tiger Woods."

Slugger peeled off to store the clubs, and Frank walked inside to where the buffet was set up.

"About time you got here," he heard a voice say.

He looked in the direction of the voice. It was Keith Forman.

. . . . .

"How did you get in here?" Frank asked. "My dad only let me eat here because he thought you couldn't get in. Caddies and players only."

"Unless a player or caddie walks you in," Keith said with a smile. He turned to a tall, lean man standing next to him. Frank recognized him instantly.

"Jim Mackay, meet Frank Baker."

"You're Bones!" Frank said.

Jim "Bones" Mackay was almost as famous as Phil Mickelson, the player he had caddied for dating back to 1992, before the two had split the previous summer.

"I know," Bones said, smiling.

Frank knew that 1992 Masters champion Fred Couples had hung the nickname on Mackay years earlier, in part because the caddie was tall and rail-thin and in part because Couples had trouble remembering names.

They chatted with Bones for a few minutes before heading to the buffet line. By then, Slugger had joined them. Frank's head was spinning. It looked as if half the players in the field were eating with the caddies.

They found a place to sit and Frank's eyes bugged completely out of his head when he realized that Tom Watson was sitting almost directly across from him. Watson, who had won the Masters twice, didn't play in the tournament anymore, but as a past champion he had a lifetime invitation and was obviously in town for the annual champions dinner on Tuesday night.

Keith apparently knew everybody, because when he said hello to Watson, the legend bellowed, "Forman, how the hell did you get in here? Do I need to call security?"

He was grinning when he said it and stuck his hand out to say hello. Watson then turned to Frank and said, "Young man, I've heard you have a great future, but you need to be careful about who you hang around with. *Never* trust the media."

He was still grinning as Frank was trying to find his voice.

He finally did and, reaching across the table, said, "It's an honor to meet you, Mr. Watson."

"It's Tom," the legendary champion said. "And, for the record, I thought you handled yourself wonderfully during that debacle at Riviera last summer. It was a terrible moment for golf, and you were caught in the middle."

"Th-thanks," Frank managed, amazed that Watson knew what had happened. Then again, everyone in golf knew what had happened. It had been a bigger story than the final outcome of the Amateur, which Frank still thought was very unfair to John Caccese, who had, after all, won the thing. All the talk the following week had been about Edward Anderson III getting caught cheating.

Frank had just taken a bite from a fried chicken leg when Watson said, "Who've you got Thursday?"

"Um, don't know yet," Frank answered. "Waiting for the pairings. I guess they come out today."

"They're out," Watson said. He turned to the man sitting next to him, who was wearing glasses and talking intently to Andy North, the two-time U.S. Open champion who now worked for ESPN. "Neil, hand me the pairings, will you?"

The man he'd addressed didn't even look at Watson, but simply reached for a piece of paper that was under his left hand and passed it over. Watson began glancing up and down the list.

Frank had been thinking a lot about who he might play with the first two rounds. He knew the amateurs were always paired with past Masters champions. John Caccese would play with Sergio García, because the U.S. Amateur champion always played with the defending Masters champion.

Watson found his name on the sheet. He smiled. "You did pretty well: Zach Johnson and Justin Rose."

Johnson had won the Masters in 2007, beating Tiger Woods down the stretch, and had also won the British Open in 2015. Justin Rose was the international player in the group—a Brit who was the 2013 U.S. Open champion and had a reputation as one of the nicer guys in golf.

Watson handed the pairings to him. "That's a good group for you. They're both good guys and they play fast."

Watson was one of the fastest players in the game's history and was well known for not liking to play with slow players— other than Nicklaus, who was as slow as he was great, and who was also a close friend of Watson's.

Frank felt his stomach twist a little as he pictured himself on the first tee Thursday with the two major champions. Not only was Rose a past U.S. Open champion, but he had lost in a playoff to Sergio García here a year earlier. A lot of people would be watching Rose and Johnson—which meant they'd be watching Frank.

Slugger read his mind. "No matter who you play with, a lot of people are going to be watching you," he said. "Don't sweat it. Like Tom says, it's a good pairing for you."

Frank looked down at the sheet. They were teeing off at 8:48. At least it was early. He wasn't going to sleep Wednesday night, so the earlier they teed off, the better.

Watson and the man he'd called Neil stood up to go. Frank had figured out that Neil was Watson's caddie.

Watson leaned down to talk to Frank in a low voice before he left. "I've heard some stories about that agent Lawrensen running around trying to make deals for you. Don't get carried away with all this. You're a high school senior, right?"

Frank nodded.

"Go to college. If you're any good, there's plenty of time to play golf."

He shook Frank's hand, patted Neil on the shoulder, and they took off.

Slugger watched them leave, then turned to Frank and said: "You see his caddie, Neil Oxman?"

Frank wasn't paying attention. He was thinking about what Watson had just said.

"What?"

"Neil Oxman, Watson's caddie."

"What about him?"

"He's probably the richest guy in this room. In real life he's a big-time political consultant," Slugger said.

"A *Democratic* political consultant," Keith put in.

Slugger was nodding. "Yup, a commie, just like Keith. But a rich one."

Frank smiled and nodded vaguely, but all he could focus on was what Tom Watson had just said in parting: "Go to college."

He knew the legend was right. But how could he convince his father of that? He snapped from his reverie. That could wait. He had a tee time the next day with Rory McIlroy, Jason Day, and Phil Mickelson—ten major titles among them. There was no reason to think of anything else. At least for now.

27

KEITH FOLLOWED FRANK AND SLUGGER OUT OF
the caddie barn and spent a moment with them outside. He
was tempted to reinforce what Watson had said inside, but
figured he didn't need to here and now.

They were leaving. Frank was worn out from the early
wake-up and wanted to be ready for his big day on Tuesday.
Keith thought that was a smart idea.

"What are you going to do the rest of the day?" Slugger
asked his friend.

Keith sighed. "Something I'm not going to enjoy—find
some agents."

"Why?" Frank asked.

"Because I want to get more specifics on what Lawrensen's
really up to. He must be getting around if Watson's heard
stuff. I'd like to find out what you might actually be dealing
with next week, Frank. Your dad and Lawrensen certainly aren't
going to tell me, so I have to try to get a feel for it on my own."

"Well, do me a favor," Slugger said. "Don't tell us. Let's keep Frank's focus on golf—at least for the rest of this week."

"Couldn't agree more," Keith said.

Frank and Slugger turned to walk to the player parking lot. Keith went the other way, circling back to the other side of the clubhouse—the golf-course side.

He walked up the hill to the big tree. The lawn underneath its enormous branches was teeming with people. Monday under the tree at the Masters was like the first day of school. The entire golf world was there, and everyone was glad to see everyone else.

Keith said hello to a number of people, but he was on a mission now. He spotted Mark Steinberg, Tiger Woods's longtime agent who also represented Matt Kuchar and Justin Rose. The guy knew just about everyone in the world of corporate golf.

Steinberg was talking to Jerry Tarde, the editor in chief of *Golf Digest*—who was Keith's boss. That meant that Keith had a good walk-up excuse; he wasn't just interrupting Steinberg and a stranger.

"Ah, there he is, the man I'm paying to babysit a teenager all week," Tarde said as Keith approached.

"The teenager's playing tomorrow morning with McIlroy, Jay-Day, and Mickelson," Keith said.

"I hope he brings his wallet," Steinberg said.

Keith pretended to be stunned. "Mark, you know there's no gambling on the PGA Tour," he said.

The conversation continued in that vein for a couple of

minutes before Tarde said, "Well, I should probably check on my writers who are actually working this week."

As he walked away, Keith asked Steinberg if he had a minute. Steinberg shrugged. "As long as you aren't going to ask me about Tiger, I've got all the time you want."

"Actually, I wanted to talk to you about the teenager I'm babysitting."

"I hear he's pretty good," Steinberg said. "But Ron Lawrensen is all over him. In fact, I think Lawrensen's already got a deal with the old man."

"Oh, he does," Keith said. "But I'm hearing he's also trying to make deals for Frank right now."

Steinberg looked around for a second as if making sure no one else was listening. "I've heard the same thing," he finally said. "Talk to the Nike guys and to the Brickley guys. I think he's trying to draw them into a bidding war of some kind. Which, by the way, is smart. He's also talked, I hear, to Callaway and Titleist about club deals. *And* he's talking to McCarley about some kind of deal with Golf Channel."

"Deal with Golf Channel?" Keith said. Mike McCarley was the television company's president.

Steinberg nodded. "Like a 'year in the life of a rookie' type of thing."

That was the same sort of idea the agent had been pitching ESPN the previous summer. Now it appeared that Lawrensen was trying to create yet another bidding war, this one between TV networks, for Frank.

Keith realized that neither ESPN nor Golf Channel could

do such a story if Frank wasn't a rookie on the Tour. Even if they wanted to chronicle his freshman year in college, NCAA rules wouldn't allow it.

"Is he pitching this stuff for right now?" he asked Steinberg.

Steinberg shrugged. "From what I hear."

It occurred to Keith that the train might already be out of the station and the engineer driving it—Frank—hadn't even been told.

He thanked Steinberg and turned to leave.

"Hey, we're off the record on all this," Steinberg said. "You aren't going to quote me to anybody."

"Promise," Keith said.

What he needed right now was information, not quotes.

He wanted to find some of the people Lawrensen was dealing with. Even if they wouldn't confirm anything, their demeanor and body language might tell him a lot.

He circulated around the tree a while longer, bumping into Guy Kinnings, the head of golf at the sports agency IMG. The agent had heard basically the same things that Steinberg had, except he added that Sky Sports was also talking to Lawrensen about some sort of documentary deal. Kinnings was based in London, so it made sense that he might know something about a Sky deal.

Keith went inside the clubhouse to see who else might be around. He walked up the circular stairs to the second floor, where the dining room, veranda, and the champions locker room were located. As he reached the top of the steps, he almost ran smack into Mike Weir, the 2003 champ.

Weir had been the first lefty and the first Canadian to win the Masters. He had struggled with injuries in recent years but was one of the more popular guys in the game. Keith had first met him when Weir was playing some Web.com events to try to get his game back into shape.

"Not waiting in line for the shower, were you?" Keith said, nodding in the direction of the door to the exclusive locker room.

For a split second Weir looked baffled; then he burst out laughing. "No, but you can bet I'll take care of that early to-night."

He had once told Keith a story about the 2004 champions dinner—which he had to host as the defending champion. He'd been on the range, grinding on his swing, when he suddenly realized the dinner was starting in a half hour and he was a sweaty mess. He'd raced back to the clubhouse to take a shower.

"There's only one shower in the champions locker room," he had said. "I walk in and Nicklaus and Watson are waiting their turn. Palmer's in the shower. Kind of hard to cut that line."

Just for the heck of it, Keith asked Weir if he had seen any of the shoe guys, as everyone called them, lurking around any-where.

Weir smiled. "Look behind you," he said. "Billy Nevins is sitting right over there in the corner."

Keith turned and saw Nevins, the main Tour rep for Brickley, sitting at a corner table in the dining room with a very beautiful woman.

"Thanks, Weirsy," Keith said, using the nickname Weir was almost always called by everyone on the Tour.

The small dining room only had about a dozen tables. There were perhaps a dozen more outside on the veranda. Inside was packed. Keith explained to the maître d' that he was looking for Mr. Nevins, whom he pointed to in the corner. There were several members, easy to pick out in their green jackets, sitting at a number of tables. Keith felt as if they were staring at him as he moved across the room, even though he knew most—if not all—of them had no idea who he was or would care even if they did.

He reached Nevins's table. He knew Nevins to say hello to, usually on the range, but had never had any kind of real conversation with him. His interest in who was wearing what clothes or golf shoes was, to say the least, minimal.

"Billy, Keith Forman," he said, reaching his hand across the table.

Nevins smiled, but not with any warmth. "Sure, Keith, I know," he said. "This is one of our sales reps, Erica Chambers."

Erica Chambers was, in fact, quite beautiful. She had jet-black hair and matching eyes that seemed to look right through him as she extended a hand. "I've read you in *Golf Digest*, haven't I?" she said.

"On occasion," Keith said, flattered and a little bit dazzled.

Erica Chambers wasn't a run-of-the-mill good-looking golf wife or groupie. She was stunning.

"You *love* Rory McIlroy, don't you?" she added. "Every time I read you there's something in your story about what a great guy Rory is."

"Well, Rory is a great guy," Keith said defensively. "And very quotable."

"Erica's very competitive," Nevins said. "She'd rather you love some of our guys, not a Nike guy."

"Well, actually I was hoping to talk to you about someone who might be one of your guys soon," Keith said.

Nevins pointed at the empty chair directly across from him. "Join us. You hungry?"

"Thanks, but I ate in the caddie barn," Keith said. "I wouldn't mind some coffee, though."

Nevins waved in the direction of a waiter while Erica Chambers looked at him, surprise in her spectacular eyes, and said, "You ate in the caddie barn? With the caddies?"

Clearly, she found the notion remarkable.

"And a few of the players," Keith said. "It's the best food on campus."

"On campus?" Chambers asked.

"Just a phrase I use," Keith said. "This place reminds me of college, somehow. All the cliques and the endless popularity contests."

The waiter arrived, a familiar face from Keith's past trips to Augusta.

"Mr. Forman, how good to see you," the waiter said.

Keith had always found Augusta's employees to be the nicest people at the place. Joseph Andrews was one of those people.

"Joseph, great to see you, too," he said.

"Are you eating?" Joseph asked. "Need a menu?"

"No, thanks," Keith said. "Just coffee with cream would be great."

"Coming up," Joseph said.

"So, Keith, what can I do for you?" Nevins asked.

Keith decided not to beat around the bush. "Frank Baker," he said.

Nevins's eyebrows twitched. He smiled. "We on the record or off?" he asked.

"Whatever gets me an honest answer," Keith said.

"That would be off."

Keith nodded and made a point of putting the notebook he'd taken out of his pocket on the table, pen on top of it.

"Of course we're interested in the kid," Nevins said. "Everybody is."

"Nike would kill to have him," Chambers said, which earned her a sharp look from Nevins.

"Nike, Adidas, everyone is in the mix right now. But . . ." He paused and leaned back in his chair as Joseph arrived with the coffee.

"But," Keith said once the waiter had left.

"But I think we have an edge. Our biggest-name player right now is Jesse Allen. We're going to make a play for Harold

Varner III because he's got such a great personality, and if he plays well at all, he can make us a lot of money." Nevins paused for a sip of water. "Nike has Rory, who is a big number and worth it, and Tiger, who is a bigger number and not worth it—unless he actually starts racking up wins again. I think they want the kid. But they have a ceiling on investing in a teenager. We don't have a ceiling."

"You're that sold on the kid?" Keith asked.

"Everyone I've talked to loves his game, his maturity, and his personality. Look, the last sure-fire guy was Tiger. Nike got a bargain with him at the beginning. No one's ever really sure-fire, but we like this kid a lot." He stopped as if he thought he'd gone too far. "What are you going to do with this?" he asked.

"For now, nothing," Keith said. "But that might change as soon as . . ." He left the sentence hanging intentionally.

"Next week," Nevins said, finishing the thought for him. "You sure Lawrensen will deliver him?"

Nevins smiled. "Ron Lawrensen's an agent. I never trust agents. But there's a lot of money at stake for him here, short term and long term. He's told me the kid is balking a little at turning pro right now, but he'll deliver. As you probably know, Double Eagle practically owns the father. The kid will sign."

"With you," Keith said.

"Well, if he wins the Masters that could change things," Nevins said with a laugh. "Beyond that, I feel pretty confident."

Keith drained his coffee and reached into his wallet to leave money to pay for it.

Nevins waved him off. "Brickley Shoes can pay for a cup of coffee," he said. "If you can be bought for that, then you're in trouble."

Keith was about to answer when Joseph returned with lunches for Nevins and Chambers.

Seeing Keith's wallet, the waiter said, "Don't worry, Mr. Forman, coffee's on me." He put the plates down and asked if his two customers needed anything else.

"Ketchup," Chambers said, not adding a "please."

"Coming up," Joseph said. He shook Keith's hand and said, "Please stop in and have lunch with us one day."

"I will, Joseph," Keith said.

He turned to say goodbye to Billy Nevins and Erica Chambers, and then walked away.

28

FRANK WAS WIRED WHEN HE GOT OUT OF THE car on Tuesday morning.

He realized his adrenaline was almost out of control. If he felt this way for a Tuesday practice round, how was he going to feel on Thursday?

He practically sprinted to the entrance to the range—oops, tournament practice area—and had to wait for Slugger to catch up with him.

"Do me a favor," Slugger said as they were handed some range balls by one of the attendants. "Don't drink any more coffee this morning."

Phil Mickelson and Jason Day were already hitting balls, and Frank stopped to say good morning, introduce himself briefly, and shake hands. One thing golfers understood was that you didn't socialize on the range very much before playing—even on a practice day. After a round was different. That was more of a social hour than pre-round sessions.

"We're off at seven-fifty," Day said. "Earliest I could get when I signed up."

"Perfect," Frank said. "Have you seen Rory?"

Day laughed. "No, and we probably won't for another half hour. He's not big on long warm-ups."

Sure enough, McIlroy walked onto the range at seven-thirty, hit about a dozen balls, and said, "Meet you guys on the putting green."

It was on the putting green, with fans—who hadn't even been let in the gates until 7:15 but who were already at least five or six deep—that the four players all gathered in the middle of the green to settle on the day's bet.

"We do it here," McIlroy explained, "so that the patrons and green-jackets on the first tee don't hear us."

"Since no one bets on the PGA Tour," Day put in.

Mickelson nodded, with his big impish grin—if a forty-seven-year-old could be impish—firmly in place. "So, usual non-bet, right? If we were playing for money, it'd be a thousand bucks a hole, automatic presses." He turned to Frank. "Can you handle that, kid? Or do we need to play for a dollar or something?"

"He's fine," McIlroy said. "No worries."

Mickelson's crack about playing for a dollar reminded Frank of a famous story told about Jack Stephens, the late past president of Augusta National. According to legend, a friend of Stephens's had shown up one morning with a guest who thought himself quite the hotshot.

"So what are we playing for?" the guest had said on the first tee. "A thousand a hole, five thousand?"

Stephens, who was a billionaire, looked at the guest and said in his Arkansas drawl, "Around here, we usually play for a dollar."

"A dollar!" the guest said, stunned. "A dollar? What's the point of even playing?"

He continued to complain the entire round about the embarrassment of only playing for a dollar. When the round ended, the foursome moved into the clubhouse for lunch. When the guest *again* expressed dismay at not playing for some real money, Stephens looked at him and said, "Exactly how much are you worth?"

The guest drew himself up and said proudly, "Forty-two million dollars."

Stephens nodded, waved a waiter over, and asked for a deck of cards. The waiter brought the cards to Stephens, who put the deck on the table and said, "Forty-two million dollars, right?"

The guest, a bit baffled by now, nodded.

"Okay," Stephens said. "I'll cut you for it. That real enough for you?"

The guest practically whimpered as he backed down and didn't say another word the rest of the day. Needless to say, he was never invited back.

Even though McIlroy was fronting him, Frank would have preferred to play for a dollar, like Jack Stephens.

The bet made, the four of them walked between the ropes from the putting green to the first tee. There were cheers all around, people leaning against the ropes reaching out for hand slaps as the players went by. They all granted them. There were no autograph requests because club rules expressly forbade autograph-seeking on the golf-course side of the clubhouse.

As the players walked onto the tee, several fans began chanting, "USA, USA," the chant that seemed to break out anytime Americans were playing against non-Americans in anything.

"USA versus foreigners, right, Phil?" someone yelled on the tee.

Mickelson shook his head. "This isn't the Ryder Cup—it's a practice round," he said. "Rory wanted the kid." He turned to Frank and said, "Lead us off there, kid."

Me? Lead off? In front of all these people? Frank, who'd been enjoying every second up to this moment, had no choice.

He teed his ball up, stepped back to go into his pre-shot routine, and heard Mickelson say in a loud stage whisper, "Wonder if he knows about the bunker out there at about three hundred?"

This got a laugh from the crowd. The first hole's fairway bunker was impossible to miss.

"You starting already, Phil?" McIlroy said with a grin. "On a seventeen-year-old? Really?"

"You were pretty good at seventeen, as I remember," Mickelson said.

"At least I can remember when I was that age," McIlroy answered.

Oh my God, Frank thought, stalling to let the trash talk wind down. *Is it going to be like this all day?*

. . . . .

It was exactly like that all day.

With the bunker now clearly stuck in his mind thanks to Phil's ribbing, Frank pulled his first tee shot into the left rough but managed to keep it out of the trees. From there, he made par—as did everyone else. That helped him settle down.

Then, on Number 2, he bombed his tee shot over the bunker. So did McIlroy and Day. Mickelson found the bunker and had to lay up. The rest of them went for the green in two. Day hit his shot into the left-front bunker. Frank found the green and had a 40-foot eagle putt. McIlroy got his ball to within 20 feet. Day got up-and-down for birdie, making the bunker shot look easy. Frank hit a good putt to within three feet.

Frank looked at Mickelson. "Pick it up?" he asked.

"Better mark it," Mickelson said. "Just in case Rory knocks his six feet past."

Instead, McIlroy's putt went dead center for eagle, winning the hole for them. "Now," he said to his partner, "you can pick it up."

They fist-bumped.

Frank was having a blast.

That's how it went the rest of the round. Kevin Streelman had given Frank some helpful hints the day before, but his three playing companions this time around seemed to know every inch of the golf course. Mickelson had won the Masters three times; Day had finished second; and McIlroy had taken a four-shot lead into the final round seven years earlier, only to shoot 80 on Sunday. He was just twenty-one at the time. Six weeks later, he'd rebounded to win the U.S. Open by eight shots.

The level of play was breathtaking. Someone seemed to make a birdie—or an eagle—on every hole. Frank and McIlroy won the front nine one-up, when Frank, remembering what Streelman had said about needing to hit the ball 20 feet past the pin on the ninth green when the hole location was near the front, did just that. The ball rolled back to within three feet and he made the birdie putt.

"You brought a blanking ringer!" Mickelson said to McIlroy. "This kid's not seventeen. No way!"

He walked over and fist-bumped Frank. "Good playing," he said softly.

The back nine was more of the same. Day and McIlroy halved the 13th hole with eagles; then Mickelson made one at 15. They came to the 18th with the whole match—for an "imaginary" $5,000—even, and McIlroy and Frank one-up on all the various presses. If 18 was halved, Frank and Rory would win $1,000. If they won it, they'd win $6,000. If Mickelson and Day won the hole, Rory would have to pay their opponents $4,000.

Frank stood off the tee, looking down the chute between the trees, heart pounding. Mickelson and Day had the tee, and they both bombed drives past the fairway bunker on the left. McIlroy hit first for their team, and he, too, striped his drive. With his partner safely in the fairway, Frank relaxed and hit a bomb that was only a few feet short of McIlroy.

"Honestly, I can't believe how long you are at seventeen," Rory said as they walked off the tee. "I couldn't hit it close to there when I was your age."

Frank just smiled at the compliment. In truth, he normally couldn't really hit it close to that far either. He just had so much adrenaline pumping that the ball felt as if it were exploding off his club.

They all had seven- or eight-irons in. The hole was cut near the back of the green, so Frank took the seven, even though Slugger thought it might be an eight. Slugger might have been right. The ball landed hole-high, took a quick hop, and went over the green, leaving him with a difficult downhill chip back, even though he was less than 20 feet from the hole. The other three all hit the green, none of them close but all below the hole with birdie putts.

Mickelson and Day went first, each from about 30 feet. Mickelson's putt looked like it was going in before it curled right, about six inches from the cup for a gimme tap-in. With his partner safely in for par, Day banged his putt, but it hit the cup still going fast and popped out.

McIlroy was about 25 feet away. "Why don't you go first," he said to Frank. "Get it close so I can go after my putt."

Frank liked that idea. He knew Rory wasn't going to three-putt from below the hole, which meant that they would, at worst, tie the hole and the match.

He thought for a moment about putting, which he often liked to do from off the green, but the grass was a little too thick, so he took his wedge.

"You land it more than about six inches on the green, it's going all the way to the bottom," Slugger said.

"And if I land it short, it might not get on the green," Frank said.

"That's why you should have hit eight," Slugger said, which annoyed Frank a little.

He shook it off, studied the shot, and stood over the ball. The crowd was at least six-deep around the green. Augusta never released attendance figures, but Frank had read that at least fifty thousand people passed through the gates on practice days. It looked as if half of them were around the green at that moment. He hadn't seen his father or Lawrensen all morning, but that was okay—they might have been standing on top of him and he wouldn't have noticed. He was having too much fun.

It was as quiet as if it were Sunday afternoon. Frank got his club well under the ball and felt it gently pop in the air, exactly as he had intended. It landed just on the green and began picking up speed as it approached the cup. Frank realized that if it didn't hit the flagstick, it wasn't going to stop for a while.

"Hit the hole!" he yelled, in what he knew was a pleading tone.

Somehow, the ball heard him. It hit the stick, popped into the air, and then disappeared into the hole. The crowd exploded. Frank felt like he'd *won* the Masters. McIlroy was running at him, arms in the air. If they hadn't been on the iconic 18th green at Augusta, Frank might have jumped in the air for a chest-bump. Instead, they double-high-fived, and Rory hugged him.

"*You* are ridiculous!" he shouted in Frank's ear.

Mickelson and Day were standing there with silly grins on their faces. They also hugged Frank.

"When I'm Ryder Cup captain, I want you on my team," Mickelson said.

Frank knew Mickelson wouldn't be Ryder Cup captain for another six years, but that sounded good to him.

"Great playing, mate," Day said.

"We'll pay off over lunch," Mickelson said.

They walked off the green with the crowd chanting, "USA, USA!"

Frank didn't quite get it, but he enjoyed it anyway.

· · · · ·

They all had to spend a few minutes under the big oak tree talking to the media. Most of Frank's questions were about what it was like to play with the three stars. Then someone said,

"Rory just said you're the most talented young player he's seen since he came on tour."

It was a statement, not a question, but he was clearly expected to respond.

"That's really nice of him to say," Frank said. "I had a very good day today. I'm not really as talented as all that. I was just inspired, I guess, by playing with those guys."

It occurred to Frank that he had shot 67 on his own ball, which was pretty amazing, especially given the pressures of the match and Mickelson's constant needling.

"Do you think you can play as well as this on Thursday?" someone asked.

"I hope so," Frank said. "I'm sure the golf course will be set up very different and there won't be as much joking around going on, so we'll have to see, I guess. I'm certainly psyched for it."

Oh jeez, he thought, *that sounded like a seventeen-year-old.*

"So how much was that last chip-in worth?" someone asked.

The others had already coached Frank up on this one. "Worth?" he said, smiling. "It was worth a double-high-five from Rory. There's no gambling on the PGA Tour, right?"

Everyone laughed at that one, and Frank was excused. He saw Keith Forman watching from behind his colleagues.

"We need to talk," Forman said. "Not here, not now, but later today. Without the Bobbsey twins anywhere in sight."

Frank nodded. "I'll text you after lunch," he said. "You can get to your cell phone in the press building, right?"

Forman nodded. "No rush. Go have fun."

Frank did just that. The four players had lunch in a corner of the upstairs dining room. Mickelson had wanted to bring them into the champions locker room as his guests, but the few private tables were already taken.

As they sat down amid a sea of green jackets, Mickelson looked around, then quietly slipped a fat wad of bills into Frank's hands. Frank looked and saw they were all hundreds.

"This is wrong," he said. "Rory should get this."

"No way," Mickelson said. "You earned it. And believe me, if you'd lost, the minute you turned pro, I'd have collected."

Frank had never seen so much cash before in his life. He looked at Rory, who nodded.

"Don't spend it all in one place," his partner said, grinning.

Frank stuck it in his pocket. It had been an amazing day.

29

KEITH AND FRANK MET AT A MCDONALD'S, ONE
that was well off the very beaten path of Washington Road,
which ran along the northeast side of the course. After the kid's
incredible performance that morning, Keith worried that going
to anyplace near the golf course would result in Frank being
recognized early and often.

He made the right decision. At three o'clock in the afternoon, the restaurant wasn't crowded. They'd both eaten at the
golf course, so they ordered milkshakes and sat in a small
booth in a corner.

Frank filled Keith in on the events of the day, finishing
with Mickelson handing him the cash. "As we were getting
up to leave, he said to me, 'Kid, whenever you turn pro, that'll
be tip money.'"

Keith laughed. "Actually, he's not lying. He's been known
to leave hundred-dollar tips at drive-through windows. He's
the best tipper I've ever met in golf. Did he ask you *when* you
were going to turn pro?"

"No, but Rory did when we went back to the locker room for a couple minutes. He said he's always wondered what college would have been like, but turning pro at seventeen had worked out pretty well for him."

Keith nodded. "Can't argue with that, but Rory's an unusual case." He paused. "You need to make your own choice, not your dad and certainly not Ron Lawrensen."

"What's Ron been up to?" Frank asked.

Keith filled him in on what Mark Steinberg and Guy Kinnings had told him and about his meeting with the Brickley people.

"So they think it's a done deal?" Frank asked when Keith finished describing his conversation with Billy Nevins and the beautiful Ms. Erica Chambers.

"Felt like it," Keith said. "Maybe I'm missing something, but they were so confident I almost felt as if your dad had actually signed something. Although Nevins did say if you won the Masters that would change everything because Nike would probably triple their offer."

Frank almost coughed up his milkshake. "Win the Masters? Yeah, right."

"It was said in the same vein as someone saying, 'If the Mets go undefeated this season,'" Keith said.

"They *are* one-and-oh," Frank said.

"Exactly," Keith said. "Only a hundred and sixty-one to go."

They both laughed, and then talked strategy for a few minutes. Clearly, there was nothing to be done the next few days except for Keith to keep his ears open for any more rumors.

Frank told Keith he was going to play nine holes in the morning and then play in the par-three tournament. The club had "suggested" he play with John Caccese, the U.S. Amateur champion, and Nathan Smith, who had again won the Mid-Amateur title the previous fall.

"They like to spotlight the amateurs as much as they can," Keith explained when Frank told him his pairing. "That's why they're doing this but, more important, why you all play with past champions the first two rounds."

"Nathan's got Bernhard Langer," Frank said.

Keith laughed. "Better bring a sundial," he said.

"What?"

"Langer's so slow the rules officials call him Herr Sundial. He's still an amazing player for a guy who's sixty, but boy is he an anchor out there."

Frank had taken an Uber to the McDonald's since Slugger was nowhere to be found. Keith gave him a ride back to the hotel.

"Just remember one thing," Keith said as he dropped Frank off. "Your dad and Lawrensen can make a hundred deals if they want to, and if you say, 'I'm not turning pro,' there's nothing they can do about it. It's your life, your decision."

"When are you going to write something about all this?" Frank said, his hand on the car door. A valet was standing there, and Frank held out one finger to indicate he needed a minute.

"No idea," Keith said, although he'd been thinking about it a lot all week. "I might write a long piece for *Digest* next week. If you win the Masters, I might try to sell it as a book."

"It could come out at the same time as the book about the Mets' undefeated season."

"Exactly," Keith said.

They shook hands and Frank jumped out of the car. Keith could hear the valet saying, "I saw you on TV today, Mr. Baker. It was very impressive . . ."

Keith didn't catch the rest. He didn't need to.

. . . . .

After dropping Frank off at the hotel, Keith drove back to the golf course. Since it was late afternoon, all the traffic was heading away from Augusta National on Washington Road and it only took him about ten minutes to get back.

As Keith drove, he heard Rory McIlroy's voice in the back of his head, again and again.

"I'm telling you, Keith, I know this is nuts, but that kid is good enough to win."

"Someday," Keith had said, finishing the sentence.

"Sunday," McIlroy had said, not the slightest trace of a smile on his face.

Before meeting up with Frank to go to the McDonald's, Keith had been headed into the locker room to see if anyone was around who would be worth talking to when he again bumped into McIlroy, who was on his way out.

They had joked for a minute about Frank's chip-in being the greatest clutch shot that had never happened at the Masters when McIlroy had blurted out his comment about Frank.

"Sit and talk to me for a minute," Keith said.

"My wife's waiting for me," McIlroy said.

"One minute," Keith said.

They walked over and sat down on one of the couches in the empty lounge area just outside the locker room. Almost no one ever sat in the lounge.

"Tell me what you mean," Keith had prompted.

"Look, he hits it just about as far as I do, and there are only a couple of guys out here who hit as far as I do," McIlroy said. "He can really putt, and he *likes* pressure."

"But, Rory, it's Tuesday. He's seventeen. He's never seen greens like the ones he's going to see Thursday, much less if he somehow got into contention on Sunday. You're a lock Hall-of-Famer, and look what happened to you the first time you had a chance here on Sunday. And you were twenty-one, not seventeen."

McIlroy was nodding in agreement as Keith spoke. "Everything you just said is true," he said. "But I've played eighteen holes with this kid now, and I'm telling you I'll be surprised if he doesn't play well. Now, Sunday is always another story, I know that, but it's not a fantasy."

"Is it, at least, a long shot?"

"Maybe. But not a hundred-to-one."

"What then?"

"Fifteen-to-one? Ten-to-one?"

"Those aren't very long odds in a golf tournament. You and Spieth are probably six-to-one."

"I know that," McIlroy said. He stood to go.

"Hey, Rory," Keith said. "Do you know how many amateurs have won the Masters?"

McIlroy smiled. "Exactly none," he answered. "First time for everything."

He walked out, leaving Keith sitting alone, staring into space.

· · · · ·

After parking the car, Keith hightailed it to a meeting he'd set up the previous night. He had called Oregon coach Casey Martin because Casey had told him he'd be in town on Tuesday and Wednesday. Under any circumstances, grabbing a cup of coffee with Martin would be something he'd look forward to; now it had become important.

Keith had met Martin in 2005 when they had played in the same first stage at Qualifying School. Keith liked and admired Martin, who'd been a teammate of Tiger Woods at Stanford. A year after their Q-School pairing, Martin had retired from the Tour and become the golf coach at Oregon. The Ducks had become a national power under him, winning the NCAA title in 2016 and finishing second in 2017.

Keith walked into the Augusta National grillroom shortly after five and found it virtually empty, except for a couple of agents he recognized but didn't know huddling at one table and Martin sitting at the other end of the room.

As Martin stood to shake hands, Keith tried to wave him back into his seat.

"I'm not a cripple," Martin said, grinning. "I just limp a lot."

Martin still knew enough people on the Tour to get a PLAYER GUEST credential, which meant he had access to the grillroom.

"Who hooked you up?" Keith asked, sitting down.

Martin grinned. "Tiger," he said. "He may not be playing this year, but he still has juice with the members. After all, he *is* a four-time champion."

The waiter came by and Keith asked for a tomato juice; Martin asked for another club soda. Keith would have loved a stronger drink, but knowing he would have to make his way through about a hundred cops leaving the premises, he didn't want to chance one—much less the two he knew he'd want.

"So, you sounded a little urgent on the phone last night," Martin said. "What's up?"

"I know you're recruiting Frank Baker," Keith began.

Martin broke in, laughing. "That's hardly a scoop," he said. "*Everyone* is recruiting Frank Baker."

"Yeah, I know. I also know he really likes you. But that's not my point. There's an agent running around trying to make deals for him because his dad wants him to turn pro as soon as he's out of high school. I'm afraid he might jeopardize his eligibility. Am I nuts to be concerned?"

Martin knitted his eyebrows and took a long sip of his drink. "You aren't nuts at all," he said. "You know how the NCAA can be. If this guy is making deals, the key might be the Cam Newton case."

Cam Newton, Keith knew, was not a golfer but a football

player. During the one season when he had been Auburn University's quarterback, stories had surfaced about his father basically selling him to the highest bidder. His eligibility had been put in doubt. Newton was on his way to winning the Heisman Trophy and leading Auburn to the national title. The NCAA did not want him taken off the field, so it ruled that if the so-called student-athlete did not specifically know that solicitations were being made on his behalf, he was still eligible to play for a college team. Auburn skated, too, since there wasn't absolute proof it had ended up paying Newton or his father.

Keith thought for a moment. "Well, in Frank's case, I don't think the kid knew anything was going on—until I told him an hour ago."

Martin shook his head. "You telling him shouldn't count against him. Technically, you don't know anything because all your information would have to be secondhand. But . . ."

"There's always a but," Keith said. "What is it?"

"The but is the NCAA. Frank's a star but in *golf*, not football. Golf doesn't make millions of dollars for NCAA schools. In fact, golf loses money. Golf Channel's college TV deal is worth next to nothing, and no one sells tickets to college golf. Cam Newton was a multimillion-dollar product for the NCAA, not to mention the awful position it would have been in if he'd been declared ineligible and then won the Heisman Trophy."

Martin went on to say the NCAA could decide to take Frank down to send a message to other kids in nonrevenue sports: "Don't mess with agents and corporations until you turn pro."

"What about Earl being on IMG's payroll while Tiger was at Stanford?" Keith asked.

"If they'd known, they might have done something. But remember, that didn't come out until Tiger was already on tour."

"So my guy could be in trouble."

Martin nodded. "It's all subjective with the NCAA," he said. "But I can tell you the fact that there's an agent involved and everyone in golf knows the father's on the Double Eagle payroll won't help."

"Technically, though, that's not illegal," Keith said, a little surprised that Martin knew about the dad's deal with Double Eagle. "Does everyone really know?"

"Yup. Remember, I said every college coach is recruiting him? Lawrensen's been telling people not to bother because he's already got the old man in his pocket."

"The kid wants to go to college."

"Then you better find a way to get the father and the agent to cease and desist." He paused. "If it's not too late."

Keith held his hand up so the waiter could see him. "I'd like a gin gimlet," he said.

He'd changed his mind about having a drink. He needed one. He'd worry about the cops later.

30

WEDNESDAY SEEMED TO TAKE FOREVER AS FAR as Frank was concerned. After the high of Tuesday, he felt as if he'd done all the Augusta preliminaries. He was ready to tee it up and play for real.

The par-three tournament was fun. He enjoyed playing with John Caccese and Nathan Smith, both guys he already knew, making it very comfortable.

Caccese was a wreck at the thought of playing with Sergio García the next day. "Do you know what kind of crowd he'll draw?" he asked at one point. "It'll be ridiculous."

People had told Frank that the par-three course, which was at the far end of the property, down a hill from the clubhouse, was the most beautiful part of Augusta National. He'd found that hard to believe, but when he got there he understood. There were little ponds everywhere, and the trees seemed to soar even higher around all nine holes.

He shot a respectable two-under-par 25 and was glad that

he came nowhere close to Jon Rahm's winning score of 22—which included a hole in one. The par-three had first been played in 1961. No par-three winner had ever won the Masters. Rahm said he wasn't worried about the jinx. There were other players, Frank knew, who had said they would intentionally hit their tee shot in the water at the ninth hole if they had a chance to win.

The real golf course was closed by the time Frank and his companions finished their par-three round. This was another Masters tradition: closing the golf course on Wednesday afternoon. It was done not only to get the course ready for Thursday but also to encourage players to take part in the par-three. Most did just that.

Frank would have liked to have hung around the smaller course to watch Jack Nicklaus, Gary Player, and Tom Watson—the legends threesome—play a few holes, but the crowds were so thick that he knew there was no chance. He decided against going back to the range. His swing felt great. Why do anything to tire himself out?

He settled for an awkward dinner at the hotel with Slugger, his dad, and Lawrensen. Frank was dying to confront the two men about Lawrensen's backroom dealings, but both Keith and Slugger had told him to leave it be until the tournament was over.

"So how do you feel?" his dad asked, trying to make conversation after their appetizers had been cleared.

"Pretty good," Frank said as he picked at a crust on his bread plate.

"Don't worry, Frank," Lawrensen said. "You can make the cut. It's the weakest field of the four majors. Only eighty-nine guys playing because it's so hard to get in, and a bunch of 'em are old-guy past champions who can't really play anymore."

"Ron, you think I don't know that?" Frank said, barely able to conceal his disgust. "Why don't you just let me worry about being able to get the ball teed up in the morning, okay? Slugger's my coach, not you."

"Frank!" his father said sharply.

"Dad, he's your adviser, not mine," Frank said.

The main course arrived at that moment. There wasn't much talk after that. Frank was grateful.

• • • • •

"Fore please. Now driving, Frank Baker."

Frank knew this was another Masters tradition. The starter—the man introducing the players on the first tee—didn't engage in the usual lavish intros players got at other tournaments. The only player in the field who was introduced with anything more than his name was the defending champion. For everyone else it was those few words. Zach Johnson, who'd won the tournament in 2007, had gotten them a moment earlier, followed by Justin Rose, who had been one swing away from being the defending champion.

The tee on Thursday morning was absolutely packed at 8:48. Many fans (patrons) had simply stayed there after the traditional opening drives that Jack Nicklaus and Gary Player had hit at 7:45. Frank would have liked to have watched that ceremony, but he'd been on the range warming up.

When he heard the starter call his name, he stepped forward and—as he'd seen Johnson and Rose do—waved a hand to acknowledge the applause, smiled, and teed his ball up. He was a little surprised as he looked down to see that his hand wasn't shaking at all.

Johnson had hit his drive in the yawning bunker on the right side of the fairway, the one that Phil Mickelson had so kindly pointed out to Frank on Tuesday. Rose had hit a perfect drive down the middle.

Frank took his practice swing, stepped back, took a deep breath, and stepped to his ball. As he looked up, all he saw was the fairway. He took the club back and *wham!*—the ball came off his club perfectly. Almost without looking, he knew he'd hit it just where he wanted to.

He glanced up and saw the ball heading in a graceful arc in the same direction that Rose's ball had gone.

"Sweet swing," Rose said.

"What first-hole jitters?" Johnson added.

Frank was so excited that he practically ran down the fairway.

"Hardest part's over now," Slugger said as Frank handed him his driver. "Downhill from here."

Actually it was downhill off the tee and then back uphill in the direction of the bunker and the green. Frank had been surprised at how hilly the golf course was. It didn't look *that* hilly on TV, but he was now accustomed to it after playing 54 holes—including 9 on Wednesday morning—in the last four days.

When they arrived, Frank saw that his ball was about three paces beyond Rose's.

"No respect for your elders at all," Rose said.

If anyone in the field could relate to what Frank was experiencing, it was Rose. He had finished fourth as a seventeen-year-old amateur at the British Open in 1998, becoming an overnight national hero. He had then turned pro and missed twenty-one straight cuts.

Frank and Rose watched Johnson come out of the bunker and find another bunker, this one greenside.

"Tough start," Rose murmured.

He took a seven-iron for his second shot and put it in the middle of the green.

That, Frank knew, was the place to aim. The flag was cut on the right side, near the back edge. If you flew your ball at the flag, you were apt to go over the green or, if you missed it right, shortside yourself and leave yourself with an almost impossible up-and-down.

"It's a hundred sixty-two front, a hundred seventy-seven flag," Slugger said, giving him the yardage. "I think Rose had it right, it's a seven."

Frank knew it wasn't a seven. He was so pumped up that the thought of hitting a nine-iron crossed his mind for a split second. He knew that was wrong, too. He pulled an eight-iron, causing Slugger to give him a look.

"Trust me," Frank said.

He aimed for the middle of the green, feeling a slight breeze coming from the left. The ball began to drift a bit right, and for a second Frank thought he'd pushed it. He hadn't. The ball landed almost pin-high and rolled to the right. It stopped ten feet from the cup.

"Guess it was an eight," Slugger said, grinning.

Frank walked onto the green to what felt like a hero's welcome from the crowd. Johnson hit a good shot out of the bunker to about eight feet, but he missed the putt. Rose's putt dove left at the last second, and he tapped in for par.

Frank looked closely at the putt and realized it was a classic Augusta National do-or-die putt. He knew the greens were like glass, even in the early morning. He also knew if he didn't put *some* speed on the putt, it would break before it got to the hole. If he gave it some speed and missed the hole, it was likely he'd have a longer putt coming back.

"Don't go crazy with this," Slugger said softly, reading his mind. "Nothing wrong with par on this hole."

Frank knew he was right. He knew that 4–4 (par, birdie) was a great start. There would be plenty of fives on this hole, as Johnson had just demonstrated.

The putt looked dead straight. He decided to just put a smooth stroke on it, and if it swerved right for a tap-in par, so be it. He checked his hands as he placed them on the putter. Not even a shudder.

He took the putter back just an inch and pretended it was a practice putt so as not to jerk the putter through the ball. Halfway there, he knew it was going in.

It did—dead center—or, as the TV guys bleated over and over, "Center cut!"

The crowd exploded.

As the three players walked through the ropes to the second tee, Johnson said, "You know almost no one makes three on that hole. And a seventeen-year-old in his first Masters *never* makes four, much less three."

"Just lucky," Frank said.

"Lucky, like hell," Johnson said. He looked at Rose. "Ever seen a seventeen-year-old that cool in a major?" he asked.

"Nope," Rose said, knowing Johnson was gigging him about the 1998 British. "Nothing close."

"One hole," Frank said.

"Your tee," Johnson said. "Get up and hit."

Having made birdie, Frank had the honor.

Brimming with confidence, he hit a high draw that bounced next to the fairway bunker and took off down the hill and out of sight.

He was so far down the hill when he got to his ball that he only needed a five-iron to the green. He left himself a 25-foot putt for eagle that he was happy to lag up to about 2 feet for a tap-in birdie.

Johnson and Rose also made birdies.

"The Perryton Prodigy is for real," Johnson said as they walked off the green.

The third was a short par-four with a dangerously narrow green. Frank laid up with a four-iron, hit a careful wedge to the middle of the green, and was happy to make par and move on. There was a giant scoreboard left of the green. As he picked his ball out of the hole, Rose said to him, "Don't look now, but you're leading the Masters."

Frank knew there were only a half dozen groups on the golf course, but he hoped someone would take a picture at that moment. He had a red 2 by his name—for two under. Rose and several others had red 1s.

Frank played the rest of the front nine cautiously, not going for anything spectacular. He knew that turning in even par or one under was just fine. He made his first bogey on the fifth when he misread a 40-foot birdie putt and sent it 10 feet past the hole. He got it back at the par-five eighth when he laid up to about 90 yards short of the green, hit a lob wedge to 6 feet, and made the putt. By then, Rose was also two under and Johnson was one under. They were all playing well.

Then, at the short but dangerous ninth, Frank got unlucky—and then lucky. His eight-iron approach was perfect—so perfect that it hit the bottom of the stick—the hole was near the back of the green—and rolled 20 feet away before stopping just before it got to the crest of the hill. Another 2 feet and the ball would have rolled off the green and to the bottom of the hill.

Instead, Frank made the birdie putt and turned in 33, giving him the lead by 1 among the early starters, including Rose and Rory McIlroy, who was two holes behind and also at two under.

The crowds following them had now swelled. It was impossible not to notice, even early on Thursday.

Frank parred 10, but bogeyed 11 when he pushed his tee shot, unable to get the trees running down the left side of the fairway out of his thoughts. He more or less laid up from there to the right side of the green, chipping to 15 feet and taking bogey. Another Masters saying: "Sometimes you have to remember that bogey can be a good score." Eleven was one of those holes.

He made a routine par at 12, aiming for the middle of the green. Then he hit a perfect drive around the corner at 13 and found himself with a seven-iron in his hands for his second shot. He hit it perfectly and, as the onlookers got louder and louder, the ball rolled to within five feet. When he made the eagle putt, he was four under par.

He made a routine par at 14 and then found the rough at 15, meaning he had to lay up. His wedge was a tad long on his third shot, but he putted from off the green—and again got lucky. He misread the speed slightly—which was enough to cause disaster on this green. But he'd left the pin in since he was off the green and the ball hit it—moving fast—popped in the air and went in the hole for a pure-luck birdie.

"I don't think I hit a good shot on that hole, and I made birdie," he said to Rose and Johnson while they waited on the tee at the par-three 16.

"Sometimes it's better to be lucky than good," Rose said.

Frank's heart was pounding. He was now five under par and was leading by 2. Most of the field was on the golf course by now. Rose and Johnson were both one under. If he could make three pars and shoot 67 . . .

Stop! he told himself. *Stay in the present.* He hit a cautious seven-iron to the middle of the 16th green and was thrilled to make par. Same thing at 17. At 18, for the first time all day, he saw a little shudder in his right hand as he teed the ball up.

Figures, he thought. *Had to happen.* Trying to hit a draw off the tee, he hit a slight push and found himself in the trees, right of the fairway. He had a shot—sort of—and tried to punch the ball up the fairway, hoping to somehow roll it up the hill and onto the green. Instead it rolled into the right bunker.

As they walked up the hill toward the green, the crowd stood to applaud. He knew some of it was for the two stars he was walking with, but it was also for the teenage amateur who, at that moment, was leading the Masters by one shot over Australian Mark Leishman and by two over Rory McIlroy and Dustin Johnson.

Sure, it was Thursday, but this was pretty cool stuff.

Frank stepped into the bunker and saw he had a perfect lie. He was 45 feet from the flag. It was not a difficult bunker shot—as long as your hands weren't shaking.

No reason, he thought, *not to get this up-and-down.*

He worked his feet into the sand, glanced at the hole, and dug the ball out of the sand the way he had done thousands of times in practice. The ball popped into the air perfectly, landed about halfway up the green between him and the flagstick, and began rolling.

The noise grew and grew as the ball rolled toward the hole. "Easy does it," Frank said aloud. "Stop right there."

The ball was five feet from the hole at that point. But it was still rolling. It slowed, appeared ready to slide just past the hole, and then, to Frank's shock, it disappeared—into the hole.

The place was going bananas. As he pulled himself out of the bunker, Johnson and Rose, both shaking their heads, came over to give him high-fives.

"Enjoy the interview room," Johnson said.

"Whaa?" Frank said, barely able to hear over the noise.

"The interview room," Johnson repeated. "That's where you're going next. You just shot sixty-six at the Masters, kid. You're about to be famous."

31

KEITH FORMAN HAD WALKED ALL EIGHTEEN holes with Frank Baker and the two major champions, his disbelief growing with every hole. He wasn't *that* surprised when Frank started birdie-birdie, but as the round continued he kept waiting for the "big number," as the players called it, that would send him sliding down from that top spot on the leaderboard.

Every year at the majors, a complete unknown would pop onto the Thursday leaderboard, sending reporters scurrying to the tournament player guide to learn something about them. Almost inevitably, within an hour, the guy would find water or out-of-bounds or the trees, make a triple-bogey, and become an Andy Warhol fifteen-minutes-of-fame footnote.

Or they might hang in there, shoot a decent first-round score, and then blow up and shoot 77 the next day.

There were certainly plenty of places on Augusta's back nine for the big number to happen. Keith breathed a sigh of relief when Frank's tee shot at 12 found the green, and while

Frank's wedge shot was in the air at 15, Keith was holding his breath again, thinking it might bounce down the hill behind the green and end up in the water.

None of that happened. Even on 18, when Keith couldn't see the lie because he was all the way on the other side of the green trying to peek over people's heads, the thought that Frank might leave his third shot in the bunker and finish with a deflating double-bogey crossed Keith's mind.

When Frank holed the shot, Keith let out an involuntary whoop—very unprofessional—causing Steve DiMeglio, who had come out and joined him on the 15th tee, to smile and say, "Aren't you the guy who gives me a hard time for pulling for Sergio?"

Keith did give DiMeglio a hard time about his unabashed affection for Sergio García, as did others. "Hey, I reacted to the shot," he said, a bit defensively. "Come on, tell me that wasn't amazing."

DiMeglio laughed. "Admit you're biased. You've been chasing the kid around since Riviera."

"Guilty," Keith answered. There was no point arguing.

After Zach Johnson and Justin Rose putted out and the players and caddies gathered for the traditional post-round handshakes, he and DiMeglio started walking in the direction of the scoring area. They had to wait while security stopped everyone to let the players get through.

"I'm going to the interview room," DiMeglio said. "I'm sure they'll bring him straight there."

Keith decided to wait outside the ropes near the scoring area. He was curious to see the scene there, even though he knew Frank would be taken to the interview room. He'd have to make a decision on when to leave because he'd have to walk about 150 yards to get a cart to take him to the Taj Mahal. The cart for Frank would be right there.

The three players were still inside signing their scorecards when he arrived. Keith saw Thomas Baker and Ron Lawrensen standing just outside the door. He didn't mind the notion that a player's father could get inside the ropes here, but it annoyed him that agents had that access. Still, there was nothing he could do.

Slugger came out first. He stopped to talk to Baker and Lawrensen, and Keith could tell the conversation was a little bit heated.

Finally, the caddie walked in the direction of Frank's bag, which was a few yards away.

Richard Stone, who had worked with the media committee for years, came over and said, "We're taking him straight to the interview room, Keith. Nothing here."

Stone was doing Keith a favor by giving him a heads-up that he was wasting his time lingering by the ropes. Often, players would stop and talk there for a few minutes even if they were going to the interview room. That was apparently not the case when a seventeen-year-old amateur shot 66 for the early Thursday lead.

Keith was about to turn to leave when he heard Slugger calling his name and saw him walking in his direction.

"Amazing, huh?" Slugger said, striding up with his hand outstretched.

"Beyond amazing," Keith said. "He's not just good—he has a flair for the dramatic."

"No kidding," Slugger said.

"Hey, what was that with you, the old man, and Lawrensen?" Keith asked.

Slugger shook his head. "The cart to the interview room is a four-seater: driver, player, and two others. Frank doesn't want Lawrensen on the cart. He's worried about how that will look, especially if Lawrensen walks in with the old man while he's talking."

"He's right," Keith said. "Lot of eyes and ears all around this place. Lot of rumors, too."

Slugger nodded. "Frank wants me on the cart instead. Old man is adamant."

"Frank needs to just tell the green-jacket who's directing him that he only wants his dad and you on the cart."

"Bad idea," Slugger said. "Last thing the kid needs right now is another blowup with his father."

Keith sighed. Slugger was right. *Choose your battles,* he thought.

"Everything they're doing is designed to force him to turn pro when this is over," he said.

"The way he's *playing* may force him to turn pro when this is over," Slugger said.

Then Frank walked outside, looking around for Slugger. Spotting him with Keith, he gave Keith a wave. The green-jacket had his hand on his back, guiding him in the direction of the cart. Keith needed to step on it to get back to the Taj Mahal.

. . . . .

By the time Keith got there, Frank was walking onto the podium to take his seat. Keith looked over and saw Baker and Lawrensen sitting to the side, a security guard standing nearby as protection—as if they needed it.

The interview room in the Taj was huge and had what amounted to a moat—no water, just flowers—between the reporters and the podium, which felt as if it were ten feet high. There was no scrumming post-interviews and no waiting for anyone outside the back door, like in the old press building.

Someone had joked that Tiger Woods was probably a consultant when they built the room because he was the one player who never, ever scrummed.

When a reporter wanted to ask a question, he'd raise his hand and his credential would automatically be read by the member on the podium who was sitting with the player and calling on people to ask questions. He would then call on the questioner by name. There was a microphone at every chair.

Richard Stone was the media committee member in charge of Frank's interview.

As always was the case when a player came in, Stone began with a formal, lavish introduction.

"Ladies and gentlemen, we have with us now Frank Baker,

one of our amateur participants, the runner-up in last year's U.S. Amateur. Frank opened the Masters today with a beautifully played sixty-six and is kind enough to join us here for a few minutes." Then he asked Frank the first question. "Did you even dream about leading the Masters in your first appearance?"

Frank shook his head. "I thought leading after two holes was pretty cool," he said. "When Justin Rose pointed to the scoreboard on three, I wanted to take a picture right there." He smiled. "But I figured if I took out my cell phone, I might get banished from the golf course."

That cracked up the entire room, except for Stone. "Questions?" he said, unsmiling.

The questions were routine: How had he fought his nerves all day? (No idea, just tried to play golf.) How were Zach Johnson and Justin Rose to play with? (Fantastic.) What was his most nerve-racking moment? (Third shot on 15.) Describe the third shot on 18. (Easy lie, normal bunker shot, just hoping to make 4.) What did he expect tomorrow? (Same as today, I hope.)

Frank was charming, smart, and humble. He said all the right things.

Stone wrapped up with a "Good luck tomorrow, young man," and everyone turned to leave.

Keith saw a swarm headed in the direction of Baker and Lawrensen. That made sense. If you couldn't scrum with the player, scrum with the father.

Walking out the door, he spotted a familiar face in the

hallway just outside the interview room door: Erica Chambers. He wondered how she had gotten into the building. It was supposed to be off-limits to the equipment reps.

"Ms. Chambers, what brings you here?" he said.

For a moment it was evident she didn't recognize him. Then she did. A smirk crossed her beautiful face.

"I just wanted to congratulate Thomas and Ron on the way Frank played," she said.

Keith thought of asking how she'd gotten in the building, then decided against it. He hadn't realized when he was talking to her and Billy Nevins on Tuesday how tall she was, because she'd been sitting down. She was wearing low heels but was looking him in the eye. Keith was six one. She *was* mesmerizing.

Before he could say anything else, he heard Thomas Baker's voice behind him.

"Erica!" Baker said enthusiastically. "I told the guard to be on the lookout for a tall, beautiful, dark-haired friend of mine. Guess he figured it out."

Okay, Keith thought, *if nothing else, that answers my question.* The old man had greased the skids to get her into the building.

Baker walked up, hugged Chambers and kissed her on the cheek. Then he pointed at Keith. "Is this guy bothering you?" he asked in his joking but unfunny way.

"I think I can handle him," Erica said, giving Keith a quick smile.

"I'm just doing my job, Thomas. Covering the amateur leading the Masters," Keith added.

Baker actually smiled.

Keith nodded at Baker's twin. "Ron, busy week for you?"

"I'm just a cheerleader, Forman," Lawrensen answered.

"Well, congrats, Thomas, and great to see you all," Keith said, giving them his phoniest smile. He needed to get away: Baker made him uneasy, Lawrensen made him nauseous, and Chambers made him dizzy.

He turned and walked off before they could respond. He was now convinced that Brickley was going into overdrive to be the focal point of Baker and Lawrensen's attempts to push Frank into turning pro. And it didn't hurt that Erica had those looks as well as so much money behind her.

He wasn't going to say or do anything to upset Frank at this moment. He did want to check in with him later to see how he felt about the spotlight he was now under and to ask him about the "Who's riding on the cart?" incident.

But that could wait. As he walked up the stairs to the media workroom, where reporters could find their desks and lots of free food, he realized that he was tired from walking eighteen holes, especially outside the ropes—and that he was starving.

He needed food and a break. He suspected the same was true for Frank.

32

AT THAT MOMENT, FRANK WAS STARVING. HE had been taken from the interview room to the small compound where Sky Sports (which televised the Masters in Great Britain), ESPN, and Golf Channel had their sets.

ESPN went first, then the other two. They all asked the same questions he'd been asked in the interview room. After the Sky interview, Frank walked out of the building to what looked like a small yard that led from the building to the cart path. A cart was waiting for him. So was a green-jacket he didn't recognize.

The guy introduced himself with a big smile, holding out his hand.

He was tall, with dark hair graying at the temples. He had an accent Frank couldn't place. It wasn't quite British and wasn't quite Australian.

"Wonderful playing today," the green-jacket continued after they'd shaken hands. "We're all very proud of you."

Frank wasn't certain who "we" were, but he nodded and said, "Thank you, sir."

"Small favor, if I may ask?" the official said.

Frank gathered that an Augusta favor was a lot like an Augusta request.

"Sure, anything," Frank said.

"Your comment in the interview room about the cell phone. Actually, it was quite amusing."

Frank suspected there was a but-line coming. He was right.

"But we'd appreciate it if you wouldn't repeat this or similar remarks. Our cell phone policy is what it is in order to protect you players. We don't want anyone to slip up and have a phone start ringing on the course during play. So we may come off as quite strict, but it's for a good reason. I think you'd agree."

Frank knew it didn't matter whether he agreed or not. "Yes, sir. I understand," he said, figuring there was no need to say anything more.

"Knew you would," the man said, giving him another big smile. "Hope to see you back in the interview room tomorrow. Cheers."

They shook hands again; then the official jumped on a cart and was gone.

Frank sighed and walked to the cart where his dad and Lawrensen were already waiting.

"What was that about?" Lawrensen asked, nodding as the green-jacket's cart headed down the path back in the direction of the press building.

"Nothing," Frank said. "He just wanted to thank me for being patient with all the interview requests."

That was a flat-out lie. At that moment, Frank didn't care.

. . . . .

Frank had eaten breakfast in the locker room at 7:30 before going out to warm up. They had finished the round at 1:15. As he headed back to the locker room, his stomach was growling.

Slugger was waiting for him on the front porch since caddies weren't allowed inside.

"You want to practice?" he asked.

All Frank could think about at that moment was eating. "Do you see any reason why I should?" he said.

Slugger shook his head. "No. Sooner you get out of here, the better. When do you think you'll be finished eating?"

Frank realized he hadn't gotten his watch or his wallet back from Slugger after the round.

"What time is it now?"

"Two-thirty."

"Give me thirty minutes."

Frank walked into the small player dining area in the locker room and found Brandt Snedeker sitting there. No one else was in sight.

"Sneds," as everyone called him, was one of his favorite players, even though they'd never met.

"Hey, great playing," Snedeker said when Frank walked in. He stood up to shake hands.

"Honor to meet you," Frank said. "Big fan for years."

Snedeker was one of those guys who had done everything in golf except win a major. He had played on three Ryder Cup teams, had won about ten times on tour, and had once won the ten-million-dollar bonus for winning the FedEx Cup. He'd been close a couple of times in majors, including at the Masters once, finishing—Frank thought—third.

"Can I join you?" Frank asked.

"Of course," Snedeker said.

"How'd you play today?" Frank asked. The last group had teed off at 1:55, so Frank knew Snedeker had to be finished if he was sitting here.

"Reasonable," Snedeker said. "One under. Nothing like you."

"Got a little lucky," Frank said, thinking about the shot that hadn't hopped in the water at 15 and the hole-out at 18.

"No one shoots six under at Augusta on luck," Snedeker said.

Throughout the week, Frank had noticed that players never talked about scores in actual numbers. They simply referenced par. Snedeker would never say he'd shot 71, he'd say "one under." The course record wasn't 63, it was "nine under."

The waiter came over, added his congratulations, and said, "You must be starved, Mr. Baker. What can I get you?"

Frank ordered and the waiter hustled off.

"Can I ask you a personal question now that we've known each other for two minutes?" Snedeker said with a smile.

Frank shrugged. He'd already answered about a hundred questions that day from reporters, why not one from someone he looked up to?

"Shoot," he said.

"Are the rumors true that you're thinking of skipping college to turn pro?"

Frank thought for a moment. He could easily duck the question, but he knew that wouldn't stop the rumors. More important, it wouldn't stop his father and Lawrensen.

"*I'm* not thinking about it," he said finally. "My dad and this agent are the ones who are ready for me to cash in now while I'm supposedly a hot commodity. Especially the agent." He still believed that when push came to shove, his dad would be on his side.

"Oh, you're a hot commodity all right," Snedeker said. "But you're nuts—they're nuts—if you don't go to college, even if you only go for a couple of years. Even Tiger went to Stanford for two years. When he left, he'd won the U.S. Am three times."

"You're preaching to the choir, Mr. Snedeker," Frank said, not sure if it was okay to call him Sneds. "I know I'm not ready to spend thirty weeks a year in hotels—even if they're all Four Seasons or the Ritz."

"Which they won't be," Snedeker said. "Even if you make it straight to the Tour, in a lot of the towns where we play, the Courtyard Marriott is the top of the line." He leaned forward in his chair, just as Frank's soup arrived. "You want me to talk to your dad? I know I'm a complete stranger, but I've been out here a long time and I know it's not a fun place to be a teenager, no matter how good a player you might be."

Frank thought that was a remarkably generous offer. But he knew his father was in no mood to listen to anyone right now—except for Ron Lawrensen.

"If I thought for a second it'd do any good, I would say absolutely," Frank answered. "But Dad's dug in on this. The only one who *might* convince him is me. And I'm not so sure about that either."

"Well then, you better be ready to dig in yourself," Snedeker said. "This could be a make-or-break decision." He paused for a second. "And I'm not just talking about your career."

Frank dipped his spoon in the soup. It was too hot to touch yet. *Sort of like my life*, he thought.

. . . . .

Frank walked outside at 3:01. To his surprise, Slugger was nowhere in sight. Keith Forman was, sitting on the porch bench talking to Fluff Cowan, longtime caddie for Jim Furyk. Frank had read once that Fluff had been on tour for so long that other caddies often asked him what Walter Hagen and Bobby Jones had been like.

Keith waved Frank over and introduced him to Fluff, whose nickname came from the fluffy mustache that was his trademark.

"Great playing today, young man," Fluff said. "I told Keith that even Tiger missed the cut the first time he played the Masters as an amateur."

"Well, I haven't made the cut yet," Frank said with a laugh, remembering that Fluff had been Woods's caddie in 1997 when he'd won the Masters by 12 shots at the age of twenty-one.

"Well, I like your chances," Fluff said. He stood, shook Frank's hand, and looked at his watch. "Gotta meet my guy on the range. Good luck tomorrow."

"Slugger will be back in a minute," Keith said to Frank as Fluff walked off. "He asked me to stay with you until he got back."

"Where'd he go?"

"Something about getting credentials for the weekend. Now that it looks like you're going to be here, he's got some folks up in Connecticut who want to come down."

Frank shrugged and checked the time. He really wanted to get back to the hotel.

Keith read his mind. "I'd take you back myself, but my car is on the other side of the grounds near the press center."

"It's okay," Frank said. At least he was fed. He wanted to tell Keith what Snedeker had said, but there were too many people around. "Actually, if Slugger didn't have the keys, I'd just leave him." He was smiling when he said it, but he meant it.

It took ten minutes for Slugger to finally show up.

"Sorry," he said. "Getting an extra credential out of these

people is like getting Commie here to admit he's wrong about something."

"On all three occasions in my life when I've been wrong, I've admitted it," Keith said. "It's just that none of those occasions involved you."

Frank wasn't in a mood for banter. "Can we get going?" he asked Slugger.

"Easy there, kid," Slugger said. "You've got the rest of the day off."

That was good news, Frank thought. It had been a very long day. Fun. Remarkable. But exhausting, too. Time to kick back.

. . . . .

Frank's tee time the next day wasn't until 11:48, but he was up by seven o'clock anyway, too restless to sleep any longer.

His phone was full of texts and emails, most of which he didn't bother to look at, since they were all the same: **Great playing . . . You're on fire! . . . Good luck Friday.** There was one from his mom: **It's on TV here,** she'd written. **Stayed up to watch. I'm SO proud of you.** As usual she signed it **xoxoxoxo.**

It was the last one, though, that brought him up short. It wasn't what the text said, but who it was from: **Got your number from Jenna,** it said. **Hope you don't mind. You're leading the Masters! OMG! You looked AMAZING on TV! Text me when you get home! Hope.**

Frank read the text five times, heart thumping. Hope Christopher was, without question, the hottest girl in the senior class at Storrs Academy—captain of the swim team and editor of the school paper. She had never, as far as he could remember, even glanced in his direction. She was all about basketball players—or so it seemed.

At last fall's homecoming dance, a teammate from the school's golf team had dared Frank to ask her to dance. He'd actually been willing to give it a try, but there were no fewer than *six* really tall guys hovering around her when he walked over. He'd chickened out.

He sat in his hotel room and thought hard for several minutes about a reply. Maybe he *shouldn't* reply. Just say later, "I was busy." He compromised: **Thanks!** he wrote. **It was just one round. Heading to golf course now.** He tried to think of something funny to add but couldn't come up with it. He stared at his message a long time and then finally hit send. Then he thought of adding something about how much he enjoyed hanging out with Rory McIlroy, Jason Day, and Phil Mickelson on Tuesday. *No,* he finally told himself, *be cool.*

This was much more nerve-racking, he realized, than playing in—or even leading—the Masters.

The good news was, he still had a few minutes to himself to read the papers—both the *Augusta Chronicle* and *USA Today* were waiting outside the front door. The *Chronicle*'s front-page headline was straight-up biblical: "And a Child Leads Them."

He thought that was kind of cool—and just a little bit odd. Then again, they were in the Deep South. He skimmed as many stories as he could, then read Steve DiMeglio in *USA Today*. DiMeglio's story was full of quotes from other players—notably Zach Johnson and Justin Rose—about his golf skills and remarkable maturity. Looking up from the paper at the Cartoon Network show playing on his room's television, he had to laugh.

· · · · ·

Slugger knocked on his door at 8:15, and they had breakfast in the hotel dining room. They left for the course at 10:00 and Frank walked on the range at 10:30. Golf Channel's Todd Lewis asked if he could stop and talk briefly. Frank's first instinct was to say no, but he flashed back to the day before when the thought that he was becoming a prima donna had crossed his mind. So he said yes. He knew from watching Golf Channel that Lewis always asked good questions.

He was right.

"What's your biggest challenge today after such a magical day yesterday?" Lewis asked.

"Trying to stay in the same place mentally that I was then," Frank said. "I know that'll be hard because the circumstances are a lot different."

"Any goals for today?" Lewis said.

"Try, *try* to stay in the present," Frank said. "If I can do that, I'll be fine."

Lewis thanked him, and Frank walked onto the range. Jordan Spieth was walking off.

"You shoot six under again today, Prodigy, and we're all toast," Spieth said, clapping him on the back. "Have fun out there."

Yeah, sure, Frank thought. *Have fun out there.* What was it Jordan had said after he'd won that Masters three years earlier? "My receding hairline is a product of playing golf for a living."

Frank's hairline was fine. For now.

33

KEITH FORMAN AGAIN WALKED THE ENTIRE eighteen holes with Frank, Justin Rose, and Zach Johnson on Friday. The crowds were so thick he had to scramble to see much.

Not surprisingly, during the first nine holes, Frank seemed to realize that seventeen-year-olds weren't supposed to lead the Masters. He didn't make a single birdie, and he bogeyed 3, 4, and 9—hitting his second shot hole-high only to watch it spin back off the green and down the hill. It was the kind of mistake he had done such a good job of avoiding on Thursday.

While the players waited on the tenth tee for the group in front of them to hit their second shots, Keith walked glumly down the hill to the right of the fairway.

Frank was now three under par for the tournament, still only three shots behind Justin Thomas, who was four under par for the day playing the 13th hole. Thomas was the kind of player who could go very low—he'd shot 63 in the third round of the U.S. Open a year ago—and with 13 and 15 still to play, a 65 or 66 was clearly in reach. Rory McIlroy and Jordan Spieth were in a group of four players a shot back.

It had rained overnight, softening the greens and making them easier to attack. That's what made Frank's front-nine 39 truly disappointing. He had tamed a much more difficult golf course a day earlier.

Keith was calculating where the cut might fall as he stopped to watch the three players hit their tee shots. He was relieved when Frank, last up after his ninth-hole bogey, found the fairway with his best tee shot of the day. At that point, Keith wasn't really thinking about Thomas or the other leaders. He wanted to be sure Frank would play the weekend. If the leader was eight under par, that would mean the 10-shot rule would fall at two over. At the Masters, anyone within 10 shots of the 36-hole leader made the cut. Or, if fewer than 44 players and ties were within 10, they all made the cut whether within 10 or not. Keith guessed the cut would be two over, perhaps one over if Thomas went to nine under, since the leaderboard was pretty bunched.

That meant Frank would have to completely collapse on the back nine not to play the next day. Still, there was lots of water ahead, and Keith knew Frank well enough to know he was frustrated at that moment, which could lead to more mental mistakes—like the one on Number 9. It was up to Slugger to keep him calm.

That didn't fill Keith with confidence. He'd had dinner with Slugger the previous night, and his old teammate appeared to be a lot more jumpy about things than Frank had been. When Keith pointed that out to him, Slugger got defensive.

"Frank's going to be a multimillionaire, if not now, then later," he said. "He's playing with house money here—which is great. But I'm not going to be a millionaire. In fact, I don't even know if I'll still be his teacher after this week. The old man is still mad at me for getting you involved, and I *know* that Lawrensen wants him to get rid of me and hire one of the big-name teachers. He wanted me gone after the Amateur, but Frank told the father he needed me and the father went along— for now. So cut me some slack."

Keith tried a joke about how Slugger could charge new players a thousand dollars an hour, like the big-name guys, if Frank won the Masters.

That seemed to calm Slugger, but not by much. "I'm sorry," he said. "I should be enjoying this. It's a once-in-a-lifetime type of thing. But you don't have a wife and two kids to worry about."

Keith couldn't argue with that. And, as Frank and Slugger walked down the tenth fairway, he hoped his family back home wasn't on Slugger's mind at that moment. Focusing on pulling the right club was far more important right now.

Frank managed to par 10, 11, and 12—which was a relief to Keith, because they were probably the three toughest holes on the back nine. If he could stay dry at 13, 15, and 16, he'd be fine—at least in terms of the cut, which, being honest, was all Keith was worried about.

Frank hit a perfect drive on 13, cutting the corner of the

dogleg, the ball bouncing way down the fairway. Keith's guess was that he had less than 200 yards to the flag. That meant he *had* to go for the green in two, which made Keith a little nervous. Any sort of mishit, and he'd find the creek in front of the green. The genius in Augusta's back nine par-fives was that they were both easily reachable for most of the field if their drive found the fairway. But there was so much danger around the greens that any sort of miscalculation could turn a potential birdie into a bogey—or worse—in a heartbeat.

Keith was standing back from the ropes because the ground between the 13th and 14th fairways was elevated enough that his view was better there than trying to somehow get position close to the ropes. It looked to Keith like Frank had a seven-iron in his hands, meaning his guess that he was inside 200 yards was correct.

He held his breath for a second as the ball flew high into the air, becoming a dot against the sun before he lost sight of it. Only the roar up near the green told him that Frank had hit a good shot. He breathed out, thinking, *Two more water holes to go.*

He couldn't get near enough to the green to see how close Frank's ball was to the flag, but when Justin Rose and Zach Johnson both putted before him, he guessed the putt was makeable. He was right—it couldn't have been more than five feet, judging by how long it took to get to the hole. Frank rolled it in for eagle, and suddenly he was only one over par for the day and back to five under for the tournament. Rose and Johnson both gave him fist bumps walking to the 14th tee.

Frank made a routine par at 14 and also parred 15—which was fine with Keith. The narrow green looked about five yards wide to him, and when the kid missed the fairway and laid up, Keith was very happy with the two-putt par he made from there.

Sixteen was the last hole with water. Frank found the green safely but misjudged his first putt from 30 feet, rolling it 10 feet past the hole. He missed coming back for a bogey, but Keith was fine with that, too. All he was thinking about was avoiding big numbers.

Frank made another bogey at 17, going over the back of the green with his second shot, but hit a perfect drive at 18, found the middle of the green, and two-putted for a final par. He'd shot 74—a far cry from his 66 on Thursday—but plenty good enough after the 39 on the front side. He'd kept his cool to shoot 35—one under par—on the back nine, helped immeasurably by the eagle at 13.

Keith checked the giant scoreboard to the right of the 18th green. Hideki Matsuyama, the gifted Japanese player, had shot 64 to go from one under par to nine under par. He had the lead. Tommy Fleetwood, a talented British player, was at eight under. Four players were at seven under, including McIlroy. Three more—including Rose—who had shot 67—were at six under. Then a group of five at five under, most notably Spieth and two-time champion Bubba Watson. Currently, there were six players at four under, including Frank. That meant Frank was tied for 15th place. It wasn't first, but it was pretty darn good for a seventeen-year-old kid.

Keith walked to the spot near the scoring area where the media was corralled. Frank obviously wasn't going to be brought to the interview room today, but there were still plenty of media people who wanted to talk to him.

He saw Ron Lawrensen and Thomas Baker standing next to Frank's bag outside the scoring room. Slugger was inside with Frank while his player checked and signed his scorecard. Again, Keith felt a little bit of anger that an agent could stand there waiting for the player while the media was literally penned in a few yards away. *If anyone should be penned in,* he thought, *it's the agents.*

Frank walked outside and spoke to Slugger briefly before he picked up the bag and headed in the direction of the caddie barn. They had teed off much later today, and it was almost five o'clock. Keith suspected Frank wouldn't be hitting any more golf balls today. *He* felt drained. He could only imagine how Frank felt.

Frank spoke to Lawrensen and his father briefly, then, guided by a green-jacket, began walking up the short hill to where the media waited. Keith walked over and stood just outside the roped-off area waiting for Frank to finish. He'd try to catch him for a minute or two in the locker room—one of the few places where his father and Lawrensen could not go.

He was jotting a few notes to himself on his pocket-sized spiral when a voice behind him said, "Hey, Forman, got a minute?"

He turned and saw Lawrensen standing there.

"Where's your twin?" Keith asked.

"Twin?"

"Frank's dad. The other Bobbsey twin. I don't think I've ever seen one of you without the other."

Lawrensen didn't crack a smile.

"So what can I possibly do you for?" Keith asked, mis-speaking intentionally.

"No, my friend, it's what *I* can do for *you*," Lawrensen answered.

"Really?"

Lawrensen moved a little closer to Keith and lowered his voice. "I know you've been poking around trying to find out what kind of deals might be on the table for Frank," he said. "Lay off."

"Excuse me?" Keith said.

"Do you know how many of our clients are on *Digest*'s teaching staff?" Lawrensen smiled. "Check the last four covers of the magazine. All our guys. One call from my boss to Jerry Tarde, and you'll be lucky to have a subscription to your magazine, much less a job."

"You're threatening to blackmail my editor?" Keith said. "That's the best you've got? You think Jerry Tarde's going to be blackmailed by the likes of you or your boss?"

"Oh no, that's just for starters. Do you think *Digest* is going to want Frank under contract once he turns pro? How do you think Tarde will react when we say we're going to go to another magazine unless he dumps you? He wouldn't be doing his job if he didn't take Frank over you."

Lawrensen was probably right about that, Keith had to

admit. The whole blackmail package might make it impossible for Tarde to justify keeping him. Still, he wasn't about to back down to this lowlife.

"What makes you think Frank will go along with that?" he said. "Just because you've got the father in your pocket doesn't mean you've got the kid."

"Yes, it does," Lawrensen said. "Especially if I already have the father's name on signed contracts. The kid is still a minor, remember?"

Now Keith was angry. "Do me a favor, Ronnie boy, climb back under that rock you live under. I've got work to do," he said. "You just gave me all the quotes from you I needed. I'm going to expose you for being the sleaze that you are. *Someone* will want to read that story."

Lawrensen's smirk turned into a scowl. He grabbed Keith's arm.

"Touch me again," Keith said, pulling away, "and I don't care where we are—I'll put you down."

Lawrensen didn't want a fight, but he wanted the last word. "You expose me, you expose Frank," he said. "If you tell people he's already under contract to an agent, he can't possibly play college golf, can he?" With that, he turned and walked away.

Keith wanted to shout something at him but couldn't think of anything. He knew the Double Eagle agent was right.

34

FRANK'S SESSION WITH THE MEDIA WAS A LOT shorter on Friday than it had been on Thursday, when he was leading the tournament. That was fine with him.

When he walked into the clubhouse, he saw his dad sitting in the lounge outside the locker room. There was no sign of his usual shadow, which was a relief.

His dad walked over and gave him a hug.

"Lot of guts on the back nine," he said. "I was just checking scores. Unless John Caccese birdies the last two holes, you're going to be the only amateur to make the cut. So, at the very least, you'll be Low Amateur."

Frank was actually glad to hear that news. Low Amateur at the Masters was a very prestigious thing. Plus, it would give him a little payback on Caccese for the loss at Riviera the previous summer.

"If the current standings hold," his dad continued, "I think you'll play with Matt Kuchar tomorrow."

Frank also liked that news. Kuchar was known as one of

the good guys on tour. He also knew a thing or two about playing the Masters on the weekend as an amateur. He'd finished T-21—tied for 21st place—twenty years ago. No amateur had done better than that since then.

"Glad to hear all of that," Frank said. "So where's Mr. Lawrensen?"

"He's taking care of some nuisance work," his dad said. "Are you going to hit any balls or are you finished?"

"Finished. Done. Exhausted. I told Slugger to take off if he wanted."

"Okay, how about we have a father-son dinner tonight? One of the members said he could get us in at a nice Italian place downtown."

That sounded good to Frank. He knew his tee time would be sometime early afternoon the next day, so he didn't need to go to bed too early. Plus, a night without Ron Lawrensen was a night *with* sunshine.

Frank felt completely happy for the first time in a while. He'd survived on a day when he didn't have his best stuff. He'd made the cut and would be back out there tomorrow. And there would be no talk tonight—he would see to that—about what was going to happen when the weekend was over.

He felt . . . seventeen. It was a good feeling.

· · · · ·

Frank felt even better the next day. For the first time since he'd gotten to Augusta, he'd slept soundly. He ate a big breakfast because his tee time wasn't until 12:34. Slugger had texted to say he'd meet him at the club, that he was getting a ride, so Frank, his dad, and Ron Lawrensen drove over together.

The car was quiet, neither man wanting to mess with Frank's head before he played the third round of the Masters.

Soon after Frank started warming up, Matt Kuchar walked over to introduce himself.

"Let's just have a good time out there today," he said, giving Frank his trademark smile. "You know, I shot sixty-eight in the third round here when I was an Am twenty years ago. We've got perfect conditions. I'll bet you can beat that."

"Tell you what, I'll sign for sixty-eight right now," Frank joked.

"Hey, you already shot sixty-six once this week," Kuchar said. "Don't sell yourself short."

Frank knew he'd been lucky drawing Kuchar at this stage of the tournament. Most guys would be extremely tight teeing it up on Saturday at the Masters, especially in contention. Being T-15, five shots back, with 36 holes to play was certainly in contention. Saturday was called "moving day" on tour because it was the day when players who trailed the leaders had a chance to make a move with a low score.

That's the way you should be thinking, he said to himself.

John Caccese had missed the cut, so Frank was already Low Amateur. *No reason,* he thought, *not to go for broke out there today.*

Which was exactly what he did. He got up-and-down for par from just off the first green—no small task—and then birdied the second, leaving his second shot just short of the green. From there, he used his putter and two-putted from 40 feet.

"Good start," said Kuchar as they walked off the green. He had started exactly the same way: par-birdie.

Frank almost forgot where he was. He was as loose as he might have been playing in the early morning at Perryton Country Club against Slugger for donuts. He decided to hit driver at the third, a risky play, but he hit it perfectly, rolling it up just short of the green. He pitched to about seven feet and made the putt. Then he went into the "par zone" for the next four holes before making another two-putt birdie at the eighth. He parred 9 and was out in 33.

Hideki Matsuyama had birdied the second to get to ten under, but Frank was now tied for third at seven under. Kuchar was in the group at six under.

"I may have been conservative with that sixty-eight call," Kuchar said as they walked to the tenth tee.

Frank laughed. He noticed Keith Forman was standing directly behind the tee as the two players walked onto it. Frank looked at him, and Keith just gave him a quick thumbs-up. He'd have walked over to chat but figured TV was probably following them pretty closely—there was a cameraman on the tee—and there was no need to draw any attention to his friendship with the reporter.

He figured his father and Lawrensen were already walking down the hill in the direction of the green.

"Driver?" he said to Slugger, even though he'd already decided that's what he was hitting.

"The way you're hitting the ball, you bet," Slugger said.

Kuchar had the tee because he'd birdied the ninth. He smashed a perfect draw that Frank knew would run forever down the hill.

"Wow," he said as Kuchar picked up his tee.

Then Frank hit it past him—same draw, just a little lower, meaning it hit and hopped. He was ten yards past Kuchar when they got to their balls.

"Wow," Kuchar said, giving him a smile.

They both made par there and at 11, but at 12 Kuchar missed a wind gust and hit his tee shot into the back bunker. Seeing what had happened to Kuchar, Frank switched from a nine-iron to a pitching wedge, found the middle of the green, and made par. Kuchar made bogey.

That was the first of what the players called the "agua holes." The 13th and 15th defined the term *risk-reward*. Any score from 3 to 7 was easily possible on both.

Frank was happy to make 4 on both with another 4 on the par-four 14th in between. He now had five birdies and no bogeys for the day. Matsuyama had made two bogeys and another birdie, and he and Frank were tied at nine under. Rory McIlroy was also nine under. A slew of players were one shot back.

There it was, though: late on Saturday afternoon, a seventeen-year-old amateur was tied for the lead in the Masters.

"Jim Nantz is composing poetry about you right now,"

Slugger said as they stood on the 16th tee waiting for the group in front of them to clear the green.

Nantz was famous for coming up with little catchphrases when the last putt of the tournament went in the hole. Of course the sportscaster's most famous phrase was "A tradition unlike any other," which he had coined in 1986. Augusta National had trademarked the phrase in 2015, although Nantz received nothing for it since the club owned anything said on-air during a Masters telecast. Nantz didn't need the money, but he probably wouldn't mind his very own green jacket.

"Something like 'Splish-splash, he took a bath'?" Frank said, nodding in the direction of the water running down the left side of the hole.

"He's better than that," Slugger said. "Sadly, you're not."

Actually, at that point, Frank was so confident he barely noticed the water. He had no intention of challenging it, especially with the hole located back and right. He hit an eight-iron onto the green, took his 20-foot two-putt, and walked happily to the 17th tee. Another par there, and he stood on the 18th needing only a par to top Matt Kuchar's 68. There was little byplay between the two players now. Kuchar was still hanging around at six under par, but Frank's round was the one drawing all the attention.

As he stood over his tee shot, Frank told himself, *Don't be nervous—it's just another tee shot.*

Of course, that was as helpful as saying, *Don't think about elephants for ten minutes.*

For the first time all day, his nerves got the better of him.

His tee shot flew right, hit a tree, and dropped. It was the first truly bad tee shot he'd hit all day.

Walking off the tee, Slugger started to say something. Frank put a hand up: "I'm okay," he said. "I'm okay."

Slugger understood.

He had no shot from the trees other than to punch out and try to get the ball as far up the fairway as he could. He managed to get it to within 90 yards of the green, although he narrowly missed hitting a tree.

Worst I can make now is five, he said to himself, walking up the hill in the direction of his ball. That calmed him. There would be no shame in finishing with a bogey for a 68.

He stepped back from his third shot for a moment. The flagstick was back-right, the usual Saturday spot. On Sunday, he knew it would almost certainly be front-left. He wanted to keep the ball below the hole so he wouldn't have a downhill putt. But if he didn't fly it almost to the pin, it would spin back and he'd have a 50-foot par putt.

"Middle of the green," Slugger said. "Two putts and we're out of here."

That wasn't what Frank was thinking. "You know what? You're right," he said to Slugger, grinning. "But I'm not actually mature enough to understand that."

He stepped back from his ball and took a deep breath. He had exactly 93 yards to the flag. He hit the ball high in the air, aiming to fly it just over the flagstick. Which is exactly what he did. The ball flew past the stick, landed just on the edge of the green, and spun backward. Frank couldn't see the ball because the green was elevated, but he could hear the crowd noise rising as the ball crept toward the hole.

He raced up the hill to get a look. The ball had stopped two feet below the hole.

He punched the air—mostly in relief—as he walked onto the green. All the spectators (that is, the patrons) were standing, giving him a whistling, cheering ovation.

"Whatever happens tomorrow, this is pretty cool," Slugger whispered in his ear as they walked from the front to the back of the green, Frank stopping to mark his ball.

Slugger was right. This was pretty cool.

Kuchar had a 20-foot birdie putt that he just missed. He tapped in for a 70. Frank took an extra few seconds with his putt to make sure he didn't do something silly because his adrenaline was so high. He knocked the putt in for 67, and the crowd went bonkers again.

He thought about something the great tennis player John McEnroe had once said: "They love you when you're young; they love you when you're old. The killer part is in between."

Kuchar came over and gave him a hug. "That third shot was about the dumbest thing I've ever seen," he said. "And one of the best shots I've ever seen." Then he added, "Go out and win this thing tomorrow."

Frank laughed at the thought.

Then he looked at the scoreboard for a moment. He was still in a three-way tie for the lead with Matsuyama and Mc-Ilroy. The way golf pairings worked, the first player to finish at a certain score was the last player to tee off the next day. He was the first one to post nine under. That meant unless two players got to ten under—which was unlikely—he would be playing in the final group at the Masters the next day.

Hope Christopher would be impressed.

"OMG," he murmured to himself. "OMG."

35

THE BUZZING OF HIS CELL PHONE WOKE KEITH Forman. He blinked at the clock radio next to the bed: 6:26 a.m. He certainly hadn't set an alarm for that hour. In fact, he hadn't set an alarm at all.

He had fallen into bed at about 1:00 a.m. There was no need to get to the golf course early, so he would sleep in. The last group, Frank Baker and Rory McIlroy, wouldn't tee off until 3:05 in the afternoon. One thing he hated about Sundays at major championships was all the waiting around for the final groups to tee off.

But there was his phone, buzzing incessantly at 6:26. He picked it up and squinted in surprise at the screen. It was Frank. If anyone should still be sleeping at this hour, it was the Prodigy. Maybe nerves had awakened him and he wanted to talk.

"Frank," he said wearily, "what are you doing up so early?"

Frank sounded breathless. "I got a call," he said. "Just now. It was from Jonathan Tucker."

Keith was baffled. Why in the world would the chairman of Augusta National be calling one of the three guys leading the Masters on Sunday morning almost nine hours before his tee time?

"What did he want?" Keith asked.

Frank had paused for a moment, apparently trying to catch his breath. "He asked if I could come to his office at eight o'clock. He said he was sorry to call so early, but he wanted to see me before anyone was on the grounds."

That sounded serious. "Did he give you a clue what it was about?"

"No," Frank said. "He just said he'd explain when I got here and suggested I bring my dad with me but not Ron Lawrensen."

"He brought up Lawrensen?"

"Yes."

Alarm bells were going off in Keith's head. If Jonathan Tucker had mentioned Lawrensen that way, it was clear he was aware that Lawrensen was in tight with Thomas Baker. Augusta National took the whole amateurism thing pretty seriously. That was one reason why an amateur who qualified for the Masters had to stay amateur in order to cash in his invitation to the tournament.

Frank was talking again. Keith had to catch up.

"I don't want to bring my dad," Frank was saying. "Whatever's going on, he'll make it worse. He won't mean to, but he will." He paused. "Keith, will you go with me?"

Keith wasn't sure that was a great idea. Augusta National

treated the media as a kind of necessary evil. They didn't mind their presence as long as they stayed at arm's length. Eat, drink, and be merry at the Taj Mahal, but don't ask us any real questions. Just write about the "tradition unlike any other."

"I'm not sure Mr. Tucker would be thrilled—"

"I don't care," Frank interrupted. "I need someone to come with me, and I want it to be you. I trust you."

"What about Slugger?"

"I trust *you*," Frank repeated. "You're the only one who has no financial interest in me."

That was mostly true, although Keith had spent a lot of Saturday night mulling his next move if Frank somehow became the first amateur to ever win the Masters. His instinct was to find a publisher as quickly as possible and start writing the book. He assumed Frank would cooperate. But he was nervous that a movie studio or a TV network might rush in and try to get Frank to sign a contract for a movie or a documentary. So he *did* have a financial interest in Frank.

Regardless, the kid needed someone there who would be inclined to look after his interests, first and foremost. He knew that wasn't Lawrensen and, sadly, it probably wasn't his father either. Slugger—maybe, probably—but his pal was worrying about his job.

"Okay, I'll meet you in the locker room at a quarter to eight. We'll walk over to Tucker's office from there."

"Thanks," Frank said. "I'm really scared."

"Don't be scared," Keith said. "They aren't going to do

anything to someone who might be responsible by sundown for the best story in Masters history."

He hung up. He knew he was right. But he, too, was really scared.

. . . . .

Keith was concerned that he might have some trouble getting onto the grounds so early since the first tee time wasn't until 9:50. But he wheeled into the press parking lot and was guided to a spot a few yards from the security entrance.

The security people made jokes about how early he was—"You gonna try to play a few holes?" one asked with a laugh as he went through the daily drill. He then dropped his computer off in the completely empty workroom and was pleasantly surprised to find one of the carts that served as a shuttle to the golf course and clubhouse area waiting outside.

"You must be a man on a mission getting here this early," the driver said. "Leaders don't tee off for seven more hours, you know."

"I'm on my way to meet one of them," Keith said, causing the man to give him a surprised look. Keith didn't elaborate, and the driver didn't ask any more questions.

Keith had his badge scanned and walked into the locker room at 7:40. Frank was sitting in the small dining area eating a bowl of Cheerios.

"Breakfast of champions?" Keith asked.

"That would be Wheaties," Frank answered.

"Oh yeah, forgot," Keith said.

He sat down across from Frank. Other than an ever-present waiter, the room was completely empty.

"Can I get you something, Mr. Forman?" the waiter asked him. Technically, the media wasn't supposed to eat or drink anything in the locker room, but most of the waiters knew Keith and didn't care—especially with the room empty.

"Got some coffee?" Keith asked.

"Right away," he said, and was back in seconds to pour him a cup.

Keith looked at Frank.

"Did you tell your dad?" Keith asked.

Frank shook his head. "No, I'll tell him when it's over—one way or the other."

Frank finished his cereal, while Keith took a couple sips of the coffee. He wished he'd asked for it in a to-go cup. Too late. They got up and walked across the empty courtyard area to the building that housed Augusta National's offices. At the door, a security guard stopped Keith.

"Sorry, sir, no media in here," the guard said.

"He's with me," Frank said. "And I have an appointment with Mr. Tucker."

The guard nodded. "Okay, then," he said.

They were met at the top of the stairs by Steve Greenspan, Augusta National's public relations director. He shook hands with Frank, then looked quizzically at Keith.

"Keith, I think this is a private meeting."

Greenspan was almost incurably polite, and Keith tried to never give him a hard time, because he knew he had one of the hardest PR jobs in the world. For a second time, Frank stepped in before Keith had a chance to respond.

"Mr. Greenspan, I asked Keith to come with me," he said. "Mr. Tucker told me I could bring my father. He's not available. I asked Keith to come instead."

"Well, it'll be up to Mr. Tucker to decide about that," Greenspan said. "Follow me."

They followed Greenspan across a desk-filled room, down a hall past several smaller offices, and to a door at the end of the hall. When Greenspan pushed it open, Keith could see the room was massive, with large windows looking out on the courtyard area and beyond that the first fairway.

Jonathan Tucker was behind his desk, dressed as if he were about to go out and play eighteen holes. It almost felt strange to Keith to see an Augusta member *not* wearing a green jacket. There were two other men in the room, one in a green jacket, the other in a suit. Keith didn't recognize either of them. They both stood back while Tucker got up to greet Frank.

"Frank, please come in," he said, standing and coming around his desk to shake Frank's hand. Then he looked at Keith. "No offense, Keith, but what are you doing here?"

This time Keith answered. "Frank asked me to come with him. I'm here as a friend, not a reporter."

He realized as he spoke the words that he had gone way past the invisible line that reporters weren't supposed to cross in their relationships with sources and people they covered. That ship, he supposed, had sailed long ago.

Tucker looked at Frank. "You invited him, Frank? He didn't ask to come along?"

"I called him right after you called me, sir."

Tucker nodded. "Okay, then, as long as we have an understanding that all of this is off the record, including the fact that this meeting is taking place."

Keith was a little uncomfortable agreeing to that, but he decided it was okay. "Unless whatever is about to happen becomes public knowledge in some way."

Tucker gave him a tight smile. "That's fine." He then turned to the other two men in the room. "Frank, I'd like you to meet Jamison Williams, he is the club's legal counsel and, as you can see, a member."

He didn't bother to introduce Keith to Williams, which was fine with Keith. He was happy to be treated as if semi-invisible.

Tucker continued: "And this is Arthur Adams. He works for the enforcement committee of the NCAA."

That brought Keith up short. What in the world was someone from the NCAA doing here on Masters Sunday?

"Why don't we all have a seat?" Tucker said.

There were two chairs to the right of his desk and two to the left. Frank and Keith took the seats to the left. Tucker looked at Keith again. "We're clear that this is completely off the record, right?"

Keith was tempted to say that he had no idea there was a

difference between *off the record* and *completely off the record.* Instead he just said, "Right."

Tucker cleared his throat, then looked at Frank. "I'm sorry to have to hold this meeting, Frank, when you have a very big day ahead of you. But it came to our attention yesterday that Ron Lawrensen, the agent, has been negotiating contracts on your behalf and, further, that your father, who at this point is your legal guardian, has signed a contract authorizing those negotiations."

"But I had nothing—"

Tucker held up his hand. "Let me finish. We'll certainly want to hear from you in a minute." He lowered his hand and went on. "The tournament, as you know, is very clear about its rules concerning amateur players. If you or your father wanted you to turn pro at this stage, that would be fine. You just wouldn't have been invited to play based on your runner-up finish in Los Angeles last summer. In fact, I should tell you there were some club members who didn't want you invited after the incident with Mr. Anderson in the semifinals. We *do* have the right to suspend our normal procedures and not invite someone. I overruled those objections.

"I believe you were starting to say that you haven't been involved in any of the ongoing negotiations. I'm sure that's true. Under the rules, though, your father's involvement makes you liable."

"So what does all that mean?" Frank asked.

"It means we have to decide whether, in fact, you were

no longer an amateur when the tournament began. If so, we'll have to disqualify you."

"So what's he doing here?" Keith said, nodding in the direction of Adams.

"It was Mr. Adams who brought this to our attention," Tucker said. "To be honest, I had heard some rumors from various people but chose not to believe them. When Mr. Adams called on Friday afternoon, I asked him to come here to lay out the NCAA's case in person."

"Case?" Frank asked.

Keith could see that Frank was pale and his voice now had a quaver in it.

"Hang on a minute," Keith said. He looked directly at Adams. "Where did you get *your* information?"

"I'm afraid I can't discuss that," Adams said crisply in the tone of voice that bureaucrats always seemed to use. It was the kind of tone that made you want to deck the speaker.

"What do you mean you can't discuss it?" Keith said. "We're here *discussing* things because someone accused Frank of not being an amateur because of actions he had nothing to do with. He has the right to know who his accuser is."

"Our investigations are confidential," Adams said, and turned to the chairman. "Mr. Tucker, I understand this gentleman has agreed to be off the record, but no one in the NCAA other than our communications department speaks to the media. So I won't answer any more questions from him."

Keith was disgusted. He looked at Tucker. "You gonna knock the kid out of the tournament on a technicality when he's completely innocent because some NCAA bureaucrat comes to you with secondhand information? You're a lawyer, Jonathan. Are you going to convict him without anything resembling a trial?"

Tucker, after looking surprised at being addressed by his first name, leaned back in his chair. He looked at Williams, the legal counsel. "Thoughts, Jamison?" he asked.

Williams hadn't once looked at Keith since they'd walked into the room. Now he did.

"Sad to say, he has a point, Mr. Chairman," he said. "Technically, we have enough evidence to disqualify him since Mr. Adams says there is plenty of documentation to prove the actions of his father and the agent. But, if you believe he's telling the truth about not knowing what's been going on, I think we should let him play. We can always vacate his finish later if we learn he's lying. I'm sure the NCAA will be investigating this further."

"You bet we will be," the little snake Adams said. "Young man, you may get to play today, but if the information we already have is even a little bit accurate, you will never play college golf or receive any kind of NCAA scholarship."

"You're really enjoying this, aren't you?" Keith said, glaring at Adams. "I'll find out who your source was, I promise."

Tucker gave Keith a look and held up his hand. Then he leaned forward in his chair and looked directly at Frank. "Are you telling the truth, Frank? Understand, if we find out later that you're lying, your entire future in golf will be in jeopardy."

"I'm telling the truth, Mr. Chairman," Frank said.

Tucker leaned back in his chair. "I think Jamison's right. You go ahead and play today. For your sake, however, I hope I don't regret this decision."

He stood up. The meeting was over. Frank stood and shook hands with Tucker and Williams. Keith was glad when the player didn't shake hands with Adams. Snakes could be poisonous.

Keith shook hands with no one.

He and Frank left.

"What do you think?" Frank asked as soon as they were out the door.

"I think you should go kick everyone's butt today," Keith said.

Frank actually smiled. "Even your guy Rory?" he asked.

"Yeah," Keith said. "Even him."

36

FRANK KNEW THE SMART THING TO DO WAS probably go back to the hotel and see if he could steal a few more hours of sleep. But he was too wired and upset to even think about it. Plus, he wasn't ready to talk to his father or Ron Lawrensen about what had just taken place. He knew they'd soon figure out he wasn't at the hotel, but he needed as much time as possible before he had to talk to them.

Keith suggested breakfast and said he knew a place that was far enough up Washington Road that there wouldn't be many golf people in there—especially this early. "Very popular with the locals," he said. "Most of them are in church right now. Place should be quiet."

Keith was right. When they walked into the Sunshine Grill, it was about 80 percent empty. The place was brightly lit and probably had seating for a hundred, including a long counter. They grabbed a table in back and both asked for coffee.

"Don't drink too much," Keith said. "You don't want your hands shaking on the first tee."

Frank laughed. "My hands will shake on the first tee no matter what," he answered.

Keith nodded.

"So what do we do about all this?" Frank asked. He'd been silent in the car ride over.

"You don't do anything," Keith said. "You eat breakfast, go back to the club, and stretch out on the couch in the lounge outside the locker room. At least shut your eyes for a while. I'll try to figure out who did this to you."

"It had to be Lawrensen," Frank said. "If he jeopardizes my college eligibility, or ruins it, then I have to turn pro."

"That makes partial sense," Keith said. "He knows Augusta, though, and he would have to know that if he brought the NCAA into it, they would probably contact the club. If this were tomorrow, I'd say Lawrensen was a good bet. But going to the NCAA Friday, not when Tucker might very well have DQ'd you, makes no sense. Plus, Ron wants you to turn pro—absolutely. But I don't think he wants to sully your reputation unless he feels he has to, and I don't think he is anywhere near that point yet. He was still trying to threaten me yesterday. If he'd played the NCAA card, why bother?"

"He threatened you?"

"Yeah, wild stuff about getting me fired at *Golf Digest*. Nothing for you to even think about. I'm fine."

"Can the NCAA really declare me ineligible?"

"Oh yeah, they absolutely can," Keith said, remembering his conversation with Casey Martin. "The only thing that might save you is the Cam Newton case."

"The Panthers quarterback?" Frank asked.

"Yeah. When Newton was at Auburn, word got out that his father had, basically, sold him to the highest bidder. Several schools were involved. The NCAA eventually ruled that Cam knew nothing about it, and so wasn't subject to punishment.

"Here's the problem: Football is big bucks for the NCAA. Cam was about to win the Heisman Trophy and take his school to the national championship. The NCAA didn't want all that to come crashing down, so they basically made up a rule on the spot to keep him on the field. You, however, don't play football—you play a nonrevenue sport. Most people outside the golf world have no idea who you are, at least right now. The NCAA might want to make an example of you—or, more specifically, your father."

"They can do that?"

"They can do just about anything they want. And, if they know your dad signed a contract of any kind on your behalf, they've got you pretty much nailed."

Frank sighed. He didn't want to see his father later that day; in fact, at that moment, he wasn't sure he ever wanted to see him again.

"So if it's not Lawrensen, then who?" he asked. "Not that many people knew any of this."

"Probably more than you think," Keith said. "If Lawrensen made a deal with, say, Brickley, you can be sure he was negotiating with the other apparel companies. Same with equipment or anything else. The rumors have been all over. It isn't a well-kept secret."

"I'll tell you one thing for sure: when I do turn pro, he won't be my agent."

Keith shrugged. "He's probably not a lot worse than the rest of them. But I don't think he's as smart as he thinks he is."

The pancakes Frank had ordered arrived. Keith had ordered eggs and bacon.

"Hope this isn't too heavy," Frank said.

"You don't play for six hours," Keith said. "You're carbo-loading. That's good."

. . . . .

They had taken Frank's car, with Keith driving. As they turned in to the club, Keith said, "Hey, I've never driven up Magnolia Lane before. This is pretty cool."

It occurred to Frank that, seven days after gawking at Magnolia Lane for the first time, he had barely noticed where they were when the guard waved them through the gate.

They parted at the clubhouse door, Keith saying that unless he came upon something extraordinary, he wasn't going to bug Frank with any information he might dig up during the day. Frank's major concern was how to deal with his father and Lawrensen. His father had been calling and texting, and he knew he needed to respond to him.

"Just get it over with when they get here," Keith said. "Don't point fingers—at least not yet. Does you no good right now. Tell them what happened with Tucker, and say that you

340

can all deal with it tomorrow. Lawrensen will probably be thrilled—even if he didn't do it."

Frank called his father back once he was inside the locker room; cell phone use was allowed in there.

"Where the hell have you been?" his dad said. "We've been worried sick about you."

"Who is 'we,' Dad?" Frank asked. "You and your business partner?"

His father ignored the crack. "Where are you?" he asked.

"At the golf course. In the locker room."

"Okay, we'll meet you for breakfast in the grillroom in twenty."

"I've eaten. I'll meet you in the lounge outside the locker room."

. . . . .

When his father and Lawrensen turned up, Frank calmly walked them through his morning—except for Keith's involvement.

"That's shocking," Lawrensen said when Frank finished. "They gave you no clue who contacted the NCAA?"

"None at all," Frank said, watching Lawrensen for any sign that might indicate he was the leak. "Anything to this?" he asked, now looking directly at his father.

"This isn't the time or the place to talk about it," his father said. "You need to get ready to play."

If there was any doubt about whether the story was true, it vanished in Frank's mind at that moment.

He told his father and Lawrensen he wanted to try to sleep for a while. Amazingly, stretched out on the couch, he actually did fall asleep. He awoke to find Slugger standing over him.

"What are you doing sleeping here?" he asked. "Your dad told me you came out here very early. Are you okay?"

"What time is it?" Frank asked.

"About one-thirty," Slugger said. "We need to get going."

It was clear that his dad and Lawrensen hadn't said anything to Slugger about what had happened. Probably too embarrassed. Frank thought about filling him in, but he decided against it. He needed to warm up and get his mind on playing golf.

Frank was in the last group with Rory McIlroy. Hideki Matsuyama, also at nine under, and Jason Day, who had made a big move on moving day with a six-under-par 66 to get to eight-under, were right in front of them. Jordan Spieth and Justin Thomas, both at seven under, were in the third-to-last group.

Frank stretched, thought for a moment about taking a quick shower, and then dismissed the thought. Once he got on the range and started to feel the adrenaline, he knew he'd be fine.

The range seemed empty when he and Slugger walked out there. Sundays are different at a golf tournament. No one goes to the range to hit balls when they finish their round. Playing in the last group meant there were only a handful of players still warming up.

McIlroy spotted him and came over to say hello. "Bet you never thought a week ago when you couldn't find the clubhouse that we'd be in the last group together today, did you?" he said.

"Never crossed my mind," Frank said.

"Crossed mine when I saw you play," McIlroy said. "Good luck out there today."

Frank understood why Keith liked McIlroy so much. If he'd been sitting at home watching today, he'd be pulling for him to win.

But he wasn't sitting at home—he was playing. And he was going to do everything in his power to try to win. Or at least play as well as he possibly could. If someone—Rory or anyone else—was just better than he was, that was fine.

At 2:45 Frank walked to the putting green. The fans—patrons—were screaming his name as he made his way, surrounded by security people, to the other side of the clubhouse. He also heard a few chants of "USA!" that he could have lived without. This had nothing to do with where you were from. It wasn't the Ryder Cup.

Fifteen minutes later, he walked onto the tee to wild cheers. He and Rory formally shook hands and showed each other their golf balls. Frank's red circle was clearly drawn.

McIlroy was up first and hit a perfect drive that bounced

left of the fairway bunker and just kept going—or so it seemed—over the crest of the hill. Frank had to wait a moment for the cheers to quiet when he was introduced. He smiled, touched his cap once, then again, and finally put his tee in the ground. He hit the exact same shot he had hit on Number 1 all week—a draw aimed at the corner of the bunker.

This time, though, the ball stayed dead straight, never moving. It plopped into the bunker, drawing a groan from the crowd. Frank was shocked. The ball had felt perfect coming off the club.

"No worries," Slugger said. "We can make a par from there."

Except they didn't. Frank found the left bunker with his second shot, hit a good bunker shot to about eight feet, but missed the putt. It was the first time all week he'd bogeyed Number 1.

"It's just one hole," said McIlroy, who'd made par, as they walked to the second tee. "Just play golf."

Frank managed to birdie the second from the front bunker, which calmed him down. At Number 3, still feeling a bit shaky, he laid up with an iron and was happy to make par. Then he bogeyed the tough par-three fourth. He was at eight under. McIlroy and Matsuyama were at ten under, and Spieth was tied with Frank at eight under.

Still, it wasn't as if he were collapsing. He made a good up-and-down at the fifth, then drilled a six-iron to ten feet at the sixth.

"Make this, and we're back in the ball game," Slugger said. "It's dead straight. Don't overread it."

He didn't, and Slugger was right. The putt went in, the crowd roared, and the "USA!" chants started again.

As they stood on the seventh tee waiting for Matsuyama and Day to hit their second shots—Day was a notoriously slow player—Frank turned to McIlroy and said, "You must get tired of the 'USA' stuff."

McIlroy shrugged. "This is nothing," he said. "Wait until you play Ryder Cup. They never stop."

They both parred 7, bringing them to two holes that Frank knew would be critical to his chances—8 and 9.

Eight was the most difficult par-five to birdie because it was the most difficult to reach in two. Except for McIlroy, who hit two perfect shots to 30 feet and two-putted for birdie to take the outright lead at 11 under. Matsuyama had bogeyed the seventh to drop to nine under, tied for second with Frank.

Frank missed the fairway to the right—finding the rough, or as it was called at Augusta National, "the second cut." (Nothing at Augusta National was "rough.") Whatever it was, it wasn't very deep, but Frank decided to lay up rather than try to hit a wood out of it. From there, he hit a solid wedge onto the green to within ten feet of the flag, but the putt turned right at the last possible second.

Still, he was tied for second—two shots back of McIlroy.

At Number 9, the pin was in its very famous Sunday position: front-left. It was an absolute sucker pin, even with no water involved. If you landed the ball pin-high, there was almost no chance for the ball to stay on the green. If you tried to simply fly it safely to the back of the green, you'd have a brutal downhill putt.

Both Frank and McIlroy hit their drives to the bottom of the hill. Surprisingly, McIlroy pulled his second shot into the left bunker. Frank aimed for the middle of the green—hoping to land no more than 20 feet behind the hole. The ball landed on almost the spot he was aiming for. It spun back in the direction of the hole, and for a split second Frank thought he'd spun the nine-iron too much and it was going off the green. But it stopped hole-high, eight feet right of the flag.

"That's a great shot," McIlroy said as they walked up the hill to the building applause toward the green. "You give me ten shots from that spot, I doubt I'd get it closer."

Frank was thinking if he had a hundred shots from there he wouldn't get it any closer.

McIlroy's bunker shot skipped 15 feet past the hole, and he missed coming back for his first bogey of the day. As he lined up his putt, it occurred to Frank that if he made it, he'd be tied for the lead with nine holes to play. He needed an extra moment to gather himself, so he circled the hole a second time. He got over the putt, reminded himself that putts on this green always broke more than you thought, and then managed to get the putt to just glide over the right edge—and in.

The "USA!" chants were now getting very loud. He and McIlroy were both ten under. Matsuyama, Spieth, and Day were a shot back.

"The Masters doesn't begin until the back nine on Sunday," McIlroy said with a grin as they walked between the ropes to the tenth tee.

"There is no back nine," Frank said. "Just a second nine."

They were both laughing as they walked onto the tee. It occurred to Frank that he was actually having fun. How was that possible?

37

KEITH FORMAN WAS STANDING IN HIS NOW-
usual spot directly behind the tenth tee when Frank Baker and
Rory McIlroy arrived. Both were laughing. Keith found that
amazing. There were nine holes left to play in the Masters, they
were tied for the lead with a posse of great players chasing, and
they were laughing?

He hadn't seen a single shot on the front nine. He had decided his time would be better used seeing if he could get some
kind of fix on who might have tipped off the NCAA about
Ron Lawrensen and Thomas Baker. He figured if Frank played
well enough to stay in contention, he'd pick him up on the
back nine. If not, he didn't really want to watch him collapse.
He had to admit he was a little surprised when he checked
the scoreboards and saw that Frank was hanging in with
McIlroy, Matsuyama, Spieth, and Day. If you added Dustin
Johnson to the list, you'd have the five top players in the game.

So it was four stars and a seventeen-year-old kid. Amazing.

Not having any idea where to begin his search, Keith

wandered up to the tree. There wasn't nearly as much activity there now as there had been early in the week. Many of the sport's corporate rainmakers had already left. Same with a lot of the agents. There were media guys hanging around because the thick crowds made walking the golf course with the late groups on Sunday almost impossible without inside-the-ropes access. Although Augusta never announced official numbers, the consensus was that at least forty thousand people were on the property. Keith was almost dreading walking the back nine if Frank was still in contention.

For a while, he wandered aimlessly, not even sure who or what he was looking for. He could hear the roars coming from the golf course as the leaders moved around the front nine.

The first person he saw worth talking to was Steve DiMeglio.

"Can you imagine the rating CBS is going to get with this leaderboard?" DiMeglio said. "No Tiger, you got four of the big five, plus your guy, who is the best story of all. I think Nantz will explode if the kid somehow wins."

Keith knew DiMeglio wasn't exaggerating—at least not by much. He'd watched some of the CBS highlights show the previous night, and Nantz and the entire CBS crew—or as Nantz liked to call it, "the CBS golf family"—had more or less been comparing Frank's 54-hole performance to the invention of the wheel and the iPhone.

"It would be one of the great sports stories of all time," Keith said.

"Yeah, only problem with it is that Ron Lawrensen gets rich, and not only do those phonies from Brickley get the kid, but he becomes the most valuable property in golf. Hell, as it is, he's a gold mine."

"How do you know about Brickley?" Keith asked.

"I haven't been in a cave all week," DiMeglio said. "Hell, Erica and Ron are upstairs on the porch right now—probably working out just how to make the announcement tomorrow."

"What?" Keith had figured that Lawrensen was out on the golf course with Thomas Baker.

DiMeglio pointed upward, and Keith could see Ron Lawrensen and Erica Chambers sitting across from each other at a table he knew was just to the left of the door leading to the dining room.

"Gotta go," he said to DiMeglio.

"Why?" DiMeglio asked. "You think you're going to stop any of this?"

Keith didn't answer because he was bolting in the direction of the clubhouse door, which was a few yards from where they were standing.

He hustled up the circular stairway—too fast by Augusta standards—and walked through the almost-empty dining room to the porch. It was four o'clock in the afternoon. The only people there were Lawrensen and Chambers. Both looked surprised to see him.

"You aren't out watching the golf tournament?" Lawrensen said. "Isn't that what real reporters do—watch the golf?"

"Save it, Lawrensen," Keith said. The time for niceties and dancing around had passed.

He sat down in the chair between the two of them.

"Please join us," Chambers said sharply, without a trace of her luminous smile.

"You can save it, too," Keith said. He was done gawking at her. He probably hadn't been aggressive enough trying to find out exactly what Brickley was up to because he'd been dazzled by her.

"I assume you two are finalizing—or more likely celebrating—a deal that Frank knows nothing about and wants nothing to do with."

"Oh, he'll want something to do with it when he sees the numbers involved," Chambers said.

"*No*, his father will like the numbers. You don't know this kid."

"Oh, and you do?" Lawrensen said.

"Very well," Keith answered. "That's why he asked *me* to go with him to see Jonathan Tucker this morning. Not you. Not his father. Me."

Keith knew—because Frank had texted him—that Frank had told his father and Lawrensen about the meeting. So he wasn't giving anything away—except for his presence.

For once, Lawrensen looked caught off guard. "You're lying," he said lamely.

Keith shrugged. "No need to lie. You can read my story about it later."

Now Lawrensen was concerned. "You could ruin his image if you wrote about that," he said. "I thought you said you cared about him."

"Unlike you, I do," Keith said. "If I write about this, you

will look like a sleazebag, and so will his father. The kid's an innocent bystander."

Chambers looked at Lawrensen. "If this damages his image—and I'm sure it will—we might have to reconsider some of the numbers in the contract."

Keith almost laughed. "Figures that's what you'd care about," he said. "Trust me, Erica, I'll make sure your image and Brickley's image will take a hit, too."

"Your friend was right about him," Chambers said to Lawrensen. "He really doesn't take a hint, does he?"

"Friend?" Keith said.

"Thomas Baker and I aren't friends," Lawrensen said, looking directly at Chambers. "We're business partners."

"Coming from you guys, that's a compliment," Keith said. "So, Erica, do me a favor and give me your cell number. I might need it if I write something to give you a chance to tell Brickley's side of the story. Or should I talk to your boss, Billy Nevins?"

He was telling the truth, but that wasn't the only reason he wanted the number. The germ of an idea had just come into his head—a long shot, he knew, but one that might be worth checking into at this point.

"Sure," Chambers said. "Always glad to talk to the media." She rattled off a number. Then she leaned forward and smiled. "If need be, we could do it over dinner."

Keith smiled. "You're a beautiful woman, and, trust me, the notion is tempting. But no thanks. I also know you guys are located in Connecticut, and that sounds like a switchboard number to me."

"It's not," Chambers said. "Call it right now. You'll get my voicemail since my phone's in the car."

"I don't have mine either," Keith said. "It's back in the press center."

"Call it later, then," she said. "I've got no reason to hide from you." She gave him her stunning smile. He decided he'd check later, when he had a chance. Which wasn't now.

A roar was coming from the ninth hole. He looked at the scoreboard right of the ninth green. Frank and McIlroy were playing there now. One of them had just hit a great shot. It was time for him to make like a real reporter and go watch some golf.

"This isn't over—not even close," Keith said.

"Yes, it is," Chambers said. "At least as far as you're concerned. All you've got is a lot of innuendo. Believe me, Forman, I've handled better than you."

"So have I," Lawrensen echoed. "You're way over your head here, Forman."

"We'll see," Keith said, turning to leave.

· · · · ·

Frank was happy to see Keith on the tenth tee. He hoped it meant he'd figured out what was going on.

"Everything okay?" he asked, walking to the back of the tee for a moment.

"All good," Keith said. "Golf tournament starts right now."

Frank wasn't sure if Keith was just trying to reassure him

so that he'd focus on his golf or if he'd actually figured something out. Either way, he had nine holes to play, and he knew worrying about what might come after that was foolish. He wondered for a moment where his dad and Lawrensen might be among the throngs of people.

He had the tee after the birdie at Number 9 and, feeling completely calm, he hit the ball perfectly, the ball drawing to the fairway and taking a big hop down the hill.

"I'm going to have you drug-tested when this is over," McIlroy kidded as he teed the ball up.

His drive was just as perfect as Frank's. The Masters—the back nine on Sunday—had begun.

For the next three holes, nothing changed. Both players had birdie chances at 10, both were happy to escape with par at 11 and 12. As they had walked off the 12th tee, Frank heard a roar coming from the 13th green.

"Jordan birdied," Rory said. "That's not an eagle roar."

Frank knew he was right. He'd heard that you could actually recognize roars at Augusta, especially on Sunday. If Jordan had eagled, the roar would have echoed off the trees. This was loud, but not *loud*. That meant he, Rory, and Jordan were now tied for the lead.

The 13th had been Frank's favorite hole all week because it suited his draw perfectly. Once again, he hit a perfect drive and, once again, his ball was within 200 yards of the flag. There was just one thing: McIlroy's drive was 30 yards past him.

"Talk about drug-testing," he said when he saw where McIlroy's ball had come to rest.

"Little pumped up, I guess," McIlroy said.

It occurred to Frank that for all of McIlroy's friendly chatter, he desperately wanted to win the tournament and complete the career Grand Slam. Who could blame him?

Frank had 192 yards to the flag, and he hit a seven-iron. He pulled it a little bit, but the ball took a fortuitous bounce, rolled on the green, and stopped about 35 feet from the flag. McIlroy couldn't have had more than 165 yards to the flag, and Frank heard him say, "It's no more than a nine," to his caddie. Frank was amazed—driver, nine-iron—to a par-five. He was long, but simply not in McIlroy's league. At least not pumped up.

McIlroy's shot was close to perfect; it landed a few yards short of the pin and rolled so close Frank thought it might go in. It stopped about two feet away. A kick-in eagle.

"Great shot" was all Frank could manage.

McIlroy just grinned. "Needed it, didn't I?" he said.

Frank was able to two-putt for birdie. That meant he and Spieth trailed McIlroy by one.

They both reached the green at 14 safely, managing to get their second shots over the ridge that separated the two levels of the green. As Frank was marking his ball, he heard something resembling a gasp. He looked at the scoreboard and saw a red 9 going up next to Spieth's name on 15. Somehow, he had bogeyed the par-five. Now McIlroy led him by one and Spieth by two.

McIlroy's lead grew by another shot at 15. Again, he bombed a drive and he hit a midrange iron to about 20 feet. From there he two-putted for birdie. Frank was just as uncomfortable on the 15th tee as he was comfortable on the 13th. He just couldn't seem to find the fairway. He thought he'd done it this time, but the ball kept kicking left and almost rolled into the trees. From there, he had to lay up and, holding his breath, barely held the back of the green with his third shot. He was happy to settle for par.

Except now, McIlroy led by two with three holes to play. Spieth had parred 16 and was three shots back. No one else was in contention.

The flag at 16, as was always the case on Sunday, was tucked left, near the water. It wasn't as much of a sucker pin as it appeared to be because if you caught the slope in the middle of the green, the ball would roll in the direction of the pin. McIlroy, knowing he was pumped up, took a nine-iron. But he wasn't quite *that* pumped up, and the ball stopped on the front of the green 50 feet below the hole.

Frank, knowing he had to make something happen to have any chance, went with a seven-iron. He figured it was really an eight-iron for McIlroy and he was about a club longer than Frank most of the time. He hit it just the way he wanted to, right-to-left, drawing to the middle of the green. It hit and began to roll toward the hole. It stopped eight feet away. He had a real birdie chance.

McIlroy hit a wonderful putt, leaving the ball inches short of a miracle birdie. He smiled and tapped in. Frank knew he was playing slower than he ever had in his life. But he needed deep breaths as he looked at the putt. He finally got over it, took one more deep breath, and hit the ball dead center.

McIlroy's lead was one. It was a two-man golf tournament.

McIlroy was smiling as they walked off the green. "You just don't want to go away, do you?" he said. "Have I ever done anything to offend you?"

Frank laughed. He was almost beginning to feel guilty about "not going away."

He was so relaxed he smashed a perfect drive at 17. McIlroy's was pushed and, for the first time all day, he showed a little frustration, letting out a soft profanity as the ball flew right. His second shot found the left bunker. Frank's second shot was about 25 feet short. The 17th was not a green you attacked. If you went over the green, you were all but dead. It was the place that had inspired CBS golf analyst Gary McCord's infamous 1994 comment "There are body bags back there," which had gotten him banned by the Augusta members.

Frank was thinking a par might mean he'd be tied for the lead going to 18. He was wrong. McIlroy hit a brilliant bunker shot to about three feet and made the putt. Frank's birdie putt was wide right all the way. They went to 18 with McIlroy still up one.

Frank was figuring he had to make birdie to have a chance. Slugger had gotten so quiet he was almost afraid to ask him anything. The look on his face told him he was terrified. Frank took out his driver and said to himself, "One more time, please?" He got what he asked for, the ball bouncing beyond the fairway bunker. He'd given himself a chance.

McIlroy was silent now. He was clearly totally focused on

what he had left to do. His drive was just as good as Frank's, a little farther left, a little closer to the green.

The crowd was going nuts as they walked up the fairway. They were going to see history one way or the other: either a seventeen-year-old amateur was going to win the Masters or Rory McIlroy was going to complete the career Grand Slam. If nothing else, it was great theater.

When Frank got to his ball and asked Slugger for the yardage, Slugger looked at him blankly. "Yardage, Slugger?" he asked again.

"Sorry," Slugger said, his Masters-green yardage book in his hands.

Frank noticed they were shaking. *Good thing I'm the one playing,* he thought.

"You've got a hundred sixty-eight front and a hundred seventy-four flag," he finally said.

The flag was in its traditional Sunday spot: front-left.

It was a perfect seven-iron distance since it was uphill, but Frank knew his adrenaline was almost out of control. He pulled an eight-iron from the bag.

"You can't get there with an eight," Slugger said.

"Watch me," Frank answered.

The crowd began screaming as soon as the ball was in the air. It hit on the front-center of the green and rolled hole-high, perhaps 15 feet right of the flag. Not a great shot, but a good one.

McIlroy was perhaps five yards closer. His shot, no doubt a nine-iron, was right at the flag. But the ball didn't spin, and it rolled about 30 feet past the hole. Advantage, Frank.

They walked up the last hill onto the green with everyone on their feet. Frank realized he would probably never feel like this again, no matter where his golf career went from here. He took a moment to drink it all in.

McIlroy slowed so Frank could catch up to him as they went up the last hill.

"What're you doing?" Frank said. He'd slowed to let McIlroy walk on the green first. That was the tradition: the leader went first.

"We're walking up there together," McIlroy said.

"But—"

"No buts. Walk."

Frank did as he was told. The "USA!" shouts had died out, and fans were now screaming both their names.

McIlroy was a notoriously fast player, but he took plenty of time looking over his putt, which was almost straight downhill. Finally, he putted, and, for an instant, Frank thought he'd left it ten feet short. But Rory knew what he was doing. The ball picked up speed and finally died about 18 inches left of the hole.

McIlroy was clearly disappointed he hadn't made it, because the door was still open for Frank to make his putt and force a playoff.

McIlroy walked to his ball and marked it. Then he looked back at Frank. "Am I in your line?" he asked. "You need me to move my mark?"

Frank saw that he did. "Can you move it one left?" he said. His putt would break right to left, so moving the mark to the left of the hole should take it safely out of his line. McIlroy put his putter head down and carefully moved his coin to the left the width of his clubface.

He moved out of the way. Frank knew the putt was going to break hard left when it got close to the hole. He remembered watching old footage of Mark O'Meara making almost the identical putt in 1998 to win the Masters and saying he had played the putt one ball farther right than he read it, because he knew the break was harder than his eyes told him.

Frank did the same thing. Five feet out, he was convinced he'd made it. Then, at the last possible second, came the dive to the left. The ball stopped an inch—literally an inch—left of the hole.

Frank felt all the air and adrenaline go out of him.

He had missed a playoff with McIlroy by that inch.

He tapped the ball in.

As Rory was putting his ball down, he said softly, "I can't believe that didn't go in."

He stood to tap in and finally clinch his green jacket.

Frank started to step away to give him some space. Then he noticed something . . . something terribly wrong . . . and a warning flew out of his mouth. "RORY, STOP!"

McIlroy looked at him as if he'd lost his mind. "What?" he said, stunned to hear Frank's voice at such a climactic moment.

"You didn't move your mark back!"

McIlroy looked at him blankly for a split second, then understood. "Oh my God!" he said. "You just saved me."

He put his mark back down and picked up the incorrectly

placed ball. Then he stepped away, gathered himself, and moved the mark back, the width of his putter face. He put the ball down, glanced at the hole for a moment, and then tapped in.

The cheers were coming from everywhere as he took his cap off and wrapped Frank in a tight hug.

"Saying thank you doesn't begin to tell you how grateful I am," he said in Frank's ear.

"You won fair and square," Frank said, shaking with emotions he couldn't begin to describe. "I wouldn't have wanted to win on a technicality."

Frank realized that only a few people in the crowd understood what had just happened. It didn't matter. He'd given Rory McIlroy everything he could give him. And he'd done the right thing. He felt great.

As an amateur, he wouldn't receive a dime of the eleven-million-dollar purse. But what he had won was priceless.

38

REMARKABLY, KEITH FORMAN HAD A PERFECT view of everything that unfolded on the final green. He was able to push his way through the people standing to the left of the green by saying repeatedly, "Really sorry, Frank's my nephew, I'd like to see this if possible."

One man said angrily, "Why didn't you get here sooner?"

Keith was ready for that one: "I've been walking with him all day."

By then people were starting to say, "Hey, uncle coming through, help him out."

Keith ended up standing directly behind the rows of lawn chairs where people were seated.

He thought Frank had made his birdie putt, so he was about to push his way out to go back to the 18th tee for the start of the playoff when he saw the ball dive left and just miss the hole. He was waiting for Rory to tap in so he could watch the handshake when he heard Frank shout, "STOP!"

He turned back to see McIlroy step away from his tap-in

putt and then re-mark his ball and move the mark. Realizing what had happened, Keith set out to get to the scoring area the second the two had finished hugging.

He circled to the right to avoid the area that had been blocked off to get the players through and actually arrived just before they did.

Frank, Rory, and the two caddies went inside. A moment later, Slugger came out and took his phone from Frank's golf bag and made a call. Since the tournament was over, taking his phone out was apparently okay. Keith was trying to get his attention, but his college teammate wasn't looking in his direction.

Keith desperately wanted to talk to Frank before he and McIlroy were carted to Butler Cabin for the TV green-jacket ceremony. After that would come the formal green-jacket ceremony on the putting green, and it would be a solid thirty minutes—at least—before he'd have any chance to get close to him.

Slugger finally got off the phone and Keith shouted his name, a no-no, but he didn't care at that point. Slugger saw him and walked over, phone still in hand.

"Who were you talking to?" Keith asked.

"Just now?" he said. "Amanda."

That was his wife. Something in the way Slugger answered the question made Keith think he was lying.

"What an ending, huh?" Keith asked.

"Yeah, I guess," Slugger said, without much enthusiasm.

Frank walked outside and was instantly surrounded by

green-jackets pointing him at a cart. Keith called his name, figuring it was futile. TV waits for no man—or teenager.

Keith saw one of the green-jackets talking urgently to Frank, pointing at the nearby golf cart. Rory hadn't come outside yet. Frank put up one finger and walked quickly to where Keith and Slugger were standing—Slugger inside the rope, Keith outside it.

Keith reached over the rope to hug him. He didn't really care who saw him at this point.

"I couldn't be more proud of you," he said. "The way you played, and then what you did for Rory at the finish."

Frank frowned and looked at Slugger. "Did you tell him yet?" he asked.

"Tell me what?" Keith asked.

"Slugger said I should have let Rory putt from the wrong spot," Frank said.

Keith shot Slugger a look of surprise.

"Heat of the moment," Slugger said. "All I could think was, if Rory putts from the wrong spot, Frank wins the Masters."

Keith knew that failing to move your mark back was a two-stroke penalty. "You'd want him to win *that* way?"

Slugger looked sheepish. "I guess not."

"You were pretty mad when we walked off," Frank said, clearly not buying Slugger's back-off. "Hey, they said I have to go as soon as Rory comes outside, so what's up?"

Keith snapped back to what he wanted to get done.

"Slugger, I need to make a quick phone call—really

quick—and my phone's back in the press center. Loan me yours for a second."

"You can't make a call from here—"

"Yes, I can. Your phone's authorized in the scoring area, and the tournament's over. I gotta let Jerry Tarde know what I'm up to. Take thirty seconds."

Slugger was still shaking his head. "What *are* you up to?" he asked.

"Give me the phone," Keith said. He knew McIlroy was going to come outside at any moment.

"No," Slugger said firmly.

Keith reached out and tried to swipe the phone from Slugger's hand. His ex-teammate quickly switched it from his right hand to his left, watching Keith all the while. As he did, Frank reached out and grabbed the phone from Slugger, who—uncharacteristically losing his cool—tried to grab it back.

Frank tossed it to Keith, who spun away from Slugger so that he couldn't pry it from his hands.

Slugger hadn't locked it after his phone call. Keith went to recent calls, and there it was: the last call was to the number he expected. Erica Chambers hadn't been lying about her cell number. He scrolled down and found a dozen calls to that number. Then he found the other one he was looking for, a different number in the 317 area code—from Friday night. He knew 317 was the area code for Indianapolis—which was where the NCAA's headquarters were located.

Frank was hanging on to Slugger for dear life to keep him from getting to Keith. McIlroy came outside. The green-jackets, looking confused by the sight of Frank wrestling with his caddie, were coming for him.

"We need you right *now*, Mr. Baker," one of them said quite firmly.

"Coming," Frank said. "What'd you find in there, Keith?"

"Tell you later," Keith said. "Go take care of the ceremony."

As Frank was whisked away, Keith tossed the phone back to Slugger.

"You want to tell me about it?" he said.

"No, not really," Slugger said.

But then he did.

. . . . .

More than an hour passed before Frank got a chance to talk to Keith. He had gone through the Butler Cabin ceremony, where he'd been given the medal as Low Amateur, and then did the same thing on the putting green. McIlroy had gone on at length about Frank's "remarkable act of sportsmanship," thanking him over and over for saving him from losing the Masters because of a mind block.

"I guess, given my age and Frank's age, you could say I had a senior moment," he joked.

Frank was brought to the press center before McIlroy and the questions were all about his cool under pressure and when he planned to turn pro.

"Not for a good long while," he'd said, even knowing he might not have a choice in the matter.

Finally, someone asked if he thought he might someday regret stopping McIlroy from putting because it was possible he'd never have a better chance to win the Masters.

"You think I'd want to win the Masters *that* way?" he said. "I'd much rather be remembered for not winning it this way than for winning it that way. I would only have regrets if I hadn't stopped him. Right now, I haven't a single regret. Not one."

As Frank stood to leave, he heard applause. Keith had told him reporters didn't applaud at the end of press conferences. Apparently some—many—had decided this was a moment for that rule to be broken. He waved a hand in thanks and realized the applause was getting louder. Then, many—most? all?—were on their feet. Standing in the back of the room, Keith got misty-eyed for a moment.

It was pitch dark when they drove Frank back to the clubhouse. He'd told his father he'd meet him at the hotel. He needed some time alone with Keith before he faced his father or Ron Lawrensen. Or, for that matter, Slugger.

His father was waiting for him in the lounge. There was no sign of Keith.

"I asked Keith to give me five minutes alone with you," his dad said, reading his mind. "He's out on the veranda. I'll send him in as soon as I'm finished. I promise this won't take long."

Frank sat down on one of the couches. His father sat across from him.

"I'm so proud of you right now, I don't even know how to

express it," he said. "I'm proud because you played so well, but I'm *so much* more proud because of what you did on the eighteenth green." He paused. "I wish I was half the man you are."

"Dad, come on—"

His father held a hand up. "No, I mean it," he said. "This last year, I've been the teenager blinded by money, letting Lawrensen lead me by the hand. I was willing to basically sell you. Ron didn't walk today because he was trying to seal a deal with that Brickley woman. Gave me a lot of time to think as I watched you play. By the way, she's now offering double the money that was on the table after what happened. If you want it, it's yours. I'll sign on your behalf."

"I don't want it, Dad."

"Good. Neither do I." He paused. "I just want to go back to when we played golf together for *fun*—although now I'm going to want a *lot* more shots than in the past." He smiled. "You tell me where you want to go to college, and if the NCAA declares you ineligible to play on a college team and you can't get a scholarship, I'll pay your way."

"Dad, you don't have to do that."

"I know," he said, and stood up.

Frank stood, too, and they hugged.

"I'll send Keith in," his father said. "You two have a lot to talk about. He's the other hero in this story."

They hugged again.

"I love you, Dad," Frank said.

"I love you too, son."

He walked out.

Keith walked in a few seconds later.

The guard at the door started to say something, but Frank said, "He's with me."

The guard just nodded.

. . . . .

They walked back to the table in the dining area where they had sat thirteen hours earlier before going to see Jonathan Tucker.

"So?" Frank said.

Keith nodded, the way you nod when you have to tell a story but would prefer not to tell it.

"It was Slugger who called the NCAA on Friday," he said. "He's also been working with Brickley to make sure you sign with them—right now."

"But why—"

Keith held up a hand.

"It's always about money, Frank," he said. "Your dad and Lawrensen had told him a while back that he was done once the Masters was over. They had lined up interviews with all the big-name teachers."

"But Slugger should know I'd never—"

"*Should* know is right, Frank. But he didn't. He was worried, and then Brickley showed up. Lawrensen was putting you up for bid, and Brickley was worried if you played well here— as in top ten or something—that Nike would come in with a blow-away bid. They've been known to do that. They told

Slugger if he delivered you to them *now*—not after two years of college but *now*—they'd pay him two million dollars as a finder's fee."

"Two million dollars?"

"Lot of money for a guy with a wife and two young kids, a mortgage, and a salary of eighty-five thousand a year." Keith let that sink in, then went on. "When you kept insisting to him and to me that you weren't going to turn pro no matter what, he got scared. So, for insurance, he called the NCAA on Friday and told them what Lawrensen had been up to. He knew they'd come running because they love to take down stars in nonrevenue sports: it lets them show how tough they are, but it doesn't cost them any money, the way taking down a star football or basketball player would."

"But wasn't he afraid I might get disqualified for not being an amateur?"

"He felt comfortable that Augusta wouldn't want the scandal in the midst of the Masters. And he was pretty confident Tucker wasn't going to take you off the golf course Sunday with the potential for record TV ratings because of you. Plus, he knew Tucker has a soft spot for amateurs because he won the U.S. Amateur himself. It was worth the gamble."

Frank sat back in his chair.

"Still, how could he do that to me? I mean . . . that sucks."

"For what it's worth, I think he genuinely feels awful. He knows he's ruined the most important relationship he's ever had outside his family."

"I don't know if I can ever look him in the eye again," Frank said. "What do I do now? If I can't play college golf, then—"

Keith cut him off. "You might still be able to play. The Cam Newton case works in your favor, since you knew nothing about what your father and Lawrensen were doing. There's also what happened today. If I were the NCAA, I'd want you playing college golf. You stand for everything that's right about sports. They like that stuff."

For a moment, Frank said nothing. "But you said this morning there's no way to predict what the NCAA will do. That guy didn't seem inclined to cut me—or anyone else—any slack."

"True," Keith said. "It could go either way. But it's not his decision. It will go much higher than him."

"But what if they rule against me? Guess I have to turn pro in college, then, right? My dad says he'll pay my tuition, but I'm not sure he can handle that even if he wants to."

"Best part of this story is, it looks like you got your dad back," Keith said.

Frank smiled and said, "Yeah, I think I did." His voice caught for a split second.

"I don't think he'd have to pay your tuition, though," Keith said. "I have an idea."

"What do you mean?"

"You know how you've been asking me the last eight months if I was ever going to write anything about you?"

"Yeah."

"Well, guess what? After today, publishers will be pounding on your door wanting a book. There will be a bidding war, and someone will pay a lot of money for your story."

"And you'll write it?" Frank said.

"I'd like to," Keith said. "Unless you've got somebody else in mind."

Frank laughed. "Yeah, right," he said. "Split the money fifty-fifty?"

"Yup. Which should leave you with plenty to pay for college until you're ready to turn pro."

"Can I pick the title?"

"Sure," Keith said. "What have you got in mind?"

"Do the Right Thing."

Keith knew that was the title of a Spike Lee movie from the '80s, and he suspected that more than one book author had used it as well over the years. But he could see why it was a title that appealed to Frank.

"Perfect," he said.

"Let's celebrate," Frank said. "Let's go crash the dinner for the members and the champion upstairs."

"They might kick us out," Keith said.

"You think Rory would let them do that?" Frank said.

"Come to think of it, I doubt it," Keith said. "Let's go."

Frank stood up. He would have liked to have been at that dinner as the champion. But, under the circumstances, this was even better.